Cormac mac Art [was a]
one. Well-born a[nd ...]
was the Gaelic pirate who plowed the waters of the Narrow Sea, though he never raided the shores of his native Eirrin. Yet time came when Cormac mac Art was captured and flung into a filthy, rat-infested dungeon—an event more fortuitous than Cormac would have believed at the time, for it was here that he met the tall Dane, Wulfhere Splitter of Skulls.

Together the two escaped their captors and joined the crew of another renegade who knew no fear. Trailing a wake of blood, their pirate ship returned from sorties having burned fear into the hearts of the ravaged peoples of Britain and Alba. With time, Cormac and Wulfhere went a-roving on their own and it was thus that Cormac returned to the isle of Eirrin and to the confrontation with the death-giving wizard who served the serpent god. At last, Cormac mac Art would face the entangling grip of death's head wizard—DEAD yet ALIVE!—under the silvery shimmer of

Other Ace Science Fiction titles by Andrew
J. Offutt:
   KING DRAGON
   WHEN DEATH BIRDS FLY
   THE MISTS OF DOOM

THE SIGN OF THE MOONBOW

ANDREW J. OFFUTT
KEITH TAYLOR

SF

ace books

A Division of Charter Communications Inc.
A GROSSET & DUNLAP COMPANY
51 Madison Avenue
New York, New York 10010

THE SIGN OF THE MOONBOW

Copyright © 1977 by Andrew J. Offutt and Glenn Lord

An ACE Book

First Ace printing: November 1980

Published simultaneously in Canada

2 4 6 8 0 9 7 5 3 1
Manufactured in the United States of America

Prolog

A cadaverously thin man stood close against the ship's mast, his back to it. His robe flapped in the breeze that drove the one-sailed craft across the sea that lapped south and east of Britain. Night-dark was that robe; tall was its wearer. He was bound in place, though not with ropes. Cords could not hold such a one able to assume slithering forms other than his own. Nor could he be prisoned with leather, or with chains of iron or steel.

Two sword pommels stood out from his chest and abdomen. He was held fast in the only way he could be held: impaled and pinned to the mast, motionless and unmovable. The swords nailed him to the mast.

No blood flowed.

He writhed, snarling.

It was not from lips those snarls emerged, for the doubly impaled man had no lips. Nor mouth, nor face

5

he had; there was neither cartilage nor skin nor hair on the shining, grey-white skull that was his head. Yet within the shadowed holes that had been eye sockets, red lights burned, more like hellish and ever-maleficent flames than eyes. He writhed, and snarling sounds emerged from his lipless mouth.

He saw; he felt; he complained of cold, but not of pain.

He was neither alive nor dead. Dead, he lived. Yet he could not be slain, for he was not truly alive. Un-dead he had been for eighteen thousand years, escaping all the means that had slain so many others, the countless deaths he had personally wrought and callously caused. He could only be held—and only by this ghastly means.

The skewered man in the dark robe rode the foremost of two ships that slid over little known seas.

Each could loft a single sail, though the gentle breeze filled only the sail of the first. Each was constructed of overlapping planking in the clinker style. Each could ship over thirty oars, though neither did. Neither had as many as twenty aboard to man her oars, nor even ten. Many men lay dead in their dual wake, all victims of the power and machinations of the baneful captive with the skull for a face.

The second ship was without crew at all. All those who had sailed her hence down from Britain were dead; all she had borne out to sea now provided food for the plants and creatures on its floor. Unmanned, bearing the name *Amber Rowan* along her blue-painted side, she wallowed along at the end of thick plaited cables of rope, doubled and tripled. Her greyed sail was furled against a sudden change in the light breeze, whether of direction or force.

The towing ship was heavy laden, though it bore six persons—and one of those was the repugnant creature nailed to her mast. Not for so few was the using of oars. Green-streaked *Quester* was no merchant vessel, but bore considerable cargo.

The fine fabrics and the gold, the silver and jewellery of precious stones, the arms and armour and wrapped personal possessions of some twenty men were not trade goods.

All had been stolen—if aught could be called stolen that had been paid for in the scarlet coin of so many lives. The cargo had been the booty of murdering Norse reavers, all four months dead; it had been sought by three-and-twenty Britons, all dead over a fortnight. The cargo had been taken from the Norse pirates' cache, and that on a tiny isle where stood a castle raised by men dead these hundred and eighty centuries.

The undead man was of long-sunken Atlantis. The survivors and possessors of the rich plunder, his captors, were four of the Eirrin-born and one of the land they called Loch-linn, home of the Danes, Dane-mark.

The Dane was a giant, red of hair and bushy unkempt beard, huge of chest and broad of shoulder. His arms were the size of the thighs of other men. He lounged at the tiller, his ax, shield, and coat of scale-mail nearby. Little effort was required of him. The sun was bright, the breeze steady and not swift, the ship slowed by the similar long boat she towed. When the sun was lower, he would use the sun-stick to check their course. By day, there was no other means.

One man was speaking. Like the fell writhing captive he was robed, though in the green of nature, and girt with a length of rope. A lunula hung on his chest, a half-moon of gold that returned the sun's light in dull flashes. Above, more closely fitting, he

7

wore the twisted necklet of the Celts, a torc. He it was who had promised fair skies and good winds. His companions had learned to believe this servant of Behl and Crom, and to believe.

"In times more ancient than we count," the green-robed druid told the others, "an exile from Atlantis found employment as weapon-man in a land called Valusia. Time came when he made challenge to the king, and brought defeat and death on him, and the Atlantean was king over Valusia. His name was Kull. Trusted counsellor to him was a man named Tu. Just that: Tu. I am. . . I was Tu, as I have been others since, in the endless cycle of birth and death and rebirth. And you, Cormac, who have been others as well, are and were Kull. For it is all the same, Celt and Keltoi and the Keltii of the Romans; Kull and Cormac, Cull and Kormak."

The others looked at the man the druid addressed as Cormac.

Dark of hair and skin he was, like the druid, and with the same grey eyes though the druid's held more blue; both men were Gaels, of Eirrin. A life fraught with hacking swords and venomously whining arrows and rushing battle axes had left scars that, with his narrowed deepset eyes, imparted a rather sinister aspect to the face of the man called Cormac. Yet he was loved by four of the six aboard, including the woman, and hated by one—the captive.

"I. . . remember," Cormac said.

The Dane frowned, giving ear in silence. Their talk was alien to that which he had been taught, but others among the beliefs he'd held true had been shaken in this company, more than once. *Father Odin. . . will I not dine and drink with you, but return once more in another body to live another life on this same Midgard?* The redbeard looked not

8

happy; one-eyed Allfather Odin made no reply.

"A great enemy and plotter against King Kull," the druid said who had been Tu of Valusia, "was the mage and master of illusion, *Thulsa Doom*. In no less than four plots did Kull foil the wizard and put defeat on him, though in each wise Thulsa Doom prevailed for a time. On two occasions did the king like to lose his life to this unrelenting enemy. And eventually Kull and Tu and a mage on Kull's behalf won the final victory—on the isle where we're just after being."

The others glanced back. But the isle of sorcery-wrought dread and evil, that isle of Kull's sorcerously preserved castle, was long since left behind and lost to sight. Hours ago they had consigned to the sea the comrades they had lost to death there, of the power and plottings of their captive and the iresome illusions he created.

"There Thulsa Doom was left," the druid said, "trapped by sorcerous bonds: the bondage of a body without hands or feet or voice."

"The serpent Cormac slew!" the Dane rumbled. "Four months agone that was, when he and I rescued Samaire from the Norsemen."

Redbearded Dane looked at the red-maned woman he called Samaire. She was in her second decade of life and wore strange tall boots of black leather that rose up her thighs to vanish under her folded tunic. Her long hair gleamed orange and gold in the sunlight.

"And the vanishing?" she asked, this Samaire. "Those several times Thulsa Doom vanished, Bas, whilst we laboured to load our ships, and his disappearing even when impaled?"

"And returned, still impaled," the youngest aboard said, and he glanced at the undying wizard.

The youth sat on a rowing bench, near Cormac. His hair was very fair.

"Of old," Bas the Druid made reply, "Thulsa Doom effected escape into another dimension, a sort of world parallel to ours and not unlike it—and yet *different*. There he is invisible to eyes from this world of ours. Frown on; I can explain no better. This explains his disappearings. He seeks similar escape from us. But his body holds him. Sword driven through him into shield held him ashore, pinioned in the only way he can be held. Even then he took my form, and yours Samaire, and that of a serpent—and aye, he sought escape by disappearing. Was Cormac saw the key to this, holding captive even Thulsa Doom, and thus we must keep him pinned still."

"Forever, if need be," the other Gael muttered.

"He will. . . attempt again?" This from the young man, a youthful weapon-man with flaxen hair and pale eyes.

"Yessssssss," Thulsa Doom hissed in rage, and he vanished from *Quester*.

"He be still here," Cormac son of Art said grimly.

Awestruck silence cloaked the little ship, despite Cormac's words of certainty. The vanished wizard could assume the form of any man he had seen—or woman, as Cormac had learned in a night of horror on the island they'd quitted. Too, they had learned in manner dismaying that he could gain control of the very minds of some, so that they dully carried out his will. Yet none of those now aboard *Quester* had succumbed, though they'd been forced to slay their former companions—which was why only these five survived.

And why had none of them fallen under the illusionist's mind-control, neither Bas the Druid nor Wulfhere the Dane nor Samaire Ceannselaigh nor

10

Brian na Killevy whom Cormac called I-love to-fight?

"Mayhap we were too determined of purpose," Bas said.

"Too staunch," Cormac suggested.

"Too loyal to yourself," Samaire said.

Young Brian nodded, for he adulated the tall and rangy Gael who had been a noble of Connacht in Eirrin, and weapon-man for the King of Leinster though not of age, and then of the King of Dal Riada in Alba when he was exiled from Eirrin's shores, and then riever or reaver: pirate, and then Champion of Eirrin welcomed home by the High-King on Tara Hill and then captain of this expedition on behalf of Samaire and her royal brother; finally it was Cormac mac Art who had somehow conquered the unconquerable, slain again the dead men raised by Thulsa Doom—and at last he had conquered the undying wizard himself.

Brian I-love-to-fight saw Cormac as the man he hoped to emulate though knew he could never equal; Cormac mac Art saw Brian as the youth he had been, before the years had laced him, body and mind, with so many scars. Brian of Killevy was glad and proud to know the man and be in his company, for surely Art's son of Connacht had been Eirrin's great hero of old, the legendary Cuchulain himself of Muirthemne.

Samaire looked asea and pensiveness was on her. Loyal, she had said, but it was more.

Though it was companion she called herself, and weapon-companion to Cormac mac Art she was, she loved the man. Too, she *knew* that the words of Bas were true. Sureness was upon her that she had known Cormac in a life or lives lived out before this one. Though actual memory was not there, certain knowledge was.

Cormac glanced up at the mast. Thulsa Doom was there once more, and the eye-spots in the deeply cratered sockets glowed rage-red. Almost, Cormac smiled. Then he directed his gaze at Bas.

"Bas—what have you done? We've seen your powers prevail over his, in the matter of the wind and clouds. What know ye now that we must needs know?"

Bas's black hair blew in the salted breeze. "I was able to protect us all during our waking hours. And *Quester* and all aboard, despite Thulsa Doom's wizardry. For it's of Eirrin this ship is, and my own powers are strongest on our own soil and with those that were born there, human or no. And. . . there are other things. Let me keep that knowledge. The telling of them will avail ye naught and may weaken me—and empower *him*."

They looked at the death's-head apparition at the mast.

He writhed, snarling.

He did not bleed.

"I will tell ye what I read on the walls of the castle of Kull," Bas the Druid said, and the gazes of his companions returned to him, leaving the wizard's dreadful aspect and plight with more than willingness.

"Those pictures *did* speak, then!" Wulfhere glanced at his longtime weapon-companion and fellow reaver, for Cormac had stared at those thrice-ancient walls as though preternaturally held fast by them. It was then the Gael's *remembering* had come upon him. From time to time, confused and fearful until Bas had made explanation, Cormac mac Art *remembered* events of long, long, incredibly long before his birth.

Before his birth this time, the huge Dane mused, for how could he disbelieve the endless cycle of

12

return, of death and rebirth, in which the sons of Eirrin held belief? Were not they living evidence of that theory alien to the adherents of Odin/Woden and Thor/Thunor?

Aye, and Wulfhere Hausakluifr gave listen to the servant of Behl and Crom of Eirrin. With a great sigh that expanded his chest a prodigious number of inches, the Dane slid a horny fingernail up into his beard. Listening, pondering, Wulfhere scratched at the crust left by sea-breeze and salt spray.

"I read the pictures on the walls," the druid said, "and certain markings. Runes. Some of what I learned I will tell you of, later. But this—this I shall enjoy speaking in *his* presence, that *he* will know we know the means of destroying him. For it's only vengeful and hate-filled I am toward you, Thulsa Doom, who exist only in vengefulness and hate. The wall told of how ye may be slain *again*, Skullface, and permanently."

The death's-head mage snarled like a predatory beast. The teeth of that faceless, skinless skull clashed and ground in frustration and overweening hatred.

"That skull," Bas said, staring not at his companions but at Thulsa Doom, "severed and wrapped in good leather, must be put into the hands of a crownéd woman. She—"

Thulsa Doom writhed and strained and gnashed his teeth with a clack and clash. The ship was suddenly amove, rocking with much noise of slapping sloshing water. Yet the wind had not risen. Such was the fury-heightened strength of the sorcerer from the past. Another sound came from him, a hiss—and an enormous serpent replaced him at the mast.

The reptile sought to writhe and whip and tear itself free of the impaling swords. Cormac came hurriedly to his feet, pulling steel partway from scabbard. But the snake was no more able to escape those bonds like gigantic nails than the man-shape. That form the mage resumed—

And again, Thulsa Doom disappeared.

"It is strange," Brian said, and there was a quaver in his voice he sought to conceal. "In such a short while have I learned to accept the impossible. I do not even gooseflesh now at his vanishing."

The boat lurched so wildly that Samaire slid along the rowing-deck and groaned at the leap of pain in one bruised leg. Cormac staggered. Water splashed high and white. The Gael looked about. The other ship was placid, stirred only by *Quester*'s bucking; there was no wind and the sea lapped softly.

"He is not gone from us," Bas the Druid said.

"A crownéd *woman*, though," Wulfhere said. "Of what value be that information—no such exists!"

"More sorcery," Brian said, little above a whisper.

Bas only looked upon the youth with coolly wide grey eyes. "Will ye hear the rest?"

"We will," Cormac said.

Samaire added, "Please."

"This crownéd woman must then pound the skull into dust, with a hammer of iron."

"Iron?"

"Aye, so I believe the ancient picture-writings tell us. Mayhap there was no steel in the days of Atlantis."

Cormac's face was grim and not hopeful. "But—a crownéd *woman*! Where rules a woman?"

"Nowhere," Samaire said, with a sigh. Her face went reflective.

"Then—"

"Then—" Bas began.

He gave pause at renewed turmoil. Their craft

rocked violently. Water spumed high. The sky seemed to shimmer. When all abated, eyes were fearful and knuckles white from gripping handholds as though to keep from being hurled off the ridge of the world.

Bas commenced anew. "Then we must keep our prisoner, as our duty to all humankind, for dead Thulsa Doom cannot otherwise be slain."

And he was fixedly, madly bent on horrid vengeance against Cormac mac Art—or him he had been in the distant past.

As they sat in tight-lipped silence, the ship on that calm sea rocked as though gale-struck. Groans rose as stomachs seemed to be wrenched, seemed to somersault. Then all was still but for the gentle breeze that swept *Quester* away from Kull's isle they'd named Doom-heim, toward distant Eirrin. Thulsa Doom reappeared, helpless at the mast.

"Da-a-m-m-mnnn ye!" he ground out, and he was still.

Two ships that were in truth long boats slid across the sea in a gentle breeze, bearing history and horror.

The eyes of Bas were signally bright and wide, and he looked skyward. His hands fingered the symbols of his gods and their powers, which were those of nature, like the green of his robe. The others realized that he wrestled now with Thulsa Doom, whose powers were of darkness and illusion, rather than nature and the light.

Then Samaire was calling out. "There was a rocky little island—there! It—it's gone!"

Her companions looked about, and in a babble of voices they agreed. The exiled princess of Leinster was right. The sea had changed; the world had changed. Bas turned from them, paced in his woods-green robe to the wizard.

"May ye be damned! It's again and again ye've tried, tried amain and it's both failure and success ye've grasped, isn't it? Ye did break through into your other dimension—but ye've brought us with ye, into a different world!"

PART ONE

The Isle of Danu

Chapter One:
"I slew Wulfhere years ago!"

The ship wallowed slowly along, towing *Amber Rowan* seaward on a northwesterly bearing, away from the isle of horror and death.

Aboard sat its pitifully tiny crew: a druid in lunula of gold and soiled robe of green; a weapon-woman whose hair blew orange in the sun of autumn, and three weapon-men—one of them but little past his first beard-growth. The woman bore a lurid bruise on one thigh, gained while wielding sword as few women had done.

These were the crew of *Quester*; the passenger stood bound to the mast in the only way he could be held. The picture he presented was monstrous and horrible. The owner of any onlooking eyes not aware of the prisoner's nature and powers would surely have been shocked at the seeming cruelty of his captors.

He writhed, and now and again he complained of cold, the cold of steel blades piercing his body and holding open its wounds.

But he did not bleed.

The lovely little breeze had grown now, riffling the sea and tugging at their hair. *Quester* slid smoothly over the nigh flat plane of the sea. *Amber Rowan* followed like a dog at leash, in turn seeming to lead a long white trail of foam.

The second ship was empty, crewless, of no present value. It only slowed them, and already they had had to swing wide, to avoid the Wind Among the Isles that had once wrecked Cormac and Wulfhere, and to avoid too the isle the Gael had named after the sea-god of his people: the Ire of Manannan Mac Lir. But Wulfhere Skullsplitter and Cormac called *an Cliuin*, the Wolf, had spent long years riding the breast of the sea, a-reaving. Wulfhere was not capable of leaving behind a perfectly good seaworthy craft. Cormac was not capable of leaving behind a perfectly serviceable ship either—unless it was absolutely necessary.

Fortunately, necessity had not risen. An it did, the son of Art hoped with sincerity that the necessity was direfully pressing. Else it was argument there'd be, between impetuous overconfidence heightened by headlong, bulling strength, and the practicality and ever-thinking mind of mac Art. There had been many such arguments. Nor had Cormac always won his way, and he bore scars and the memories of intimate acquaintances with death as mementoes of those times he had yielded to the Dane's boyish inclination to bull forward regardless of odds or terrain.

Now, however, sea and wind were good, Thulsa Doom was their prisoner, and ahead lay the unnamed

19

isle that was their immediate goal.

Cormac well remembered it. Here they had landed to tarry briefly afore, he and Wulfhere and Samaire and her brother Ceann mong Ruadh. As now, there had been then the need to take on water. Wulfhere had groaned when good ale had been emptied from leathern bags that they could be filled with fresh sweet water. Too, it was much in love with personal cleanliness the people of Eirrin were. Samaire and Ceann had insisted on bathing. At that Cormac had groaned—and climbed high to keep watch. Apparently the forested island was unpeopled, and Cormac had taken his turn abathing, whilst Wulfhere kept the needless lookout.

Now, cleverly making use of the wind and daringly defying it all at once, the Dane brought them skimming in to that same paradisic isle. It rode the sea south of Britain like a floating emerald, fragrant and richly green.

Trees still rose high and full-leafed from the high stony banks standing over the water, and birds still sang their joy of the place that seemed made for their kind. Crystal water still tumbled many feet from a pile of steep grey rocks to splash into the little inlet that formed a perfect sheltered harbour. Into it, with an expertise hardly equalled on the Narrow Sea or any other, Wulfhere of the Danes brought *Quester*.

Amber Rowan proved rather more difficult; laughing and splashing despite the horrid presence of their prisoner, they accomplished it.

Wulfhere aided Cormac into his mailcoat while Samaire reminded them both that this green spot on the sea had proved uninhabited. Her own jacket of leathern armour lay on the deck; she wore only a soiled tunic of blue, and the usual boots that rose up under it.

20

Cormac gave her a dark look.

"So was Doom-heim unpeopled," he told her, and he buckled on his sword. He turned to Brian, who had his own coat of small-linked, Eirrin-made chain ready in his hands and was obviously preparing to accompany the man he adulated. Cormac raised a staying hand.

"I will climb up there, above the waterfall, and keep the watch. I have done it here afore. Do you help them take on water, Brian—and bathe."

Brian frowned. He looked up at the tree-crowned cliff, back to Cormac, and glanced at Samaire. Bathe? Three men and a woman?

Cormac smiled. "The matter of bathing here has been accomplished afore, Brian I-love-to-fight. Surely ye can work it out, as we have the matter of answering calls of nature, four men and a woman aboard ship!" Cormac looked at Bas.

"I will remain aboard, with—*him*," the druid said.

With a nod, the Gael turned and made his way to the prow. There he slung his buckler onto his back, girt high his sword, and squatted, measuring distance with his eyes. He sprang several feet onto a shelf of rock that sprouted curling roots like listless serpents. Mail jingling, his buckler thumping his back, he scaled the cliff's face as he had done four months previous. It was not a difficult climb.

Samaire stood watching, shaking her head. Ever the so-cautious and ever-watchful pirate, her dairlin Cormac!

She sighed, watching him with a pensive smile. It was not that she had been instantly attracted to this hardly handsome man, back when she was but a girl and he a boy who concealed his age to fill the role of weapon-man in her father's employ twelve years agone; she had *recognized* him even then, as did those

21

others who liked or loved inexplicably at what they thought of as first sight.

It was first sighting only in this life, this one of many, last but not final in a long line of lives, an unending and unbreakable chain of carnate existences extending into the time that had been and aye, into the time that was yet to be. Samaire *knew;* whether Samaire Ceannselaigh of Leinster had been of Atlantis or Valusia, or indeed had even known this King Kull they spoke of, she was not certain. It mattered not. She was certain that afore now she had known the life-force or soul or *ka* that had been incarnate as Kull, and as Conan, and Cormac, and others between. The when of it was unimportant. The names they'd borne in past lives were unimportant. Now was important. This time, and the time to come, the beyond-Now. Cormac, and Samaire, and Tu, linked across the millennia that sprawled like the star-strewn skies.

Nor did Samaire of Leinster in Eirrin assume that there had been ease or would be; this life-force to which hers was connected throughout time was a key one, a volatile one. And now he was Cormac mac Art, and he was safely up the cliff, this man she loved and had loved—throughout time.

She smiled, and turned to join Wulfhere and Brian in collecting the containers to be filled with that which neither Doom-heim nor the sea offered: clear sweet water for drinking. Only Wulfhere made complaint that waterfalls bore not ale.

The rocky cliff, rearing forty or so feet above water, was so rough of face as to afford easy climbing. Cormac soon scaled it. His breathing was hardly accelerated when he squirmed on his belly over the lip of the cliff and onto level ground. The grass began a few feet away; the trees just beyond. He moved onto the grass and looked down the long incline that was crowded with trees and brush. It swept down and down, into the forest that seemed to cover all the island.

A beautiful place, he mused.

Small, grown up completely in greenery, fine oaks and nut-trees rearing high above lesser neighbours. Perhaps half their leaves had fallen with the onset of autumn, to strew the ground already richly carpeted with grasses, moss, creepers, weeds, bushes, and wildflowers that had long since bloomed and gone to seed. Back in the summer just past, it would have appeared as an enchanted isle of eternal summer, all richly green and colour-splashed by the blooms of weeds and wildflowers.

Now autumn had come, and it was little less beautiful.

Such a land, he thought, to be without people!

Then he saw that he was wrong.

There were people.

He froze, staring, a man who had barely heard the myth of Eden told by the adherents of the Dead God but who stood now overlooking paradise—and discovered the serpent. The humans he saw were engaged in the ugly business of their kind—his kind.

A youthful couple, boy and girl or perhaps young man and woman of small stature, were beset in an oak-bound clearing by four weapon-men. These wore round helmets and armour, two in coats of scalemail and two of leather. One was sword-armed; the other three wielded axes. All bore round shields and all four were bearded with flax or gold. The youths were prey, not opponents, for they were neither armoured nor armed—at least not with steel.

In truth they were doing well for themselves with nought but staves, which they plied with uncommon

23

expertise. An ax flashed at the boy in a great half-circle, missed, and a swiftly plied stave, nigh the height of the youth himself, rushed so that the attacker only just interposed his shield.

The long-haired youngsters defended themselves well—but would of course fall before steel in the hands of skilled, armoured men. Nevertheless, Cormac mac Art set his lips and forced himself to turn his back.

Where there were four of the men of Norge, there were more. Their ship was drawn in somewhere on this island's coast. Perhaps the pair under attack below were escaped captives—temporarily escaped. *They are none of my business or concern.*

He stared down at his own companions. They had nearly finished collecting their water and transferring it onto the long boat that was their ship, and the men were elaborately—and ridiculously—turning their faces seaward. This so that Samaire could bathe. As Cormac looked down, she doffed her last garment and glanced upward. The slim woman waved gaily and flashed him a smile. Then she plunged into the pool to betake herself in under the waterfall. If she had called out, its roar and splash swallowed the words and her voice.

She'll not be tarrying, he mused. *A few hundred heartbeats and it's back on the ship she'll be, swirling her hair in the sun, and the others in the water. Nor is it long they'll be. I'll take no turn; it's dirty and smelly they can accept me! These others. . . this be no fight of mine, no concern. No. And four Norse on this isle means a ship, and that means twoscore and mayhap more, and—we are but five. We have fought enow! We must needs be going on, and about the business of ridding the world forever of Thulsa Doom!*

24

He knew dismay at that thought; ending the menace of an illusion-spinning mage of eighteen thousand years' age were bad enow—but to find a woman who *ruled,* to set him forever at rest—as well seek a serpent amid the green green grass of Eirrin or a shamrock growing from the solid rock of Doom-heim!

He looked all about, with care.

He saw no other ship. Below, Samaire was doubtless splashing and laughing, though the falling water isolated him from sound. No. He'd climb down and tell them now. They'd be off. They'd been at the sword-reddening combat enough and more than enough. An he interfered with the attack of four Norse on seeming innocents, they'd doubtless have then to face the Norsemen's comrades, and surely in overwhelming numbers. Pretty young men had been slain afore ere they'd shaved and sown their seed, in thousands, in millions. Pretty young women with flying hair had been bruised and raped and slain or left moaning and bleeding, time and time again, time without end. It was the way of the world, and its history. It was no business of a harried weapon-man of Eirrin, and him with awful responsibility on him as well as a woman to cherish and watch over.

No. He'd merely not look. One need not have concern over that which one saw not.

Norsemen. . .

It was Norsemen their own brother had intrigued with, to have Samaire and her brother Ceann snatched from Eirrin's own sod. *The bloody dogs would rather leave their cold land and slay and steal than eat!*

Aye and aye, but this time was no concern of his.

Below, Samaire emerged nude and glistening from the pool, her water-darkened hair falling past the middle of her back. Cormac smiled on the whiteness of her buttocks and the jiggle of bare white breasts, but try as he might it was a different urge he felt. He felt the ache in his jaw, too, and heard the gritting of his own teeth.

Deliberately he looked away from Samaire, who waved up to him again.

He looked again inland, down the long green hill.

Axes flashed silvery menace in the sun that struck through half-leaved oaks into the glade. Backward the young man fell, against the base of a great-boled oak, and his quarterstaff dropped from unfeeling hands. He lay still. The young woman, moving lithe as a cat and built with the same economy of bone and flesh, rapped a Norseman's helmeted head with her stave, which she held before her with both hands. She aimed almost instantly at the face of a second with the staff's other end.

Grinning, the four men dropped their steel. Retaining their bucklers in necessary defense, they closed on her. The boy lay still.

Girl or woman, she was valiant and her hair a fine cloak of black spraying out from the yellow band at her nape. Almost, she might have been Samaire in days past. Or Brian's sister of Killevy, if indeed Brian had siblings. Or—

Cormac turned and lunged down. Flat on his belly, he hung his head over the cliff and shouted. His companions did not hear him above the waterfall. At the mast, Thulsa Doom stood like a ghastly statue. In her shift, her hair wrung and close-bunched like a sheaf of gold thread, Samaire looked up. Cormac shouted; he saw her smile and shout in return. He heard only the hint of her voice above the sound of rushing water and its splashing below, sweet water into salt. The men turned, hearing her. Their gazes followed hers upward.

Shoving himself up onto his feet, Cormac drew his sword, pointed inland, and waved sword and buckler.

Cormac turned and plunged down the long green hill, sure his companions had understood his silent message.

He ran as best he could, avoiding trees and berrybushes and entanglements of viny plants. Once he fell, instinctively flailing wide his sword-arm so that he did not come to grief on his own blade. He rolled and slid, grunting. Getting his body turned crosswise to the slope, he stopped himself, lunged cursing to his feet, and hurried on. Behind him the sound of downrushing water dwindled. Now there were only the calls of birds and the wind of his own swift passage.

He heard the girl cry out, for girl he had decided she was, and her so tiny.

A shout from him would cause her attackers to turn from her to face him. Aye. . . and to be thus well prepared for him. *Suffer a bit, girl, and it's of more value I'll be against unarmed men wearing tall horns!*

He ran on in silence, hearing the sound of male laughter and shredding cloth.

So rapt and enwrapt were they in their own lust, laughing and calling encouragement to him who now had their prey down, that none heard either the passage of a rushing man between rustling bushes nor the jingling clink of his mailcoat.

Then the dark man was bursting from the forest into the glade, and one tow-bearded reveler turned in time to see his own coming weird before it was on him in a swift sword-slash that shivered the air and opened his throat and windpipe in a moment. Blood

27

leaped from a severed caratid. The Norseman staggered, his eyes huge, his hand rising ineffectually to his throat. Already his knees were loosening; already his silent rushing attacker was half-whirling to thrust at a second of the pale-haired men of Norge, the one with the dragon knife-etched and red-outlined on his round shield.

Driven by an experienced arm backed by rangy though unusually powerful muscles, the sword of the Gael split apart scalemail links and drove them before his point into the man's belly, nigh the length of a hand. That raider, so far asea on the Viking trail, stopped short, shuddering. His mouth was wide as his eyes. Moving sidewise without interrupting his initial action, Cormac gave his sword a strong twist and a swift tug. It came free, scraping on destroyed scales of steel and followed by a spate of scarlet.

There had been four men of far cold Norge. Now two lay dying quietly, if not silently. There was a moment for Cormac mac Art to scan about, rather than attack as he had, slashing one man blindly and reacting to the movement of the second with the reflexes of a longtime weapon-man.

The slender girl with the long, midnight hair lay on her back, and her skin was much exposed and dark as Cormac's own. Between her thrashing legs, mailcoat and all, lay a man from under whose helmet escaped a single thick braid that was almost yellow. Though she was kicking, writhing, flailing, he was getting his way with weight and strength. Nor could Cormac end that man's efforts and his life; the fourth raider, buckler on right arm, had snatched up ax and was lunging at the Gael. At the same time, he called a warning.

Cormac mac Art had oft avowed that he killed only when necessary. Challenged on the matter of the

28

bloody wake of his past, he admitted that it was often necessary. . . . it was necessary now. Where there were four raiders from the sea, there were others. None of these must go free to warn their fellows, wherever on this small tree-grown island they lurked.

A left-handed foe could be difficult. His disadvantages were his advantages. His shield was on Cormac's shield side, his ax aligned with Cormac's sword. Interpose a shield quickly across the body at his slash, and strike back at—what? Yet there was no time for difficulties and normal circle-and-feint this day. Cormac swung in a way that appeared wild. Nordic eyes gleamed at the invitation, and ax came arushing. The Gael was not there to stop its edge, either with buckler or flesh. He dodged and moved in, swinging his shield over and up to smash the wrist just back of the ax-wielding fist. Then he was past without waiting to watch the ax waver, lower, drop from fingers that flexed open.

The Norseman whirled. Cormac's sword was a streak of silver that lifted the hem of a leathern coat of armour and plunged upward from groin into intestines and the floor of the man's stomach. With the ugly noise of a sick rooster, the raider clutched at himself, bending, bloodying his hand on the skewering blade. The Norseman fell backward off Cormac's point, still staring.

The Gael turned to face the fourth man—their leader of course, as he'd got first turn with the captive. He was up. He had his buckler, and his sword. And he was no small man, crouching so expertly with sword held just so and buckler at the precisely proper height and distance from his body.

Over their shields, the two men stared at each other, the scarred, black-stubbled Gael of Eirrin and the fully bearded blond of Norge.

"Cormac! It's Cormac the Wolf—again! And *here,* both of us far from familiar haunts! Well, Cormac, well. . . it's here you meet your weird, *Skraeling* of Eirrin! It's here I do death on you at last, as I slew your fellow sea-thief Wulfhere of the Danes *years* ago!"

"*Thorleif,*" Cormac said, and he gasped the name.

O gods, would it never end? This was Thorleif Hordi's son, whom Wulfhere had slain years agone, on the isle of Kaldjorn when he and Cormac had been at the matter of regaining the kidnaped sister of Gerinth of Britain.*

"Wulfhere slew *you,* Norseman! Must I spend my life facing dead men risen to challenge me anew?"

A frown darkened the wind-etched face of Hordi's son of Norge.

"It's madness on you in your declining years and last moments of life, Wolf," he said. In a crouch, he twisted his buckler and waggled the powerful wrist of his sword-arm.

Blood of the gods! Cormac's brain lurched. *First it was those illusory men Cutha Atheldane of Norge set against me, in the passage beneath Kull's castle—all men I myself had done death on in years past. Then a fullscore and more dead men, Danes and Norse alike, enemies and former comrades raised by Thulsa Doom's horrid arts in that same castle less than a fortnight agone, and them not to be slain by mere steel. And now it's Thorleif I face—whom Wulfhere slew!*

Will steel prevail this time? Is this some trick of Thulsa Doom who is somehow also Cutha Atheldane? Can I put darkness of death on Thorleif's eyes—again, with point and edge? Or need I mistletoe

---

* See *Tigers of the Sea,* Zebra Books.

and holy oak to lay this life-like lich?

   Or—is it mere illusion?

Thorleif lunged; Cormac dodged and cat-stepped aside without trying a counter-blow. If this were illusion, only the face was; the ringing blow on his shield and the jolt to that arm were real enow!

Thorleif turned, a big man light on his feet, to keep his eyes ever focused on his foe.

"You want this skinny little wench with the darkness of your own hide on her, *Skaeling*? Take her then—you have only to come through me!"

"I wear no horn for her, mad dog—but it's two I'll have, once I've sliced yours off!"

With an enraged cry Thorleif swung; Cormac's buckler took the blow and his point leaped—to thud into the other man's shield and be turned aside with a hideous scraping sound. Prepared to strike again, the Norseman saw his foe's readiness and glittering eyes and thought better of it.

It was then that a slender leg whipped up from the leaf-strewn sward and a bare foot struck flat, hard-driven, into the back of Thorleif's left knee.

The Norse raider lurched, staggered, sagging to leftward, and Cormac stabbed past his shield into Thorleif's armpit. Thorleif gasped loudly, vocally. Gone suddenly all shivery, he tried an offensive swing of his buckler. Cormac was better at it; shield smashed the other man's face and he showed his mercy by ending the Norseman's misery: the point of his glaive leaped through blond beard into throat.

Breathing through his open mouth, Cormac went to one knee to wipe his sword on Thorleif's leggings. The leg twitched. The Gael turned then to the girl for whom he'd acted so foolishly—and who had aided him in turn.

"It's well we team," he said, "and be easy—I seek

31

no strength-taken woman."

She blinked, frowned slightly—as if she did not understand—and then swung her head to her fallen companion. Without reply she went to him.

She was tiny, less than five feet in height, and passing slim as well. Her clothing had been torn away considerably more than half by her assailants, and certain attributes proclaimed her woman, though she appeared just to have come into her nubile days. Yet her startlingly dark eyes said otherwise. Mayhap she was not yet a score of years in age, Cormac mused, but it would not be long ere she observed that birthday.

She went down beside the fallen youth, murmuring. He looked much like her, the Gael saw; her brother, sure, lying asprawl on his back with a bloody gash on the right side of his head. He breathed, and the gash was not deep. Ere Cormac was to them in that glade of corpses, she was away into the edge of the woods, plucking the leaves from plants Cormac did not know.

He looked on while she pressed them to the youth's head, murmuring, and the Gael saw that she knew what she was about. He could not help but note how dusky they both were. Black of hair both were too, like himself, but with a shortness of stature that surely could not mark Gaels. Their skin *could* be the result of much sun. . . but not those raven locks.

The youth groaned, muttered, groaned again, and only her hands stilled the movement of his ax-struck head. Cormac saw his eyelids flickering.

Her rescuer started to touch the girl, decided against it; she'd enough of the hands of strangers this day. "It's no death-wound he's taken," he said, squatting beside that pair of dark slim youths. "Your brother?"

They spoke, both of them, as the young man gained a hold on consciousness and wits. Cormac was startled. He knew now why she had frowned and blinked at his first words; his reaction to hers was the same.

The words they uttered were recognizable, aye, but only just. Different. Old; they spoke in the old way. He had heard the druids pronounce the language of Eirrin in such a wise. They were of Eirrin, but as if from her past, or as if raised apart by some unchanging oldster without ever hearing others speak their tongue.

"It's slowly we must speak," Cormac said, enunciating carefully, with his hand on the boy's arm and his gaze on the girl's great eyes. They were brown as good walnut. Seldom did a man see such eyes, who—what were these people? "Slowly and with care, to understand one another. I am Cormac mac Art of Connacht—and ye be not of Eirrin as well, but know her language."

She gazed long into his eyes, then looked down at her brother.

"He saved us," the youth said. His eyes were brown as good walnut. . .

"We are not enemies," Cormac said, and added, *"tongu do dia toinges mo thuath."*

She looked at him again. She nodded, touched his arm. *"Tongu do Dana',"* she said quietly.

Cormac's eyes narrowed. He had spoken ritual to her: I swear to the god my people swear by. And she had replied that she swore by. . . Danu!

She went on, in her quiet voice, whilst her brother struggled up into a sitting position and looked about the blood-splashed clearing among the oaks. Her name was Sinshi, she told Cormac, and it was a name he had never heard. This her brother was Consaer, and he repeated it after her to be sure. Aye, Consaer. Far more familiar, that; "Con" was a common enough name-sound among the people of Eirrin, with

others, including even Conn, of the Hundred Battles. And "saer" meant wright; carpenter. Yet her accent and inflections and even the turning of some phrases remained unfamiliar, as she told him that she and her brother were of a city or village inland, Daneira. And the eyes and hair. . .

"Of this isle? You are—of this land?"

She nodded. "Aye," she said, and her brother echoed, "Aye."

Cormac started to ask. He gave his head a jerk; questions born of astonishment could wait.

"Then it's to Daneira we'd best be taking Consaer and yourself, for these men from a far land, enemy of mine, cannot be alone on this isle."

Again Sinshi looked nervously at her brother—though her hand remained trustingly on Cormac's wrist. Mayhap it was not a trusting touch at that, the Gael mused; the diminutive hand was after all on his sword arm.

It was then came the great crashing and jingle of mail in the brush to hillward, and even as Cormac sprang backward and up into a fighting stance the bushes burst inward to admit a rushing form to the clearing. A huge man he was, bigger than big and taller than tall, wielding ax and buckler and on him a great lurid beard the colour of dancing flames. Blue eyes darted a swift look about the glade, taking in the four fallen Norsemen. His face went disconsolate.

"Ah, ye gods-abandoned son of an Eirrin pig-farmer," Wulfhere cried accusingly, "could ye not have saved so much as one of these dogs for your old weapon-comrade?"

34

Chapter Two:
The People of Daneira

While Consaer of Daneira both steadied himself and comforted his sister with an arm across the shaky girl's bared shoulders, she pressed close to Cormac. Her small hand remained on his arm. Wulfhere Hausakluifr examined the sprawled Norseman, one

Hausakluifr examined the sprawled Norsemen, one by one. He kept his eyes carefully from Sinshi, who was more than half naked. Then the Dane came to the man last slain.

"Thorleif!"

The Gael nodded, grim-faced. "Aye."

"But . . . Thorleif! Odin's name, I slew the man, Cormac! My ax split this skull to the chin! What Loki-sent horror is this! *More* dead men to fight and slay again?"

"He was very alive, Wulfhere, and vaunting it that it was he slew *you*—years agone, he said."

35

The two men stared frowning at each other. Then of a sudden the answer came to the Gael.

"The—the other 'dimension' Bas spoke of, whatever that means. Thulsa Doom's refuge-world, like ours and yet unlike. . . blood of the gods! Mayhap in this dimension—och, we have much to talk on, and to learn, about this business of being in another dimension."

"What? Think you that here. . . wherever here is. . . things are indeed different? Even the past? Dead men are not?"

"And mayhap living men are, Wulfhere. Consider. It would seem that here, in this . . . world, Thorleif killed *you*, old friend."

"But. . ." Wulfhere broke off, struggling with the concept, visibly worrying it about in a mind that none had deemed overly speedy. "Does this mean . . . " He broke off again. "Could there be. . . have been. . . two of me here? Another Wulfhere Hausakluifr? Another *me*?"

Cormac shook his head. "Who knows? Mayhap Bas can tell us—and mayhap we must learn of ourselves, with time and experiences. But just now, Wulf—it's other matters we must be giving heed to. It's treasure we have on *Quester,* and Thulsa Doom—and were better sure to lose the booty than have *him* loosed again! Only Samaire and Brian and Bas be there with him—and there are Norse about."

"Ye allowed some to escape?"

"I did not. Can ye imagine four alone?"

"Oh. No, no of course not. Ha! Enemies here on *our* island, is it! Well, they'll find no easy road to Thulsa Doom or treasure or even ship!"

The Dane gave his ax such a ferocious sweep that it moaned in the air. Both Sinshi and Consaer drew back. Cormac felt her hand on his arm, suddenly clamping.

"Och, ye bullish madman, Wulfhere! A woman and a druid and a green weapon-man and him not even a Dane? Suppose the Norse discover them now, with you here?"

That ploy was instantly effective. "Aye, But—yourself, shipmate?"

Cormac looked at the youths of Daneira. "Wulfhere, there is mystery here. Let me be going with them. I will join ye soon. Do you remain with the ship."

"Mystery? Hmp! Cormac, Cormac. The mystery is how she stands before the breeze, and her with so little womanly meat on her."

Cormac gave him a look and spoke with his lips tightly together. "It is not, Wulf, this girl."

"I know." Wulfhere looked down and heaved a sigh. "I know, blood-brother. It's just the prospect of climbing this accursed hill I descended for naught that makes me more than hesitant."

"And surly."

"Aye. Ye've noted how much longer hills are when one is climbing than when one is coming down?"

"Why—it's scant attention I've paid, Wulfhere. Could it be age coming upon ye, man?"

Wulfhere stiffened, stared, turned with dignity, and re-entered the woods on the hill side of the glade. Cormac heard him muttering. So were Sinshi and Consaer; they were struck by the colour of Wulfhere's hair.

Cormac considered the corpses; he decided it were better to gain Daneira swiftly than to attempt to conceal the Norsemen and all signs of their deaths. One trace of blood, found on a blade of grass, would set off a thorough search by their comrades. The people of Daneira could come and dispose of these, later; at present his efforts were better spent getting to them with the warning of danger he and these two would bear.

"Your people have armour? Where are your daggers? Swords?"

She looked at him with large eyes of soft dark doe-brown, and her voice was soft, gentle as that of a frightened or chastised child.

"We have no need, Cormac mac Art." She was staring—at his eyes. Were grey eyes as unusual to her as her brown glims were to him?

"No *need*—Blood of the gods! But you must have *axes*."

"My sister and I were not on a woodcutting expedition, Cormac mac Art."

Cormac clamped his teeth in exasperation. Consaer, asking his sister for help in drawing his tunic up over his head, started to undress. Already nonplussed, Cormac for a moment thought they must both be insane. Then he realized that the lad meant to clothe his sister's near-nudity in his own garment.

"And then we can strip off at least one of these leathern coats for you, Consaer," he said, indicating the bodies.

The youth chuckled. His tunic came off to reveal a lean dusky torso, with long stringy muscles that Cormac knew held considerable strength, if only the fellow were not so little above five and a half feet in height.

"I'd not wear such clothing of such men," Consaer said, and he had to repeat it ere Cormac understood, for the Daneiran youth had forgot to speak with slow care against the difference in their accents and phrasing. "And what fits any of them would be far too large, anyhow." He slapped his leg.

"These leggings are leather, Cormac mac Art. I need no tunic—and Sinshi does."

Hardly, Cormac thought, but he held silent with only a nod.

His sword sheathed, he gathered the Norsemen's bucklers and burdened Sinshi with them, once she was enveloped in her brother's tunic; he was both bigger built and a full eight inches taller than she. An ax the Gael handed to Consaer, who was none so steady on his feet and showed by little winces and the way he held his gashed head that it was a-throb. Cormac carried the other two axes and Thorleif's sword, with five daggers in their sheaths fastened to his belt.

Lead me to Daneira. At least four of your people will have shields, and decent weapons. These."

Consaer and Sinshi but looked at him, whether in pity or incomprehension he could not be certain. Without speaking, they entered the woods. Long black hair trembled and swung down their backs. Cormac followed, but not too close, that there would be space for maneuvering if there was need. About them rose lofty trees in grey and black. A few leaves were green; most were the colourful hues of autumn. No one had ever swung ax here, Cormac knew. Insects flitted and buzzed; birds called and trilled and warbled—and now and again fluttered in bushes so that Cormac looked sharply that way.

He asked; no, there were no animals on this island, save those brought with them here by the Daneirans long and long ago; pigs and goats and sheep, for meat and milk, fleece and silky hair, and hides.

Paradise!

Cormac could hardly believe it. Serpents? Aye, they made reply, there were reptiles . . . though throughout all the history of Daneira none had got

39

his death from a serpent's bite. Cormac could but shake his head. Paradise! The enchanted land of a chosen people!

Aye. An innocent and naif people, menaced by naught and thus unprepared for any menace; open to attack, the perfect prey for a score or two Norsemen unimpressed with gentle people living in idyllic circumstances. There would be no battle. There would be rape and butchery, and none left to know or to keen the red death of Daneira and its gentle people.

Possibly the Daneirans had naught worth coveting or stealing—save the isle itself and their very existence, their lives. No matter to the men of Norge! Their god was War; their gods were warriors. He who was chief among those nigh-guileless warrior-deities had but one eye and hurled lightning, while his simple-minded son used his hammer to create the thunder. He who was most intelligent among them was the villainous and crafty Loki, loved by none. Once the men of ice-ruled Norge got their crops out in the short growing season, they deserted their steadings, leaving the work of growing food to their women and children and oldsters. The younger men fared forth in ships laden with arms to go a-viking: a-reaving; a-killing.

For such, Cormac thought grimly, the Daneirans had enough of value: flesh for the cutting and buildings for the burning . . . and women and girls.

Following the weaponless, armour-less pair of sheep for Norse slaughterers, Cormac gritted his teeth. He should have stayed away. Did such foolish people deserve aid, rescue?

A short distance into the wood, the trio came onto a clear and well-trod trail, and Cormac realized how woods-wise were Sinshi and her brother. They went swiftly then, the youths in soft buskins and he bare above the waist—aye, and reeling a bit from the wound in his head. Cormac followed cautiously, alertly, marveling at people who were not cautious because they'd never been so—because they'd never had reason to be cautious or alert!

No beasts, he thought. *No enemies. No swords!*

They wended through the woods, two sheep and a wolf who trod a carpet of leaves in orange and yellow and scarlet, and Cormac wondered whether he felt pity for them—or envy. As for them—what felt they for him, a scarred and blood-splashed man of weapons who clinked when he walked for he wore steel, and whose narrowed eyes were constantly amove, seeking an enemy not there?

Cormac did not know. He could not imagine their lives. His had been a life of arms and combat, all his days. It seemed that he had been born with sword to hand.

In the time when Laegair's son Lugaid was High-king in Eirrin, Art mac Comail was a member of the powerless bear sept of the clan na Morna of Connacht, though he was kinsman of the *ua-Neill,* the descendants of that great Niall, High-king. This same Art got a child on his wife, and it was a son. Cormac remembered Art's telling him of his name.

"He was the greatest king that Eirrin ever knew," the boy's father told him, of that son of King Art the Lonely of a time long gone by. "In power and eloquence, in the vigour and splendour of his reign, he has not had his like before or since. In his reign none needed bar the door, no flocks need be guarded, nor was anyone in all Eirrin distressed for want of food or clothing. For all Eirrin that wise and just king made a beautiful land of promise. His grandfather was Conn of the Hundred Battles; his father was Art the Lonely; he was King Cormac. Like you, son, for I have given you the greatest name in the history of our land: Cormac mac Art.''

The training of mind and body of that second Cormac, son of Art, began almost at his birth.

It was a proud name he bore—and it was the undoing both of himself and his father. For it made even more nervous the *Ard-righ* or High-king who sat his throne at Tara Hill with the shakiness of fear on him, for he ruled ever fearful of being toppled and slain. And Cormac mac Art was a magic name. And so mysterious death had come upon Art of Connacht, and his son had fled lest he suffer that same fate. Too, he concealed his great name.

Though far too young for the skill he had with arms, he was tall and strong for his age so that he could pass for one older. As "Partha mac Othna," of Ulahd, he betook himself to Leinster. There, concealing age and name, he was employed as weapon-man in the service of the king.

Eirrin's High-king was no emperor. Each kingdom ruled itself. Nor was the kingdom of Leinster a friend to its northerly neighbour Meath, where rose Tara, the Seat of Kings over Kings. Partha mac Othna served well and distinguished himself, and was given command—which gained him enemies, envious men. As none knew his age, none knew of his trysts with a girl who was his first love and he hers—Samaire, daughter of the king in Leinster.

Too well did "Partha" distinguish himself, and it was both Leinster's monarch and High-king Lugaid did treachery on him. Was they saw that he was goaded until he slew a man at Fair-time, when the Peace of the King prevailed. Having broken that peace by doing arms-death, Partha/Cormac had no defense and no choice: he must die.

Again Cormac fled.

An exile from Connacht he had been; now he was exiled from all Eirrin, where among his ancestors had been rulers.

Northward on the Plain of the Sea he made his way, to Alba, land of the Scoti and the Picts. There he found employment on a farm—until there came a Pictish attack. His weaponish skills then showed themselves to the astonishment of all—and to the consternation and death of the attackers. Having thus betrayed his skills, he was recruited into the service of the king of Dal Riada of Alba or Scot-land. Again he fared well and distinguished himself—too well. Again was treachery done on him, and again by a crowned man, his own king. Betrayed to the Picts, he languished in a cold and filthy cell, an object of hatred and mockery. Nor was he fed; he was to die, and slowly.

He survived only because of a Pictish woman who had recently been bereft of both husband and babe; she gave him nourishment as only she could.

Eventually, Cormac mac Art escaped.

Alienated, hating kings and trusting none, he took up his career as a reaver or pirate of the Narrow Sea. Right well the well-born exile of Eirrin fared at piracy, with his own ship and his own crew. Yet there was that he would not do: never did he raid the shores or ships of Eirrin.

Time came when he was captured—and this time, flung into a cell even more cold and more filthy, he had a companion. The other's name was Wulfhere, and he was a giant even among the tall Danes. Each was the only companion available to the other, the only voice and listening ears; they became friends. To him Cormac lied about his age. Wulfhere Splitter of Skulls was older, and must not know how young was this stout weapon-man whose brain was so keen and whose counsel so wise that Wulfhere gave listen, and was guided by it. It would never have occurred to Wulfhere to keep back a bit of their meagre food, that they might use it to lure and entrap more food: the rats of that prison in which they were to die. Thus they kept up their strength, though their warders knew not.

It was bloody their escape was, and not long after the two were again asea. Both joined the crew of a renegade Dane, a-reaving.

Their ship streamed a wake of blood, for their captain feared nothing and raided the shores of Britain and Alba as well. Nor could he listen to counsel, and he got his death in Britain of that arrogance and stupidity. Indeed it was the skill and wiles of Cormac and Wulfhere enabled the others to escape, and all knew it. Natheless the dead captain's second took command, and him a man of foul disposition who showed considerably less than gratitude or respect to the two best among them, the Gael and the giant Dane.

It was Wulfhere slew that abominable man a few months later. A fair fight it was, and the dead man loved by none, and Wulfhere Hausakluffr was captain. He was counseled by his friend from Eirrin, and his so dark and scarred and dour, a man whose life had been laid out for him by the treachery of kings and whose scars went all the way in, to the brain.

They two achieved a measure of fame, and infamy. Their ship was everywhere and undefeatable. Years passed, with them friend to few and feared by many. Yet they achieved no wealth and saved little. It was the weather itself, the wrath of Eirrin's seagod Manannan mac Lir, that defeated them. Thus were they swept ashore on that nameless isle whereon they found Kull's castle, sorcerously standing intact after so many millennia, now the keep for booty-storing of a band of renegade Norsemen.

And there was more slaying to be done.

There too, after so many years, Cormac found Samaire and Ceann her brother. Both were victims of the treachery of a king—their own older brother. Cormac and Wulfhere, with those few of their crew who had survived the wrath of Manannan, freed the two of Leinster from their Norse captors. It was Samaire who persuaded Cormac to return to Eirrin—and that only at night, apart from the others.

Long months later, having trekked across half of Eirrin and fought his way through Picts and highwaymen so that his exploits gave rise to legends, Cormac reached Tara in Meath.

By dint of arms at Fair-time, he won the title Champion of Eirrin—though under a false name. It was after that series of contests that he announced his true identity, before the great triennial meeting of all the kings of Eirrin. He was Champion; he had slain the highwaymen of Brosna Wood on whose hands was the blood of many; he had saved a fisherman and his family and doubtless others from a Pictish attack, so that none survived. (And in all these adventures had Samaire wielded arms alongside him). Yet death was demanded on that old charge—by Feredach, king in Leinster, the older brother of Samaire and Ceann. Despite him, Cormac was offered a single chance to save his own life, to prove his worthiness to the god Behl. He accepted instantly.

Under his own name at last, Cormac mac Art survived with honour the Trials for Him Who would be of the Fiann—though both a druidic mage—of Leinster—and two hired killers—of Leinster—

attempted to slay him while he was unarmed and unsuspecting. And after twelve years he was Champion of Eirrin, and pronounced free and welcome both by High-king and druidic council—for the latter said that by passing the Tests of Finn he had been exonerated and welcomed by Behl of the sun, Himself.

Cormac soon interrupted his rest and his basking in the light of fame. With Samaire and Bas and an Eirrin-born crew, he returned to the isle of Kull. They would simply pick up all that Norse booty and return to Eirrin—to finance the maneuverings of Ceann and Samaire against their ruling brother—who had got the throne by the murder of his older brother. The isle they called Samaire-heim, of Wulfhere's gallant naming.

It became Doom-heim, for there Thulsa Doom awaited, plotting blackest vengeance on him he knew to be Kull reborn.

During that time, so recently past, Cormac knew horror unequalled even in his extraordinary life. And more blood flowed. And eventually they had escaped, so few now of the two ships' crews that had fared to the awful isle of bare stone. Now he was come here, to this tiny island of green and peace, for water—and once again Cormac had reddened his sword and added more deaths to his list of deeds.

Aye, was true; Cormac mac Art said that one should never kill save when it was necessary. And aye, it was distressingly true that in his thrice-hard life it had often been necessary that he deal death—lest it be dealt him.

He followed the lambish siblings he had rescued. Understand them? Understand Daneirans, conceive of Daneira and those who walked without wariness and caution and without weapons? Cormac mac Art

46

could not, and it was no happy man who followed the long black hair of Consaer and Sinshi through the forest.

They came to Daneira.

First there was a vast sprawling field that had borne corn and flax. In a huge sickle-shape it was laid out, connecting far ahead of Cormac to a tall and steep hill. At its base lay Daneira, a sprawling town all of wood. It appeared to have grown naturally there, among trees grown up over the years or left standing long ago. The hill backed the village; to its left a stream ran, coming down and around the hill and burbling off into the woods that, apparently, otherwise covered the island. The land across the stream had been cleared but for a few spaced trees; there these people had their gardens.

No wall or even palisade enclosed Daneira. It was open to the breeze and the sun—and to attack, Cormac mused grimly. The only enclosures were for the animals they kept, and these Sinshi told him were pastured on around the hill, which was mostly rock and scrub behind the village.

Strange, Cormac mac Art thought; there were no dogs. Nor saw he either cats or fowls. Well inland these people had laid out their settlement, though surely some trekked to the sea to fish, and mayhap others brought down birds in the forest. And gathered birds' eggs?

Sinshi and Consaer had thrown him constant glances, all along the way. Now all stared at the approaching trio—at the tall man in mail.

Daneira, Cormac saw, was beautiful. It gave pleasure just from the looking on it. The buildings were beautiful, superbly constructed with never a nail, and intricately adorned with carvings and with shells, with enamels and paints that were bright and

47

bespoke happy people. He recognized the style and pattern of the decor, but only from relics of Eirrin's distant past and on weathered rocks. How long had Daneira been here? Had there been no influx, no newcomers at all to bring trouble or new ideas, decorations, tools?.

He saw naught that resembled weapons.

The people stared. They were small, no man above five and three quarters feet in height and most nearer five and a half. Black or dark brown was the hair of all, *all,* and brown or seemingly black their eyes, while their skin was as if deeply tanned. Aye, Consaer and Sinshi were typical. Could they be of Rome? Surely not Gaels, with their dark soft eyes. The Daneirans stared in silence at the tall man with his deepset pale eyes and his twinkling metal clothing. Aye, for there was no armour, though he saw leather aplenty; this was not armour but superbly tanned, softened hides of their goats and their sheep and their pigs. Feathers he saw, worn as decoration, and shells and crafted things, and dyed wool and flaxen linen coloured in hues drawn from sea creatures and the plants of the woods, pleated and wrinkled.

The people of Daneira seemed healthy enough, and happy as well, though it was hard to be sure of the latter; all froze to stare at the clinking stranger whose coat and helm and burden of axes caught the sun's light.

Daneira was small. Less than a thousand people were here, all of one race and looking indeed as if sprung from a single family, one dusky, brown-eyed family whose hair ranged in hue from blackest night to medium brown. Oh, and aye—all were short of leg and unusually long of face.

The houses were sizable all, not peasantish or skimped in construction or, presumably, in inner space. He saw new decor, but no new homes. How long had the population been stable or declining? He had no idea. Of the answers to many questions concerning these people, he had no idea.

Consaer and Sinshi led the Gael—the *only* Gael, as there were no Germanic peoples or fair Celts—to one of the homes. A murmurous crowd followed, staring but without clamour. A calm, complacent folk.

A man in a long blue tunic, without leggings, came hurrying and intersected their course as they reached the house. Cormac saw swiftly that this was a physician, concerned with the wound to Consaer's head. Dark hair, dark skin, dark eyes. He entered the house of blue and green and brown with them, onto flooring that was gleaming, finely fitted hardwood planking strewn with rugs of dyed sheepskin and one that was intricately woven of coloured woolen yarn. A warm home it was, to mind and body both, with gourd-pots and pottery pans and a lute or something similar, a set of pipes, and various other utensils of the household of a farmer who was not starving.

Cormac mac Art saw no weapons, no armour.

The ax within the door was long of handle—a woodsman's tool. There were other such tools, on nicely wrought and braced shelves.

The stranger with the odd grey eyes was welcomed by parents and the brother of Consaer and Sinshi, while the physician sat Consaer down and examined him. After congratulating Sinshi on her swift application of the proper herbs, he applied more, and a thick oil of some sort. Consaer's younger brother Lugh helped him press together the edges of the wound and wrap his head tightly, around and around, with a cloth of undyed linen. Sinshi meanwhile vanished through a doorway into one of the house's two other rooms.

49

Duach and his wife Elathu were neither ruddy nor fat, and it occurred to Cormac that he had seen no truly fat people among all the villagers. Too, most of these people's longish faces held an elfin or birdlike quality, with no fleshy deposits lying beneath the skin, so that it was stretched directly over the bone. No one was round of face, or square either, like some of the blond northerners.

"You have saved my son and daughter from death and worse, Cormac mac Art," Duach told him, a short rangy man with a beard of black-shot auburn. "Anything that is Duach Fedach's son is yours." His brown eyes unashamedly aglisten with tears, Duach son of Fedach of Daneira swept his arm in a gesture that included all his household.

"I would ask naught in recompense, Duach mac Fedach," Cormac said. "But I would beg that which ye have that I've tasted not in many, many days—I see milk and I smell roasted pork."

A hand came onto his arm then, a small hand whose skin was cooler than his, though of the same hue. Large walnut eyes looked up into his face from a pretty elfin visage in which the bone structure was unusually defined, even among the Daneirans. Already Sinshi was back from another room, having changed from her brother's tunic into one of her own, blue linen over a pair of russet leggings of leather so soft it looked like wool. The girl was lovely, pretty as a tiny and fragile woods-flower.

"Sit, Cormac mac Art who saved me. I will serve you milk of the freshest and pork enow for ten, and be the milk not fresh I shall go and coax more from one of the goats, for we have seven!"

He caught the emphasis, and knew that Sinshi spoke with pride. In Eirrin, wealth had long been measured in cattle. Here, he realized, it was goats.

50

Though seven was hardly a herd for the bragging of.

"It's happy I'll be with it, Sinshi, freshest or no, for I'm long without: Duach," he said, instantly shifting his gaze to her father and dropping his pleasant expression. "Daneira is in danger, all Daneirans. Aye, and goats and sheep and hogs. Those men who attacked yours and whom I slew—they cannot have come here alone. Your people must prepare."

Duach looked uncomprehending—or as if he thought Cormac did not understand. "We have seen none from outside but yourself, Cormac mac Art, not in any lifetime or in my father's. Never have I seen such eyes, the colour of steel. We will offer these men what we have—food and drink. There is naught else, and what more can they want or ask?"

Cormac felt desperation on him. It was as if he talked to a child—no, for even a child knew of danger. . . except on Daneira.

"Duach," he remonstrated, "these are *Norsemen*, my friend, and them on the viking trail!"·

For a long moment Duach was silent, gazing curiously into the excited eyes of the other man. At last, he spoke. "What are Norsemen?"

Chapter Three:
The Wizard of Daneira

Cormac stared at the father of Consaer and Sinshi, and Duach Fedach's son gazed mildly back into the dark, scarred face.

"What are Nor—blood of the gods, man! I answer Daneira? Your life, Duach! Your wife and your daughter! It's savages we talk about, man!"

Duach gazed at him, having merely blinked. He could no more understand the concept than Cormac mac Art could understand Daneira and Daneirans. Close to hand, Sinshi bustled, with many glances from her pretty elfin face at her tall savior, the strange, sky-eyed man in the steel coat who stared speechless at her father.

It was then that another came to the house of Duach.

A very old man, he was deferentially welcomed and bade to enter. Like snow was his plaited beard, and his scalp was nigh onto hairless, shiny and deeply tan. The staff he bore was capped by a moon-sign of considerable age. Cormac's eyes widened at sight of that gold emblem, for it was like unto a bow, the old man's moon-sign. Cormac knew it but hazily; it was the ancient symbol of a goddess few thought of in Eirrin. Dana or Danu her name, she whose people were in Eirrin long before the Celts came—for what many said was the second time, after a thousand years—the bow because in addition to her being moon-connected mother goddess, she was warrior as well, remembered among Cormac's people only as the Morrighan. The Morrighan was believed in, and spoke of—but none worshiped her on her moon-mother identity. It was the goddess Bridgid that had supplanted her, and who was herself worshiped in Eirrin long before that silly follower of Padraigh and the Dead God, Bridget the Gentle, called "Saint."

Cormac marveled. As astounding were the old man's clothes: he wore a robe of leaves of the forest, all shiningly enameled so that they made little clacking noises when he moved. Shown much deference, he accepted it with grace, in a manner clearly accustomed. After a glance about the main room of Duach's home, he came to Cormac.

For some time he but stood there, gazing with fascination into the Gael's icy steel eyes. Then, the old man spoke.

"You have come to our city from outside to save two of ours from other outsiders, tall man. Ye came here not with those who attacked Consaer and Sinshi?"

Cormac thought: *City!* But his inner smile did not show when he said, "No. They are of the Norse,

53

from a far land called Norge. Ye know them not?"

The old man shook his head. His almost black eyes swiveled their gaze on Sinshi, who had come to stand close beside the Gael—and to cling to his arm. "No. And yourself?"

"It's Cormac I am, son of Art of Connacht, in Eirrin—a Gael."

"Eiru? With that hair and skin? But ye be no Celt—ah! It's our blood ye bear! I do have knowledge on me of your kind. A Gael—the dark Celts."

Cormac showed the oldster a wintry almost-smile. He thought of the fair-haired, fair-skinned Celts of Eirrin as pale Gaels.

"Aye," Cormac said, for it was politick. What meant the oldster, "*our* blood"? Too, it was disturbing that it was his right arm to which the girl clung, for what knew these naif, unmenaced people of a weapon-man's discomfort when his sword-arm was not free?

"Cormac?"

Her voice was soft and tiny, gentle as a spring zephyr that hardly riffles the new leaves. He looked down into her upturned face, and thought anew that she was less a child than he'd first thought. Those clever, womanish eyes. . . calculating? She handed him goat's milk, in a beautifully wrought and intricately carved goblet of smoothly polished wood. The symbols with which it was indited were not familiar to him.

"With thanks, Sinshi—and it's begging you I am not to hang on my. . . drinking arm."

"Oh!"

With a contrite look, she released him—and immediately transferred her small self and her grasp to his left forearm. Cormac curbed his sigh and

54

accepted what had become the inevitable and unavoidable. But now he would not drink, in the presence of so respected a man as the bald oldster with the plaited beard and lively eyes dark as peat-bogs.

Cormac returned full attention to the old man, who was staring at him. There was much quickness and intelligence in those old eyes; they seemed to sparkle with life.

"These Norsemen, Gael of Eirrin. What sought they?"

"That which they will seek here, in far greater quantity. It is their way. They sought Consaer's life and Sinshi's body."

The words were brittle and ugly, and so Cormac intended them. *Someone* had to be shocked into belief, into fear or anger or both, and this man was manifestly a respected leader—a priest, likely.

"They carry axes," Cormac said into the silence. "They are short of haft and slim of blade, for they are not for the chopping of wood, but of flesh and bone. They carry swords, and they wear metal as I do, or leather with padding beneath and the leather itself hardened as armour against blades. Like those," he said indicating the Norse blades he'd brought, "and this."

With his left hand he plucked a Norse dagger from his belt, showed it to the leaf-robed man. The latter only glanced at it.

"And their hair is *pale!*" Sinshi put in, as though that were all that was different about those who'd sought her rape.

"Not a flensing blade," Cormac said desperately. "Not a skinning blade, or one for the scraping of vegetable skins or animal hide either. This is for killing, for murder."

The man of Danu looked more doubtful than affrighted. "Ah. Never have I seen such men. But. . . my mentor passed on to me a story of such. I had nigh forgot: there's been no need to remember. Such men came here once, pale-haired men wearing tunics that clinked and carrying axes not for the chopping of wood. They slew. Aye—they slew even goats, my mentor told me." He shook his head. "For no reason."

"But Daneira is here," Cormac said swiftly. "The Norse were repulsed then, driven off. You—may I be knowing your name, father?"

"I am Cathbadh."

That was all; this man stood high, Cormac knew, and needed no other. Too old and too well known on his own reputation was Cathbadh to bother appending the name of his father to his own.

"It is Cathbadh who makes thanks to ye, Cormac, for the saving of Consaer and this nubile girl, so valuable to our people. And now—"

Cormac interrupted in growing frustration. "Cathbadh! Cathbadh, servant of Danu whom Eirrin's all but forgot—it's responsibility ye have here. Ye must prepare! Daneira has not so much even as a wall—Daneira must prepare. The Norsemen—"

From outside, a shriek arose in interruption, and then other cries.

The Norsemen had come to Daneira.

More cries rose from the other end of the sprawling lovely village of complacence, and they spread. Shrieks and screams and yells of warning and horror seemed to move closer. Grey eyes flashing like a lightning-lit sky, Cormac seized Cathbadh by both shoulders. His sudden movement hurled Sinshi's hand from his arm, and the fine goblet of polished wood went rolling over a sheepskin rug tinted a deep red. Rich yellow milk splashed.

"Cathbadh! They are come! They will rape, and slay and slay, and it's your homes they'll be burning. Believe me man, I know! Your men who hew trees in the forest must come with their axes, and those who spear fish, if there are such here. I cannot defeat a shipload of Norsemen alone!"

Releasing the man, Cormac whirled to the door and stepped outside. From there, hardly aware of the small hand that almost instantly closed on his arm—his left arm—he stared the length of Daneira, at the invaders.

Not a mere score was their number, but nigh onto twice as many.

They were tall, grimly warlike men of frostbit Norge, who paused just within the village perimeter, staring about at the strangeness of its buildings and its people. Axes and shield-bosses glinted with sinister flashes. Cormac saw a blooded ax, another. Aye, and already there were captives, a girl squirming by her hair in that man's big red-furred paw, her clothing torn to the waist, a young boy tugging at the grip around his wrist, the grip of a captor who hardly noted his struggles. A child of eleven or twelve squealed for her mother, for she too was held by the hair and tugged this way and that to keep her off-balance. A woman ran toward her, dark hair streaming and arms outstretched, and was struck easily away by a negligently flicked shield. One Norseman broke from the group to rush a house on the outskirts, and returned grinning, dragging a shrieking young woman by the ankle.

Cormac's teeth gritted and he snarled. He was but one; they were nigh twoscore. What could he possibly do? And these Daneirans—he had found the complacently peaceful, childlike refugees from old Eirrin just in time to witness their removal from the earth—and to share it.

A bony hand fell on his shoulder, and he felt its strength through his mail.

"Do not move or speak, Cormac," Cathbadh's voice said, with a surprising firmness.

He moved past the Gael, out into the village. Trembling like a leashed hound, Cormac watched the old man in his weird robe, enameled leaves flashing, as he paced a few steps toward the invaders. Still they remained paused, poised, staring, unable to believe that none fled or came banding with arms. Cathbadh's staff with its golden three-quarter moon bobbed along, carried in his right hand and pacing his left foot.

He stopped. His voice carried well. Every gaze was on him, Norse and Daneiran—and the single set of grey Gaelic eyes.

"I am Cathbadh, servant of Danu and protector of Daneira. Why have ye come to Daneira?"

The Norsemen looked at each other. One stepped forward, spoke to their leader. Cormac wondered; had Thorleif been their leader afore? This new man, his beard the colour of cheese, gave listen to his companion, and then he laughed. Laughing, he pointed at the old man who stood alone in the center of the village's main open area. He bawled out words, in his own language.

"He sneers," Cormac muttered. "He says that—"

But the man beside the Norse leader was interpreting, grinning, yelling out the words in staggering Gaelic.

"Protector? A spindly man with beard like the mountaintop snows? We spit on you, protector of Danererr. We spit on Danu, whatever that be! The

Norsemen have come to you, *Protector* of Danererr, the men of Thorleif and Snorri."

He gestured at the cheesebeard beside him, and that man braced his legs well apart and planted both hands on his hips. He looked upon Cathbadh as only a powerful and self-sure young weapon-man with no respect on him can stare at the old and helpless.

"We have eyes," Cathbadh called back. "We see the men of. . . Shorleaf and Snoaree. We beg you to beware Danu—and we ask what it is you would have of us?"

A swift brief conference, and Snorri's Gaelic-speaking lieutenant bawled back a single word.

"Everything!"

Snorri spoke more; the other man shouted his bad Gaelic. "We would have of Danererr all its gold and jewels, and its best food, and all its arms—and all its WOMEN-N-N!"

At that last bellowed word, the men of Thorleif and Snorri called out their echoes and their ayes, waving their axes and beating upon their shields. He who had fetched the blue-tunicked young woman from her very home hauled her to him by her ankle, rested his ax-haft against his calf whilst he grasped her between the legs. She cried out. From her home, a child screamed. Then a man came running, yelling hoarsely, his unbound hair streaming out behind. He waved both arms; in one hand was a quarterstaff. Two men he passed at the run on his way to his wife or sister, and the second swung his ax after him so that he bent in an impossible way ere he slid from the steel and lay on the ground. He did not so much as jerk with his back and vertebral tree and every nerve destroyed, but lay absolutely still.

Now it was Cathbadh who roared out one word, while he held his staff braced horizontally before him with both hands.

"GO!"

"Blood of the gods!" Cormac gritted, through clenched teeth. "Crom's beard—a city of children with a madman as father! Let—go—me, girl, it's my buckler I must have on this arm—ah gods, the filthy bloodhanded bastard!"

The invaders' shock at Cathbadh's incredible command, the roar of a wolf without teeth, lasted but a few seconds. As Cormac jerked at Sinshi, who gripped his arm now with both hands, the man who held the child by her hair lifted her until her little feet left the ground and her eyes bulged. In one perfectly calculated sweep then he sheared her head from her body. His ax swept through, clear, hardly blooded by the swiftness of its slicing. The girl's head remained dangling by its black sheaf of hair from his fist, enormous eyes staring: the pitiful little corpse dropped to the ground with blood fountaining from between headless shoulders.

Sinshi clung, weeping. . . Cormac started forward, dragging out his sword, lifting his unshielded left arm to hurl the girl from him. . . Cathbadh cried out and raised his face and staff to the sky, calling out words in a language Cormac had never heard. . .

And a streak of flame leaped up from the ground, all at once in a line across the village just before the Norse.

Even as they cried out and drew back, the yellow fire sprang up into a wall of dancing red and gold and orange. . . and *extended itself,* racing along the ground like two serpents that swept about either flank of the massed invaders. As that line rushed to encircle them, it grew swiftly up to form a wall, whipping around to encompass the yelling Norsemen as if it were a sentient creature, a live creature with a brain and purpose, an encircling serpent of living dancing licking flame—that made no sound.

The flame closed its circle. The Norsemen were prisoners within a ring of fire that danced up to twice the height of a man. It became an inferno.

Cormac stood trembling and staring, Sinshi hugging him, her face averted and pressed to him. Within the ring of awful flame there were shouts and shrieks, ghastly cries of horror and panic and suffering. A Norseman burst through, a falsetto-shrieking apparition with flaming hair and legs. Delirious in a frenzy of pain, he ran staggering, blinded, up the center of the village toward Cathbadh. The protector of Daneira stood unseeing; he stared at the sky, a seeming statue with uplifted staff. The gold Moonbow at its end flashed like fire.

Heedless of her falling, Cormac wrenched free of Sinshi. He ran straight at Cathbadh's back, and past that living statue, at a dead run. He did not hear his cry; did not feel his arm when it drove his sword forward. A few feet in front of the wizard, Cormac took considerable pleasure in putting the fiery Norseman out of the misery no man should have to endure.

Like all others then, Cormac stared at the awful circle of fire.

The flames roared now, bellowed, and sprang higher, tall as the trees of the forest. The cries from within lessened in number and volume. The nauseous odour of burning cloth and meat drifted over Daneira, and Cormac heard wretching. His own belly heaved and rumbled and he was glad he'd had no time to partake of food.

The flames leaped, trembled, seemed to execute a ghastly dance of death, appeared to flow like some horrid liquid in halfscore everchanging hues. The constant roar of well-fed inferno rose to the sound of booming surf, of steady thunder closeby. Now no cries came from within the fiery circle. Silent too was the grim statue that was Cathbadh, his robe of enameled autumn leaves no longer ludicrous, but a symbol both of life and of death-dealing flame.

The old man stood silently, rigidly, and Cormac saw that he quivered all over in his stiffness. Not even his so-pale pupils showed now in their sockets; the eyes of Cathbadh the protector of Daneira were rolled back so that he had become something from which children would flee.

The protector of Daneira was Protector indeed. The wolf was far from toothless.

Sorcerous flames lapsed. The wall of dancing fire lowered. For the first time as he turned again to stare at the doom-fire of Snorri's band, Cormac realized that he had felt but little heat. Yet it was fire. The man at his feet was burned; the ring looked like fire and sounded like fire, and beyond the lowering flames the Gael could see how treetops seemed to shimmer. Billowing gouts of black smoke boiled up—and up, lofting into the air without rolling over Daneira.

The sorcerous inferno died.

Cormac mac Art stared, paced forward, stared.

The Norsemen were gone. In the space of a few minutes, close onto twoscore men had been consumed. More, they'd been turned into *ash*—and the puddles of hideous bubbling smoking slag that Cormac realized with a chill horripilation of every limb was formed of melted axes, and swords, and the armour boiled from living men as their skin and hair and even bones burned away to ash.

Cormac turned slowly, to gaze at Cathbadh.

The stiffly upraised arms lowered. The staff fell to

the ground. Slowly Cathbadh's head came down, and for a moment his eyes focused, or seemed to focus, on the horror he had wrought in protection of his city of children. Then the man crumpled and fell to lie as if dead.

Only the Gael was close enough to see that Cathbadh's chest rose and fell, and he knew that the wizard had utterly exhausted himself in the saving of Daneira.

Chapter Four:
The King of Daneira

It was the stranger to Daneira who carried the unconscious wizard to his own bed.

Amid the uproar of the people, a passing thin man had come to Cormac and the fallen Cathbadh. A long robe of plain homespun was upon him, undyed, and girt with a belt to which had been fastened lacquered oak leaves, all green. By this and the fact that he carried a staff surmounted by the three-quarter moonsign of Danu, though it was of yellow-painted wood rather than gold, Cormac took him to be another servant of the goddess. He bent at once to take Cathbadh's hand and place an ear to his chest.

"He lives," Cormac said. "You are a fellow servant of Danu?"

The man, perhaps in the third decade of his life, looked up. "I am his apprentice. He bade me stay behind when word came of your presence. Now he has exhausted himself." He too stared, at the strange colour of Cormac's eyes.

"Ah. Show me where to bear him, then, for this man must receive care, and live forever!"

The apprentice gazed at the tall man for a time, then nodded. He rose and watched while Cormac easily lifted the wizard-priest, whose strange robe clacked.

"I am Flaen. Follow."

Cormac followed Flaen—and by the time they reached their destination Sinshi was with them, followed by a crowd of excited people. At the door of a house set apart and decorated only with a three-quarter moon on the lintel, Flaen stepped aside, motioned Cormac within, and stepped before the doorway.

"This day has Danu saved us all, and through the power of Cathbadh. Now he is but exhausted; he lives. Go and mourn the dead—and see about the business of. . . cleaning up. The metal can be of value to us."

They dispersed, while within a dim, unlit room Cormac laid Cathbadh on a long cot set against a wall, though he noted it bore only a spread, cloth worked with moon-signs, and no padding or cushions. Wondering whether to cover the man or even to think about undressing such a one, he glanced at the doorway. Flaen entered, with two others.

One was Sinshi. She rushed to Cormac, and took his arm—the left. He patted her hand without looking at her.

The other wore a robe of fine white wool, girt with gold. Around his muscular neck he wore a golden chain, which suspended the sign of Danu on his chest. He was the first person Cormac had seen who was armed; the fellow wore a sheathed dagger slung from his belt of gold cloth. A symbol of office, or power? His hair was a deep brown, and so too his eyes; mustache and beard were auburn. No small man was he, in build, though he would be only average outside of these short, slight people.

His name was Uaisaer, and he was king over the Daneirans. Again Cormac noted the emphasis on woodworking; the king's name meant Noble Wright, Noble Carpenter. And he was the ninth of that name to rule as king over these people. With no strong hand and no pomp, Cormac decided, noting that the king was dressed relatively simply—and barefoot—and came with no guard or retinue or even adviser. Further, he introduced himself, for Flaen went straight to his master.

The room held one chair, nicely wrought but unornamented, and a table and a bench, and naught else but shelving and things of strangeness hanging upon the walls. An undoored doorway led to another room, but Cormac had the feeling that Cathbadh had few possessions. He wondered about the barefoot king.

On all the ridge of the world, surely there were no people so strange and *different* as these of Daneira!

Again Cormac mac Art was heartily welcomed and profusely thanked for having saved Consaer and "this nubile young maid who is so necessary and valuable to our people."

He wondered—was she valuable because she was nubile, or was there more he did not know? While the matter was intriguing in its cryptic nature to the Gael and thus of considerable interest, he set it aside in his mind, with other questions to be asked later.

He was hardly comfortable. He had watched at work a most potent mage indeed—and the man had

66

then collapsed and had to be carried here like one dead. Once again Sinshi was treating his arm as a possession—though at least she remembered, and confined her viny clinging to the shield-arm! Too, Cormac mac Art was not comfortable in the presence of any king. He had known several, and all had betrayed him, including that former High-king of Eirrin itself. Cormac mac Art had served royalty and he had been served badly in return. He was no lover of kings.

Sinshi crowded her rescuer. Her little hands seemed bent on piercing his armour, so closely and tightly did she cling, her hands so small against the Gael's mailed sleeve and muscular arm.

"You are twice welcome here," Uaisaer, king, said. "What would ye have of us?"

"Lord king, my thanks—"

"I am called Uaisaer."

Cormac nodded. Not such a bad king at that, mayhap—though he stood back and allowed an old man to fight his battles without so much as ordering his people to withdraw or attack. Still—with such a man as Cathbadh about, what need was there of armour and shields, walls and royal orders?

"My thanks, Uaisaer. In truth, it's others I have with me, a druid of Eirrin and a woman—" Sinshi's hands tightened— "and two men, and—"

"Such as yourself?" The king was most interested.

"Aye, weapon-men, one of Eirrin and—oh. No, Lord k—Uaisaer, not with my hair and skin. The hair of one, whose name is Brian, is flax, and the other, him who is of the Danes and taller than I, constructed like a barrel, has hair and beard on him like the red of the rowan-berry. With us too is. . . a captive. A dread mage of evil, of whom I would talk with Cathbadh."

"Ah. Well, I see that Flaen has brought his master's

chest, and is tending him as none other can. The king of a grateful people offers food and drink.''

Cormac smiled. King over a village! Aye—and food and drink. The goat's milk he had never tasted.

"Fetch milk for Cathbadh," Flaen said, "girl."

"We have grapes," Uaisaer said, "and too we have ale."

"Ale? There be ale in Daneira?"

The king looked both astonished and a bit hurt. "We are men!" he said, and it was answer enow.

Though she was obviously not anxious to depart Cormac's presence, Sinshi looked away before the gaze of her king and hurried from the little house. Cormac flexed his arm and glanced anxiously over at the unconscious priest-wizard. The old man's night-black eyes flickered open even as he looked. They fixed on the Gael.

"Now, Cormac mac Art, ye know why none was affrighted."

"Now I do, protector and saviour of Daneira! Were there more like yourself on the ridge of the world, it would be a peaceful place and it's another life I'd have led—and a shepherd I'd probably be!"

Cathbadh smiled wanely. "But understand that one out there was sore afraid, Cormac. That one was I. Today I have done what I have never done afore."

Cormac went to the cot, squatted beside it. "And—ye be not ill, Protector of Daneira?"

"Weakened. Drained, like a squeezed waterskin," the old man said. "Never have I had to call on such powers. The small pigskin bag from the chest, Flaen," he said, and looked again at Cormac. "Though those who look on see only the power, the manifestation of the goddess and ancient knowledge passed from one to one to another and so down to me, there is much labour in. . . what I did. It is exhausting. I lay

68

unconscious?''

"You did. Was I bore ye here. And it's glad I am ye be recovering, Cathbadh of Daneira. Memory will be on me as long as on the the people ye saved from the Norse this day.''

Cathbadh's face clouded. "Not quite all. A girl not quite nubile died with them—and two childbearers.'' He sighed. Glancing at Flaen's movement, the old man's eyes brightened, though Cormac had noted they had seemed not so weak as his body. The Gael turned to follow their gaze.

The chest or casket Flaen had fetched was old, very old, of unbound wood and decorated only with an etched moon-sign. From it he had taken a small pouch of russet-hued pigskin, and opened its strings.

"Master,'' he said, extending it.

"Come, I must needs sit up,'' Cathbadh said, and received swift aid from the Gael. "Ahhh. Weak, weak as an infant.''

"It's more need ye have for the ale Sinshi brings than I,'' Cormac said. "And for red meat, methinks.''

Cathbadh was dipping his fingers into the pouch. Flaen said, "For such as my master and I, intoxicants are *used*, not quaffed in the way of other men. He will soon have a bit of milk. Nor do we eat meat, at all.''

Cormac shook his head. "It is no simple matter, this business of serving Danu and protecting her. . . city. No ale and no meat either!''

Though he was no such great tippler as Wulfhere, Cormac mac Art was hardly an enemy of ales or wines—and he could not imagine living without meat.

"It is no simple matter,'' Cathbadh agreed. He looked up at Flaen. "Ye know, Flaen, that I shall not long survive this day's work. Your time approaches, and I wish for you that no such need is pressed upon you as on me today—ever."

Flaen sank down beside the cot. "Master!"

"Cathbadh!" That from the king, who stood silent and unassuming as no ruler Cormac had ever known or dreamed of. Nor did Uaisaer wear so much as a band about his head, much less a crown.

"Come, friends both—all three," Cathbadh said. "Ye well know our geas and our limits, and the rewards and penalties for such as we." Taking a pinch of finely crushed leaves from the pouch, he stared at them, muttered unintelligible words.

There was silence in that room then, and into it came Sinshi, bearing what was surely a sore insult to goats: a goatskin bag of goat's milk. In her other hand a larger, fatter skin sloshed most pleasantly. Beautifully turned and carven mugs of wood there were in the house of Cathbadh, and them smooth and shiny as sword-steel.

Soon they were lifting well-filled mugs each to the other, a king over a few hundreds of people, and the man who served their deity and protected them at peril to his own resources, and a weapon-man of Eirrin. One cup contained milk.

They drank, and soon Cormac mac Art felt of far more cheer.

"Cathbadh, there is a place I must go, and my friends awaiting. And. . . another. Now I hold hope that ye can be helping us, an ye be recovered enow to hear of the evil we hold captive."

"Ah," Cathbadh said, less weakly still, having eaten twice of the herbs from the little russet pouch and having quaffed fresh rich milk. He sat up the straighter. "Daneira is in the debt of this man, Flaen, and hear him! We are fortunate that he has some need of us." He turned clear, coal-dark eyes on the Gael. "Cormac mac Art?"

"An ye can accept this, Master Cathbadh—"

"I am called Cathbadh, Cormac."

"A king called by name and a genius among wizards the same!" Cormac exclaimed. He shook his head, and his lips drew back in a tiny smile. "On all the ridge of the world is no other place such as Daneira, and may none ever find ye!"

"May your words be naught but truth," the crownless king said, from behind the Gael. And he drank again, of the ale of Daneira.

Cormac fixed Cathbadh with his slit-eyed gaze. "An ye can accept this, Cathbadh. . . on my ship is a most powerful mage, dedicated to evil. Divers forms can this one assume—and he cannot be slain, nor held by means other than the ghastliest of inhuman impalement. So is he held fast now, with my companions in constant dread lest he break somehow free. He is a creator of illusions, this one, who can assume the form of any man or woman, and a serpent as well."

Cathbadh interrupted. "A serpent?"

Cormac blinked in surprise. "Aye."

"Ah. A mage long upon the earth, is this one, and dedicated to naught but the doing of evil. Though it's the image of humankind he wears, it is all humankind he hates and plots against."

"Ye know him, then?"

Cathbadh shook his head. Black eyes glittered. "I know his kind. Many stories have come down, Cormac mac Art, over thousands of years from one servant of Danu to the next. Comal de Danann I am called, and so I am: Slave of Danu! But I had not thought that such as this one ye describe yet lived on this earth."

"He does not live, Cathbadh. It's dead he is—and thus he cannot be slain. But yet he does live, in some way not understandable to such as I. If knowledge

71

were with ye of some means by which he could be held captive, whilst we seek his final doom—"

"A servant of the serpent god and he dead and yet alive; Undead! Ah, but he can be slain!"

"Cathbadh! You can do this?"

The old man shook his head. "I cannot, Cormac de Gaedhel; Cormac of the Gaels. Nay, for of old it was said that only a woman enthroned could be the ultimate death-giver of such."

Cormac's shoulders slumped. Suddenly he wished for all of him that this damned uncrowned King Uaisaer were a woman or that he had rescued not the daughter of a carpenter but a princess, like a self-respecting hero.

"Cormac."

The Gael looked morosely into the wizard-priest's eyes.

"Be of cheer," Cathbadh said, and lifted his cup with its remainder of thick milk. "He can be held, or rendered rather powerless. I have the means. I have the means to make even such as you powerless, Cormac, or myself—*in the mind*. What boots the freedom of the body, an the mind belongs not to him who dwells in that body? Ye know that we all do but temporarily reside in these forms we wear, as a man lives in a house, and when it burns or falls into rot, he moves into another?"

Excitement was on mac Art, and he nodded several times. "Aye! Sinshi—please ye lovely dairlin'—be there more ale?"

I should not have said those words, Cormac mac Art thought, as she happily refilled his fine wooden mug—and took again his arm, pressing her hip close to his mail-skirted thigh. He glanced down at the shining top of that black-crowned little head. A sensuous little tawny maid, by Crom of Eirrin!

72

"What it is with such as this one ye describe," Cathbadh said, "is that he need not wait for action of the gods upon his death, but can transfer his mind, *himself,* into another body of his own choosing. As he has doubtless done thousands of times."

"That body he wears now," Cormac said grimly, "has no face, only a skull without flesh."

Cathbadh frowned. "I can hold him, Cormac of the Gaels. I can give ye the means to hold him. I shall. Flaen, no argument—I go with Cormac."

"Ah, Protector of Daneira," Cormac said with a grateful fervor he seldom expressed, "great wizard-priest of Danu . . . it's better news and more hope ye offer me than I've known in a moon's worth of days."

Flaen was shaking his head. "Master—"

"All of us will be most pleased," Cathbadh said, ignoring his apprentice, "to be able to do this for ye, Cormac of the Gaels—and for Consaer and Sinshi, who were lost to us but for yourself."

Chapter Five;
The Chains of Danu

Three strong young men of Daneira accompanied
Cormac mac Art and Cathbadh through the woods
of the Isle of Danu. Woodsmen's axes the three carried
in their belts, and stout staves in their hands, staves the
length of their bodies. A staff carried the wizard-priest
too, though his was for a different purpose, and tipped
with a golden image combining a hunter's bow with a
three-quarter moon-cresent. His ceremonial robe of
lacquered leaves Cathbadh had left behind, to walk
the forest in stout leathern leggings and a sideslit tunic,
green in hue, to the knees.

With them too went Sinshi daughter of Duach, for
the elf-like young woman clung to mac Art as a
grapevine clamps and entwines the tree it climbs in
quest of the sunlight. Nor would she be left behind.

Along the way betwixt village and sea, Cormac

posed the query he'd set aside till now, when there was time and no press of other business.

"It's of Eirrin I am, a Gaelic descendant of Celts who have been long on this earth. Yet so too seem to be the people of Daneira out of Eirrin. . . but not latterly."

"Aye." Cathbadh walked energetically enow for an old man, after his collapse and his partaking of his wizard's herbs and goat's milk. "And it is no brag I make in saying that my people preceded the Celts onto the world as they did onto Eirrin's shores—as Danu had her followers ere Behl of the sun was born."

Cormac saw only trouble in discussing that matter, and avoided it. "Then. . . when came the Daneirans from Eirrin'0 Who are ye; whence are ye, Cathbadh?"

"Why Cormac. . . can ye not see? We are of the goddess Danu."

"Aye, of course I know ye follow the old goddess, but—" Cormac broke off. "Ye mean. . . of old? In Eirrin afore we—ye be of the *Tuatha de Danann?*"

Cathbadh chuckled. "So I've said. The People of Danu. So ye've observed."

"Cathbadh! The Tuatha de Danann were rulers of Eirrin when the Celts came, the sons of Mil. . . there have been no People of Danu in Eirrin for nigh a thousand of years!"

"That is partially true, Cormac. In truth, the time has been less than ten hundreds of years, and it's *on* Eirrin ye mean we've not been, not in. Aye, we of this isle are Tuatha de Danann. And this walking requires my breath, as will the ford we must presently make.

Cormac saw only trouble in discussing that matter, and avoided it. "Then...when came the Daneirans from Eirrin? Who are ye; whence are ye, Cathbadh?"

Cormac walked in silence, marveling.

Revelation after revelation! These strange small people were those who anciently ruled Eirrin—who *were* Eirrin, Eiru—*and were supplanted and conquered by my people! Some think them only legend—and none has any idea that they fled here, to this tiny isle that has been an unmenacing paradise to them. The Tuatha de Danann—the People of Dana! Here, surviving!*

And too there was the other astonishment: the man walking beside him was of age eighty years and seven. The de Danann were remembered as a people of great powers of magic—*and so they have proven! Or at least this one has, striding—well, walking strongly and without footgear—through the forest, at an age well past that when most lie in their graves. Blood of the gods, what a people!*

A certain morose longing stole into the Gael's mind then, with the wistful thought: *Would that their ruler were a woman!*

Still . . . an I can control Thulsa Doom as Cathbadh said, we need not be constantly fearful of his wresting free of our bonds and destroying us with his evil. It's the rest of my life I could spend at the task of finding a woman who rules in this world of men . . .

In silence then the six made their way to their goal, and they reached the waterfall and thus the two ships anchored below, in the rockbound inlet.

Seeing the approach of Cormac and strangers who knew naught of him, Thulsa Doom instantly took the form of a slim, elfin-faced young woman—Sinshi! With a shriek, Sinshi herself drew away from her rescuer for the first time. What she saw with her own eyes was her double, writhing and moaning at the mast with two terrible swords of steel standing forth from her slim body. And there nearby was the redbearded giant, even taller than Cormac whose boon companion he was—this same Cormac was leader among the foul monsters who so tortured a girl just like herself!

"Cathbadh," Cormac said quietly, with only a glance at Sinshi who had both let go his arm and shrunk away among the three men of her own people. "It's but one woman there is aboard my ship, she there in the flaming hair and tall black boots. Samaire. That at the mast is the ancient and unslayable mage I told ye of—Thulsa Doom. In past he has approached me in the likeness of Samaire, and in the form too of the giant ye see. As him, my weapon-companion for years and years, my blood-brother, in truth, the monster attacked me so that I was forced to defend—and slay. It was then he struck grue and dismay in me, for he vanished ere I knew what and who he was. He dies not. Now he seeks to gain sympathy from you, for—"

Cathbadh was nodding. "Aye," he said, and spoke loudly enough for Sinshi and the escort to hear. "For it's no double Sinshi daughter of Duach has; I know every person of the Daneirans. And that be your precise image, Sinshi, see—even to the stain at the knee of your leggings!"

They six stood staring at that image of sorcerous horror, and she sobbed out a piteous moan.

"Danu be my light," Sinshi herself said, in a little gasp of ritual. "But she *looks* so—"

"He," Cathbadh corrected.

"It," Cormac said through tightpressed teeth.

"Cormac!" That from Wulfhere, for the six had emerged at water level and could hear and be heard, and now seen by other than the undying wizard.

Then Samaire saw, and she too cried out, and
77

Brian, while Bas smiled and lifted a hand in greeting and benison all at once. Sinshi had returned to Cormac's side as he made his way to the ship. They must wade the last few yards, and Cathbadh unblushingly suffered himself to be carried above the water by the three men of Daneira. Noting the water rose above Sinshi's chest, Cormac picked her up, bade her hold up the skirts of his mail without a thought for the weight of that linked chain, and made his way out to *Quester*. She clung close, her breath warm on his cheek. Nor was it without nervousness and apprehension that four of the five from Daneira approached that ship to whose mast was bound the image of Sinshi.

No apprehension was on Cormac's companions now. True, all had had time more than adequate to grow worse than anxious about him, and were full of nervous queries. They helped him and the Daneirans aboard. The latter stared, remarking red hair and blond; blue eyes and green; fair skin.

After a moment of consideration, Cormac raised a hand. "Wait," he said, and he removed his weapon-belt. Then he bent double. The Daneirans watched with wide dark eyes while he executed a strange little wiggle. Down onto his shoulders in a rush of clinks and jingles slithered his mail, and off over his head to form a small pile of blueblack on *Quester*'s deck. The Gael gathered it up, barely a couble handful now for all its twoscore pounds, and spread it on a rowing bench where struck the waning sun.

"Lest it be splashed," he said—and rebuckled his weapon-belt about his hips.

"Ye left long hours ago, Wolf," the Dane rumbled. "Now ye return with a regular retinue— including the girl ye wrested from the Norsemen. It's much worriment we've wasted over your worthless hide.''

"And I perceive it's no bathing ye've done, yet," Samaire said, stepping back a pace from the man in the sweat-dark tunic. He'd not been still long enow for it to dry after his race down the hill and his encounter with the four men in the forest.

Their nervousness and wonder did not abate once he'd told them of his going to Daneira, and the attack, and the power of Cathbadh. No, they'd seen no evidence of fire nor smoke, and smelled none either. They gazed with respect on the old man. It was Bas who reacted more to the identity of the Daneirans than to the knowledge of Cathbadh's sorcerous prowess.

"The Tuatha de Danann!" the druid repeated, in a low voice of wonder.

Samaire sent looks askance at Sinshi, who remained close by Cormac despite his sweat and its odour. He affected not to note the questioning glances Samaire directed at him.

The Gael was, in truth, more than uncomfortable. Sinshi's attachment to him was worse than obvious, and both cloying and embarrassing. Yet how could he be harsh with the elfin creature, so quiet and gentle and filled with gratitude—and fascination with the tall, grey-eyed man unlike any she had ever seen? She had experienced horror far beyond any other who might have been assaulted as she'd been, for elsewhere victims of attack and attempted rape by barbarians at least knew of the existence of such men and such dangers. And. . . Cormac was warmed by the flattery of her attentions.

The three young escorts from Daneira, meanwhile, were gazing upon Samaire in much the same entranced way—hovering. Only one, Cormac had learned, was a family man. That is to say he had a wife, and their marriage of two years, though they were childless.

On *Quester*'s deck and not dripping as were his escort, Cathbadh leveled a cold stare on the poor moaning figure of pity who writhed moaning at the mast.

"We be not impressed by your sorcerous illusion, ancient mage of evil. Assume your own form."

Thulsa Doom did not; instead the girl he was whimpered, "O please. . . great and kind grand-father. . . please. . . "

Clamping his jaws, Cathbadh strode to the pleading girl. He spoke words none knew, and set his staff crosswise against her sword-impaled chest. He pressed.

"Assume your true form, creature of the dark! The ancient Mother of All commands it—see her sign, the crescent of the moon and the bow of the warrior huntress!"

The skewered girl ceased her laments. Through that small body ran a quiver of rage. A little hand leaped clawing for the Daneiran—and changed in air, fingers lengthening and going all bony. The girl's form became that of a tall thin man in a robe dark as night. Her hair and the flesh of her face dissolved before the eyes of all, like obscuring fog of the night before the light of the sun.

The awful death's head of Thulsa Doom stared at them, and gnashed its teeth.

The bony hand spasmed ere it reached Cathbadh. It twitched, jerked, fell back—and then Thulsa Doom cried out in rage and pain.

Both his arms dropped limply.

The servant of Danu lowered his staff, set its end against the deck. He braced it so that the gold-wrought symbol of the goddess lay against the monster's chest. Opening the pouch at his belt, Cathbadh took forth a slender chain of silver links. Thulsa Doom quivered in fruitless attempts to move, then, whilst Cathbadh slipped the silver necklace over the shining skull.

Onto the chest of Thulsa Doom dropped the Moonbow of Danu, and there it rested, undisturbed by breathing, for he who was dead and yet not dead breathed not.

Cathbadh turned. "Cormac," he said, and he beckoned.

Cormac went to him while the others were as if frozen, staring. They were fearful in the presence of mighty contesting sorcerers—one of whom could control him they had thought more powerful than any. They saw Cathbadh clutch Cormac's arm; they heard a groan escape the Gael and saw him commence to shudder.

A terrible jolt went through Cormac mac Art at the first touch of the old man's hand. Cormac's head spun. The world rocked. Not just he, not just the ship, but sea and sky and all the world seemed to rock and shudder about him. He felt as he had not since that day on Ladhban when lightning had struck less than an arm's length from him. His teeth chattered. He shivered. Awful images and impossible memories seemed to sweep through his mind like a flurry of autumn leaves before a northerly gale. No voluntary movement was possible to him.

"Be linked," Cathbadh said quietly and without intended drama. "Be linked, as slave and master."

Over Cormac's head with one hand, his fingers propping it open, he lowered a necklace of silver links identical to that he had placed on Thulsa Doom. A few moments longer the Daneiran wizard held

Cormac's arm, and Thulsa Doom's as well. Then he released both.

The Gael staggered as full normalcy returned to him and his brain cleared, all in an instant.

Deepset, narrowed grey eyes like Nordic ice stared into the black glims of Cathbadh of Daneira.

"What have you—"

"Attend me," Cathbadh interrupted. "Him you call Thulsa Doom is bound to you. He is your creature, so long as ye live—and so long as both of ye do wear this metal of mortal power against inhumanity and the emblem of the Mother of All. For she is the giver of life and the nourisher of life, Danu of the moon—while he is of the dead and the dark that fears the moon's silver light."

Cormac swallowed, regained control of himself. He touched the pendant on his chest, then lifted the Moonbow and slid it down within his tunic. When he turned his gaze on the death's head wizard, Cormac's face was sinister. Thulsa Doom stood stiff at the mast. The blaze of hate and malice seemed to have left the red lights in the black pits of his eye sockets.

"So long as we both do wear these chains and sigils?"

"Aye. He is yours to command and hold, with mind and words alone."

"Then we must take care that he lose not his jewellery," Cormac said darkly.

The Gael stepped forward. A few twists, a knotting of slim silver links, and he had tightened the necklace of control about the mage's neck so that it would not slip off.

Instantly Thulsa Doom became a serpent that squirmed erect and lashed its tail. The huge head thrust at Cormac—who, after an instant of withdrawal, spat into its staring ophidian eyes.

82

The silver necklace did not slide along the reptilian body.

"The knot is unnecessary," Cathbadh said. "The chain of control can be removed, but not by Thulsa Doom. Command him."

"Resume your own form, filthy creature from the pits! I'd have thought over the span of eighteen times ten times a hundred centuries, ye'd have tired of the form of a serpent!"

The skull of Thulsa Doom faced him again. Nor longer did the baneful light glow in those red coals of eyes.

It was with the first real smile Cathbadh had seen on him that Cormac mac Art turned again to the wizard-priest of Danu.

"Ah, Lord Cathbadh of the Danann, this was the first foe ever I met and could not conquer and who struck horror and anguish to my very liver! And ye have rendered him powerless, and it's only great gratitude and love I feel for ye, man. Would that there were aught I could do for yourself, give to yourself, wizard!"

Cathbadh gripped the other man's arm. "Ye've done us service, Cormac of the Gaels. Nor do the Danans hate your people, nor I you. If I asked that which comes first into my mind, I'd bring misery upon ye, though, for it would be that ye remain among us in Daneira."

Samaire gasped, but Cathbadh only smiled and shook his head at the anguish in the face of mac Art. Without looking at her, he stayed with a hand Sinshi's forward rush.

"I said I'd not ask that. But I will ask one service of ye, Cormac mac Art of the Gaels, and one that is in your power to give without cost to yourself."

"Granted without the hearing of it," Cormac said,

and for a long moment the two men looked each at the other, and Cathbadh nodded.

"This night ye will remain all with us in Daneira."

Cormac blinked. Frowning, Samaire looked at Sinshi—and the way that tiny woman looked at Cormac—for Samaire of Leinster knew this little creature was no girl, but a woman looking with desire on her man. Brian started to smile, quelled it, though a glance told him the three men of Daneira were broadly grinning. Nothing sinister was there in those smiles, but only joy.

"Cathbadh—" Cormac began.

"Ye've given your word, Wolf," Wulfhere rumbled. "And—this handsome Findhu here has assured me there is ale in Daneira that wants tasting by an expert."

Cormac mac Art smiled. "This night we spend with ye in Daneira, Cathbadh. And. . . Cathbadh." He turned to look again upon Thulsa Doom. "This. . . creature. He need no longer be transpierced thus, with our swords?"

"He need not, Cormac. He is powerless, and will obey you. Nor can he remove the chain of Danu's power."

Cormac nodded. "Then to leave him thus sword-nailed is unnecessary, and needless cruelty as well?"

"I cannot judge 'need' and its lack, Cormac na Gaedhel. Cruelty to leave him thus? He feels little pain, in truth. But he does know terrible piercing cold, with the steel of this world of the living stabbing through and through his body without warmth, a body that should have lain so long in the grave as to be naught but dust." Cathbadh nodded. "Aye, would be cruelty to leave him thus pinned, and it unnecessary."

Cormac stared into the eye-sockets of Thulsa Doom. "Good," he said. "The swords remain, then."

Chapter Six:
The Problem of Daneira

Wolfhere, Brian, Bas and Samaire were happy to accompany Cormac and the Daneirans to their little city of highly decorated wooden houses.

After all their hardships in the month they'd been away from Eirrin, asea and on Doom-heim, the horror and constant tension whilst Thulsa Doom sorcerously sought vengeance on Cormac and the deaths of all his companions, and that final ghastly battle of friend against friend, engineered by the undying wizard—the companions of mac Art were more than glad to accept the hospitality of peaceful Daneira.

With them went Thulsa Doom.

It was not that Cormac relented; none wanted to leave Thulsa Doom, and Cathbadh demonstrated his confidence in the Chains of Danu by leading all of them to his "city"—the docile mage included.

A feast was set in preparation, to be served in the house of the king. It was a house, not a palace, no more ornately carven and painted than many, though considerably larger than all. Cormac bathed and enjoyed the luxury of a shave in warm water. His and the others' hair was trimmed. Dinner robes were pressed upon them. These were dyed and patterned in the way of Daneira: gaily bright. Nor ever did they see their own tunics again, for by morning they had served as patterns for the stitching of new tunics for all—and a new robe of green woollen for Bas of Tir Connail. Many women worked at that task, and willingly. In Daneira the women sewed and tended the gardens, with the children; men and women alike saw to the arable land and the crops; the men tended the beasts, felled trees and stripped and trimmed them, and created furniture and new objects and utensils, all of wood. Both men and women cooked.

In Daneira there was one class of people.

In Daneira there were no warriors.

Nor had metal ore been found on the island of Danu the Mother. Cormac and his companions were not averse to pressing upon their hosts the arms and armour they had captured, for even shield bosses and belt buckles would make hoes and rakes, parts for woodworking tools, awls and scrapers and fine-pointed knives and chisels for carving and plowshares.

Both Cormac and Wulfhere winced at the thought of laboriously wrought mail being returned to liquid and beaten into new shapes, none for warfare or defense. For Brian the concept was repugnant; both the father and uncle of Brian-I-love-to-fight of Killevy in Airgialla were makers of armour. Yet neither of the two sons of Eirrin held scalemail in high regard, and donated much of that from dead Norsemen. Superb curers of hides and workers in leather, the Daneirans had no use for hardened leather that had served as armour.

The line was drawn at swords. Those the travellers would keep. Swords were valuable, for their making was a high art and a lengthy task. One blade Cormac did pronounce of dangerously inferior workmanship; two others were too badly pitted and deeply notched for the keeping. These, with every shield of Dane and Norse, Eirrish and Briton, were given to the people of Daneira. They would soon be tools for other tasks than slaying.

Far more numerous than swords were axes, for they were more commonly carried by men who could not afford the product of the swordmaker's art and high craft. Every ax was proffered on Daneira as gift. They had only to be fitted with longer helves to become tools for the felling of trees rather than of men.

To Cathbadh his guests gave silver more than sufficient to replace the Chains of Danu that Cormac and Thulsa Doom now wore. The wizard-priest was hesitant to accept the valuable metal.

"It was stolen by the Norse," Cormac told him, "who slew the original owners. We took it from the treasure-trove of the murderers. There is blood payment on it, Cathbadh—and it will all boil away in the melting down. When it is made into wire that becomes links of chain, know that ye have it of those men of that same Norge who cost ye so much this day."

Cathbadh accepted the gift of blood-bought silver.

Nor would the Daneirans abide the departure of their strange-eyed guests without pressing on them fine gifts of magnificently wrought goblets and bowls, mugs and even belt-buckles and cloak-pins, all of wood. At the softly tanned leatherwear of Daneira Cormac drew line again, saying that animals were too few here for these people to be giving away the products of their hides. His companions looked down in silence at that announcement; none of them but coveted this finest of cured, supple leather.

On the king's insistence, each traveller accepted a Daneiran belt, soft as thickly folded silk and fitted with buckles of wood, ornately carven and lacquered again and again.

Dinner in the hall of the king was a gala feast, with many present in their brightly hued dining robes. Nor could they get enough of the unusual hues of the hair and eyes of Cormac's companions, colours none had seen ere this day.

There was no avoiding it: Sinshi was most attentive to Cormac mac Art, and so to Samaire was Findhu of Daneira. Other unwed Daneiran maids made kings of Wulfhere and Brian, whose head was soon turned. Much ale flowed. Sinshi kept Cormac's carved, enameled cup of satin-smooth walnut ever full, while the two who flanked Wulfhere and saw to his cup were far busier. The capacity of the gigantic foreigner with the vast beard of flame and eyes like the sky would be legend in Daneira for many years.

Samaire shot green-eyed glances at Cormac and at Sinshi—who returned them with an apparent sweet guilelessness that Samaire saw as arch mockery. Yet so close was Findhu, and so charming and obviously charmed by the woman of Leinster, that Samaire was able to endure the younger woman's competition.

"Tell us of the Tuatha de Danann," Wulfhere said when his belly was full of food if not of ale—already he'd made one trip outside and there were wagers as to how long ere either he went again or his eyeballs

89

turned amber.

A harper plucked and strummed and a poet of Daneira recited the old history that many of Eirrin now thought mere legend.

Long before the year that would be called 1000 BC, the Fir Dhomhnainn or Tuatha de Danann came to Eirrin—Eiru. There before them were the Fir Bholg. It was at Moytura the Danans put final defeat on the Firbolgs, and Danu ruled in Eirrin; she who was also the battle-goddess called Morrighu, and who may have been Diana, and who was to become Bhrigid and Bridget. The Firbolgs went off muttering, for they had been defeated by a people uncommonly skilled in crafts—one of which was necromancy. The Danans gained thus a name for sorcerous powers.

Long after came the sons of Mil, a few centuries before the birth of the carpenter's son of Judaea who was to become the god of the New Faith, Iosa Chriost who was hanged by the Romans as a seditious rouser of the rabble—the Dead God. None knew whether there had been a Mil or Miledh, which the Romans and Romanized Britons called "Milesius." Likely not. Likely he had been Mil Espaine—the Eirrish version of *miles Hispaniae:* soldier of Spain.

It was Celts he led, whatever his name, and Celts who had departed long ago to pass through Greece and Spain and perhaps even Egypt, so that they had gained hair of colour other than red or blond, though their eyes remained blue or grey and occasionally green. They were the Gaels; Gailoin or Gaedhel, and it was at Bantry Bay they made landing.

Naturally the de Danann made resistance, and the war was joined.

Somehow the Gaels prevailed, despite the wizardry of the smaller defenders. Yet it was not quite a definitive victory; the Danans were neither slain to the last man nor forced to depart Eirrin. A bargain was struck, and it was strange indeed. The Danans went *into* the land. Their kingdom became a subterrene one, with the Gaels retaining control of the surface. Later many claimed that the Danans, the little people, were working their magicking on crops and livestock. The Poet of Daneira swore this was not true—though some Danan renegades may well have sought a harrying form of vengeance on the surface dwellers.

Above the tunnel of descent of each of the de Danar.n kings was erected a high *sidh* or fairy mound, and to the Gaels as time went on the Danans became the *Sidhe.*'Twas said by the Gaels that the Sidhe mocked them by crying out when one of the Gaelic number was to die. This was the fearsome wailing cry of the ban-Sidhe: the Banshee. With time, the Danans slid into Gaelic legend.

By their sorceries the Danans or Sidhe transformed the underworld into a place of beauty suitable for human habitation, and they throve there beneath the earth.

There was among them a source of constant contention: ever there were those who spoke out for their returning to make war on the Gaels, to reclaim their land. These agitators pointed out that the Danans were becoming even smaller in size and more and more pale, living forever without the sun. Aye, the wizards among them, the Servants of Danu, had created a moon for the goddess and to shed light on her people—but its light resulted in no tanning of the skin. Many among the Danans were ill and frail.

Gentler and more reasoned thoughts prevailed, for few doubted that were the Danans to attack those above, the Gaels would not stop this second time until there were no more of the de Danann on all the ridge of the world, north or south, east or west.

At last the Danans decided upon a more peaceful rule—of women, that there might be end to talk of war on those Gaels above, whom had become the Eirrish. It was an enormous step, long debated and decried by many.

Some among them continued to disagree, and could not reconcile themselves to the new way. At last they were sufficiently opposed to the gynecocracy to leave Eirrin. Here to this paradisic isle they journeyed, with a few animals and seeds and much hope. Daneira was founded at about the same time that a short dark man named Caius Julius Caesar led his hawknosed soldiers onto the shore of what to them was a new land: Britain. Here was founded the "city" of Danu of Eiru: Daneira.

As the poet recited the old story, heads in the hall of King Uaisaer came round and wide eyes exchanged looks. Excitement ran through the companions of mac Art like wind through a field of grain, stirring every head.

"Then . . . it's possible there be de Danann yet, beneath fair Eirrin?" Samaire's voice had risen in her excitement.

"Aye, o'course," she was told, for why would there not be?

Art muttered.

"A crowned woman. . . " Wulfhere Skull-splitter muttered.

"Aye."

Aye!

And Cormac told of the means by which Thulsa Doom could be lain to rest, and Cathbadh nodded agreement. The knowledge passed down from one Servant of Danu to the next confirmed the Gael's belief. Cathbadh rose.

"Ye be friend to us, Cormac mac Art. Friend to the People of Danu. And the Tuatha de Danann, wherever they be, shall recognize ye as such by the necklace ye wear. An ye would seek out our cousins 'neath Eirrin and their queen—do so, in knowledge that welcome will be extended."

Cormac frowned, fingering the pendant he wore on its silver chain—which tonight he wore outside the scarlet robe pressed upon him by his hosts. "But. . . Thulsa Doom too wears one. . . "

"The Moonbow on his chain is downside up, Cormac mac Art. Think ye I chose them not with care? His brands him in your control—and an enemy of humankind!"

"Blood of the gods! Then—it is possible after all. Thulsa Doom's foul un-life must be ended—and it can be!"

"Cathbadh," Samaire asked, quietly though with intenseness, "where be the Tuatha de Danann in Eirrin?"

"Aye," Cathbadh said, "*in* Eirrin, not on. There are Doors, lady Princess of Leinster, that lead to the subterrene demesne of the people of Danu. These Doorways are disguised and invisible, no longer truly beneath the mounds called sidhe, for all do know the Danans possess powers of magic never shared with the Gaels. . . who, after all, drove our people from their lands, though it be long and long agone and all here be friends. One such Doorway lies within the two long, mounded hills in the southwest. . . "

The wizard-priest described the place, and suddenly Samaire knew whereof he spoke.

"The Breasts of Danu! I know those two hills—it's the Breasts of Danu they be called, to this day!"

Cathbadh smiled and exchanged a look of some pride with Uaisaer; the Danans and their goddess were hardly forgot, in Eirrin that had once been theirs!

"Another of the Doors," Cathbadh said, "is in the hill of Bri Leith—"

"Long-ford," Cormac snapped. "The hill at Long-ford! Why—it's but a day's walk and less from Tara Hill that Long-ford lies! Cathbadh: how find we this. . . Doorway, to the land below?"

"Cormac: ye wear Her sign. Ye have my blessing. The Door will ope to ye, when ye arrive before it. More than that I cannot say with surety; we are gone long and long from Eirrin. It is nigh onto five centuries since the founding of the city of the people of Danu and Eiru—Daneira."

Smiles flashed among the visitors, for a world that had gone dark with the presence of Thulsa Doom now brightened with the prospect of his removal. No matter what was required of him, Cormac mac Art knew that he must journey with the mage to Long-ford's hill, and find the Door to the Tuatha de Danann. Sinshi shared his excitement and his happiness, but he hardly noted, for he was grinning at Samaire like a boy.

After a time it was thoughtful Bas who was gaining Cathbadh's attention.

"It is little pride I swallow, Servant of Danu the Mother, to say to ye that ye possess knowledge and powers I would beg to know of."

Cathbadh gazed upon the druid in his snowy dinner robe, a man whose hair was black and whose eyes were blue. "It is the moon goddess I serve in truth, and the sungod ye do. It has never been the way of the sun to share its daily brilliance with the moon that illumines the night, Servant of Behl and Crom. . . nor for the moon to share its silver with the sun's god."

There was silence for a time then, for Bas's request had been rejected and the brains of Cormac and his companions churned with thoughts of Eirrin, and the land beneath and within Eirrin . . . and Thulsa Doom.

In his white robe purfled with yellow, King Uaisaer rose at the long table's head, and in this wise he differed not from other monarchs. His rising signaled the meal's end. His people began to depart, taking their leave of king and guests. But Sinshi stayed, and Findhu, and soon there were but they, and Cathbadh and Uaisaer, and Cormac and his companions—and the maids whose names he could not remember, who hovered bright-faced about Wulfhere and Brian.

"Our hospitality is open here," the king said, and he was looking at the young son of Eirrin and the thick-bearded Dane.

Wulfhere took his cue for behaviour from those words. Sitting back, he wrapped an arm about the young woman on either side of him and snuggled them close. Willingly they accepted such twofold embrace, and Cormac saw that the king looked pleased. The younger Brian was less demonstrative— it was just that his hands and those of the Daneiran maidens flanking him were all out of sight beneath the board.

King Uaisaer said, "We would have converse with you, Cormac mac Art na Gaedhel."

As Cormac nodded, Sinshi pressed close, though already her hip had long warmed his. She squeezed his hand beneath the board, and leaned close to murmur for his ears alone.

"I know what words he'd have with you, Cormac. Please, please, dear Cormac. . . agree, agree!"

His companions were bade tarry or wend their way to the quarters assigned them, as they would. With

95

Uaisaer and Cathbadh, Cormac adjourned privily to another and smaller room.

"Friend Cormac," the king quietly said, "ye've noted how few we of Daneira are—and how alike."

"Aye."

"It was but two smallish tribes of the Danans left Eirrin five centuries agone. We survive today only because this is but the second 'invasion' of our isle."

The king paused, glancing at Cathbadh; the wizard-priest spoke.

"I should not have slain *all* those Norsemen this day, Cormac. The people of Daneira are weak. We suffer no menaces, but are prey to illness and debilities that worsen as they are passed from parent to child again and again. Many die young, very young. Many women never bear. They cannot; some because the fault is in themselves, others because—we think—the answer lies in the weak seed of our men. We *linger,* but we do not thrive. Daneira may not survive another hundred years. All for lack of a new strain of blood and strength in us."

Cormac nodded, thoughtfully.

"We . . . have great need of you, Cormac of the Gaels," Cathbadh said most quietly indeed. "And of the handsome lad, Brian, and that gigantic friend of yours, he who is neither Gael nor Danan."

Cormac mac Art understood. He knew now why earlier Cathbadh had not mentioned the slain man and boy, but had mourned the potential *childbearers* dead of the encounter with the Norse. And mayhap there had been hope as well as fear with Sinshi, on yester day out there in the forest with Thorleif fighting his way betwixt her legs. Aye, and he understood why he had been thanked by wizard-priest and then king in the same manner: for having saved a *nubile* maid. Her parents had borne three, and she and her brothers were valuable to the future of Daneira.

Children were the lifeblood of any people.

The blood of relentlessly, helplessly endogamic Daneira was running thin.

And here among them for but a night were three strapping males from outside, of entirely different blood and even race! Aye, Cormac knew why he and Wulfhere and Brian were so welcome here. . . and perhaps why Sinshi was so extremely, nigh-unconscionably attentive. At that thought his ego suffered a little.

"It's our seed ye want—and direly."

King and priest nodded. "Aye."

Cormac glanced at the closed door behind him. "My lords, this need not have been said. Maidens attend both Brian and Wulfhere, who are men, and long without women. The normal course of nature will see to the sowing of their seed in Daneira, and I hold hope for ye that it falls into rich and fertile soil. An we're to be a bit . . . cold about it—"

"As we are," Cathbadh said; "as we must be."

"—a fertile plot once seeded need only lie and be tended with care, whilst the gardener moves to another part of the garden. In this wise, my lords, the gardens need only depart to be replaced in the gardener's chamber by another fertile plot . . ."

The king nodded. Cathbadh smiled.

"So much for Wulfhere and the lad," Cormac went on. "As for myself—it's with my woman I've come among ye, and her a weapon-companion as well. With her this night for the first time in so long and with privacy available to us through your kindness, no desire is on me for others. Nay—let there be no argument among us, and us friends, for that is the way of it."

97

Their faces had fallen, but his last words and raised hand stilled any pleas or demurrers.

"Methinks Sinshi's heart will hardly be broke," Cormac said, with in truth a bit of bitterness, for certainly she had turned his head, and now he knew not her motive. "But it's a coward Art's son is in some matters, and this is one. I'll not be going back into the hall where she sits waiting." He nodded to indicate a deep red curtain beyond them. "That portal I remember takes me to the sleeping rooms ye've offered, lord king of Daneira, and it's through it I go now, not back to say Sinshi nay."

And he did.

The two men stared at the drapes that had fallen together behind him, and they knew that with such a man they were unopenable.

"I must. . . have meeting with Sinshi Duach's daughter," Cathbadh said quietly and with thought upon him. "Where are the clothes of the strangers?"

"They will be brought to you," Uaisaer said. "But—what of the woman of Eirrin?"

"Mmm." Cathbadh nodded. "I must have meeting with both Sinshi and Findhu!"

That meeting was swiftly held, ere the guests could act to spoil the plan of the wizard-priest. In the darkness of a most private room of that king's house Cormac prepared for bed, while to another went Samaire, knowing he had rejected the little Daneiran and would soon come to her, and in a third such private room three people stood while only a candle burned. Above, Danu, Mother and Huntress, rode the sky in Her silver chariot. In the dim-lit room stood Her servant with his staff bearing Her sign, and with his robe of lacquered leaves on him. The candle flickered and lit fleetingly the two who stood before him, Sinshi and Findhu, entirely naked though not

98

quite as the day they were born. And he spoke, and intoned, and muttered and made gestures, speaking to his goddess. And he did place upon them garments that fit them ill, being too large, whereupon lo! Sinshi assumed of a sudden the likeness of Samaire of Leinster and Findhu seemed to become Cormac mac Art.

"Go with the goddess," Cathbadh said. "Danu be thy light."

The two departed his company in likenesses other than their own.

Soon, Samaire came to Cormac, and he smiled and called her dairlin' girl.

But at the same time Cormac went to Samaire in her room, and she smiled and held forth her arms.

On the morning of the morrow, Wulfhere made brag of how he'd had no wish to be *selfish,* and so had toiled in the gardens of no less than four delightful and delighted maids of Daneira, all of whom he swore fainted in bliss; Brian but grinned and was silent, except to say quietly that he had been. . . less industrious in the numbers of garden plots, but had plowed more than once in two several Daneiran gardens, and therein sown his seed.

Cormac and Samaire said naught, for each supposed to have spent the night with the other. And it was many a day ere they knew privacy again, and learned that each had received the other that night though neither had gone, whereupon realization came upon them that they had been tricked to no fell purpose by a great mage and two loving Daneirans, no boy and no girl. After a while they laughed on the matter, and wished Sinshi well, for she, unlike Samaire Ceannselaigh, had surely taken no precautions against get.

Chapter Seven:
Thulsa Doom

Wulfhere ruddered *Quester* around the Isle of Danu with great care—and skill seldom surpassed. Aboard were two men of Daneira, filled with wonder and going constantly from port to starboard, from stem to prow, ever looking; neither had been asea before. At last the Dane spotted that which they sought: the wolf's head ship of the Norsemen.

Ashore, the woods trailed off into a short but deep strand that sloped gently to the water. On the sparkling pale sand of that beach, the ship from Norge had been drawn up to the edge of the trees. She'd been turned partially crosswise, for there was little more than sixty feet of depth to the beach betwixt trees and surf, and the Norse vessel was little more than ten feet shorter.

Quester hove in cautiously, without sail.

Those aboard saw no sign of men who might have been left to guard the scarlet vessel; there was naught here but sea and sand and woods and the ship, left whilst those who had plied her so far went ashore—to their deaths.

Taking *Quester* well into the shallows until it was nudging the beach, Cormac swung off, with Wulfhere and Brian. They moved up the strand, treading wet sand. Aboard the ship from Eirrin waited Bas and Samaire and Thulsa Doom, with the two from Daneira. They watched the trio of weapon-men move warily up glittering sand to the beached vessel. The beach twinkled as if strewn with gems, in the sunlight that struck white fire from helms and mail.

"Oh—what a beautiful ship!"

Wulfhere nodded. "Aye. None build ships better than those Norse fugitives from Hel's domain, Cormac."

Eyesight was sufficient to confirm the beauty of the *knorr*; only a few moments' examination was necessary to ensure that it was unguarded and in perfect condition, a long curving sweep of seafaring beauty with a scarlet hull the height of Cormac's shoulders. Her name was branded along her side; *Odin's Eye*. The god of the northlands had but one, for he had given up the other in trade for great wisdom. The snarling wolf-heads of *Odin's Eye* were in place at bow and stern, which meant they had been reset after the beaching, for they were removed ere a ship of the cold lands came in to shore, lest the spirits of the land be alarmed by the fearsome gaping wolf-mouths and resist the landing. None had; it was well inland that these men of Norge had met their weird.

"Be it likely that *all* the Norsemen went inland,

101

and left none behind to mind this beauty?'' Brian asked.

Wuflhere and Cormac, their eyes as if bedazzled and ensorceled by the vessel, nodded. "Aye," the Gael said. "Such is their way, often. See you any sign of habitation on this isle? They saw none, either. But—it's sure we want to be that no reavers remain."

The two who'd sailed so long together, a-reaving, looked at each other.

"We must have her," Cormac said.

"Aye."

They shouted then, above the liquid slapping of the surf. All three men clashed the flats of their blades on their bucklers to draw any who might have been left behind by Thorleif and Snorri, and who might now have fared into the forest.

"An any come," Brian asked, "shall we tell them of the welcoming they'll be receiving of those man-hungry maids of Daneira, and bid them go inland. . . provided they leave all arms here?—And armour as well?"

"No sensible man would agree to such a mad bargain," Wulfhere said. "They'd show us refusal by attacking at once." He thrust two knobby-knuckled fingers up into his beard. "I bathed not high enough! Umm. . . such *seeming* madness, I mean; I be sore tempted to remain and return to Daneira, myself."

Cormac had shaken his head. "No, Brian. Armed or no, such wolves would soon eat the gentle lambs of Daneira, alive or dead. An any come in reply to our noise, it's but one way there is to ensure the safety of Daneira."

Beyond the ship, the trees rustled their tops in a breeze off the sea. Brian looked at Cormac, with his lip caught between his teeth.

"Aye, proper death-dealing," Wulfhere rumbled,

102

quietly for once.

"Murder," Cormac said.

"We'd slay out of hand?"

"Oh, they'd make attack," Cormac said. "But—aye. Daneira must be protected, and making sweet overtures to reavers is the fool's way. Slay a few to protect a few hundred? Aye! An that goes against your feelings, Brian, lay you back. I and Wulfhere can handle any who come. And he'll only begrudge ye those you account for, I-love-to-fight."

"Unnecessary chatter. None comes," the Dane said.

Cormac sheathed his sword and rested a hand on *Odin's Eye* by the slit that allowed an oar's slim blade to be slid down into the round hole for its sweep. He gazed at the line of trees, from which no one emerged. The only sounds were of surf and treetops that seemed to rustle in a whisper.

"None comes," he agreed. "Twoscore Norsemen fared here, on *Odin's Eye,* and all found death here. Four by my hand, and the rest died of Cathbadh's sorcery. As for yourself, Wulfhere, ye high-horned dreamer. . . remain then. It's not a month ye'd last, in such an unexciting place."

"Even a month," Wulfhere said thoughtfully, and a smile twitched his beard. "I'd be the most popular man on the island, with the girls. And what fun to come back a year hence and see all the little redheaded offspring of Dane and Danu!" He grinned broadly, gazing inland.

Cormac shrugged. "Stay then, red bear of Loch-linn. It seems there be no Norse, as ye said, and it's for Eirrin's shores I am—with this ship." "

"Salvage."

"Conquest!"

"Ye'd tow *two* craft, ye greedy Eirrisher?"

"Nay. The Daneirans want no ship. Nevertheless, it's *Amber Rowan* we'll be leaving with them, and all under the deck of *Odin's Eye*. A Briton-built ship is best being pulled apart for whatever use the Daneirans have. . . "

He turned to hand-signal *Quester*. Immediately the two of Daneira swung over the side and came hurrying up the beach, with their staves.

"Your great Cathbadh slew all who fared here on this knorr," the Gael told them. "The craft itself we take with us. All aboard her is yours. And that ship—the poor one made by the Britons, who learned naught of shipbuilding or much else in five centuries of Roman rule—it too is yours, for firewood or a clambering toy for Daneira's children. Is it a good seafaring craft, Wulfhere?"

Wulfhere had come to Doom-heim on *Amber Rowan*—bound to the mast, a captive of Britons who'd learned of the spoils there from the Dane when he was deep in his cups. The Britons had little, save what the Romans had left behind eighty years agone when great Rome fell and they withdrew. Even now those Britonish shores were raided by Danes and Norsemen, Saxons and Angles, Frisians and Jutes, along with a few more from nearer to hand: Picts from other side Hadrian's Wall, along with men of both Alba and Eirrin.

Wulfhere made reply: "Nay."

"Remember that, sons of Danu. Now ye've had a taste of the sea, and it seemed marvelous to ye. But— the Daneirans are best where they are, living in peace and with hope that none find ye. Come, give us a bit of help now. We'll see what the Norsemen are after bringing ye . . . aside from the metal melted in Daneira!"

The Daneirans stared at the painted heads on prow

and stern, each with fangs meticulously carved in wide-open jaws; none of Daneira had seen a wolf, or even a dog.

Cormac and Wulfhere swung quickly aboard and raised the deckboards to bare the shallow space in which were stored those supplies that seafarers might need ashore, and they were forced to land and tarry, but had no need of while they voyaged. There was little; the ship stood not Cormac's height from gunwale to keel and was only about twice as broad, amidships. The Gael and the Dane drew forth utensils that might or might not be of use to the Daneirans; the metal would be welcome.

Astern, the small chamber of the steering platform was empty; there had weapons been stored. Keel up on deck, a single afterboat was bound and secured with ropes of walrus hide. For it the Daneirans had no use; Cormac would leave it where it was, on his new ship.

"She seems a better craft than any we've sailed, Cormac."

Cormac nodded. "So she seems. Come; we'll be stripping. That Britonish craft will be easy to pull and push in."

It was. The matter of coaxing and manhandling *Odin's Eye* into the water was far more difficult. Samaire and Bas came to lend their strength. Without the prodigious strength of the Dane, they'd never have accomplished it and would have had to wait for the vessel to be floated by the tide. Then *Odin's Eye* was partially afloat, and they tethered her behind *Quester,* as *Amber Rowan* had been. Cormac checked over every inch of the towline.

"I tell ye again, Wolf: If we encounter weather, real weather, ye'll have to cut loose that leashed dog of a ship. She'll be the death of us else."

"The weather will hold," Bas said.

It was a statement of absolute fact that made the Dane feel gooseflesh on his bare sweaty arms. Nevertheless he asked, "For a ship named for a god not of Eirrin?"

"The weather will hold."

Cormac said nothing, but turned to the two of Daneira. "Mayhap this craft and these few things of Norge can be of use to ye," he said. "It's sure I am none will sneer at the metal ye bring home! Ye know the way to Daneira from here?"

They but smiled at that. The people of Danu's Isle knew its every inch, sure!

"Then it's leave we'll be taking of ye. May your goddess send happiness on ye both and all your people—and many children." Cormac turned seaward. He was more ready to be off and away, and no love was on him for these weaponless people who had never known travail. It put a fog and a darkness on his mind, just the thought of their easy lives, for when ever had he known ease or lack of strife or the necessity of having his sword by him—aye, and shield?

"Danu be thy light, Cormac mac Art. Danu be thy light, friends of the Danans."

"Danu be thy light, Cormac mac Art, and thou Wulfhere, and Brian. And thou Samaire—and yourself, holy druid."

From the ship to which he'd returned to be by Thulsa Doom, Bas nodded.

Cormac boosted Samaire onto *Quester* and swung up. He gave her a swift crude fondle while there was none to see, and turned to aid Brian aboard. Then the Gael looked down at Wulfhere, who had turned to look back toward Daneira. Heavy laden, the two sons of Danu were lugging Norse utensils into the woods.

"Fare ye well, Wulfhere Hausakluifr," Cormac

106

said. "Many children. Oh—and may your goddess Danu shed her light—"

Wulfhere swung to glower up at his friend. "May plague fall on ye and the restless worms infest your anus, son of an Eirrish pig-farmer!" And the Dane swung aboard with such vehemence of motion that *Quester*'s planking creaked and water sloshed.

And this time they held out again to the open sea and, with sail opened to the wind, stood forth northwesterly for Eirrin. The water gurgled past the hull as if delighted to be bearing them homeward. It was a journey that might take a few days—or months, for none could ever be certain. Reckoning was worse than imprecise, and only gods might know or control the weather—which controlled both the sea and all those aboard its undulant plain.

A wind huffed without undue enthusiasm across the sea south of Britain, so that *Quester*'s green-latticed sail stood out nicely like a merchant's belly. The Isle of Danu was left well behind and the voyagers were alone, as in a gigantic empty chamber that surrounded them on four sides with water and sheltered them only with a roof of sky that was nigh the same colour as the demesne of Manannan mac Lir.

The world was blue, green-blue, and white.

In the heavens Behl added the warm yellow of his smile. Cormac and his companions wore no armour, now. Mail and leathern coats were stored in the little compartment under the steering platform astern. They had buckled their weapon-belts on again; the sea was ever unpredictable and none wanted his most valuable possession swept overboard amid some emergency of wind and wave. . . and three aboard had survived a volcanic eruption that brought new land onto this same ocean.

Nor could they bring themselves to store away sharp-edged steel, even though their dread enemy was now a helpless captive.

Scarlet tunics made in Daneira wore Brian and Wulfhere and Cormac, and on the chest of the latter's new garment flashed the Moonbow on its silver chain. Rather higher up on the night-dark robe of Thulsa Doom rode his identical Chain of Danu, though with the Moonbow upside down; on him the goddess frowned and from him she turned away her face. The deadliest creature in the world sat at the mast. He was not bound. Nor could he change form or launch attack on mind or body; he wore the necklace. He sat still at the mast as he'd been bade by his master. The undying wizard was the creature of Cormac's will, now, as before his will had commanded theirs and brought so much horror and agony on them all.

The ship slipped rapidly across the sea under swollen sail, straining toward Eirrin. Those it bore talked of what it might mean, this being in a "different dimension." It was like unto the world they'd always known—with differences.

"What *differences?*"

They could not be sure. Perhaps in the world or dimension they had quit, the Isle of Danu was as uninhabited as they'd supposed.

"Mayhap," Bas said. "Mayhap in our own dimension all that we now know of the People of Danu after our ancestors supplanted them—did not take place. Mayhap there they are not ruled by a woman at all. Or do not exist."

"Let us hope they do," Brian said, with a glance at their captive.

"*And* that a queen rules them," Samaire added.

Wulfhere chuckled. "A niceness, if Thulsa Doom himself made it possible for us to be his weird for all and all, by bringing us here, where rules the crowned woman to end his foul existence!"

"If such does rule here," Samaire said, for she was aware of the improbability even more than the others.

"But. . . where," Brian wanted to know, "is *here?*"

"A plane of existence where at least one island does not exist," the woman said, idly fingering the dark-bordered hem of the tunic made for her in Daneira; it was an almost yellow green. "Remember the isle that was suddenly not there and thereby told Bas we had been dragged here by Thulsa Doom, in his attempts to escape us." She looked with malice on the undying mage. He sat moveless, an unwilling but helpless slave of the Chains of Danu; a slave of Cormac mac Art.

"A place where a Norseman named Thorleif, son of Hordi, once slew Wulfhere," Cormac said.

"Hmp! That I refuse to believe! I could slay such as Thorleif all day and still have time for Daneiran maidens the whole night through!"

"They are so far astern now that not even their isle is in view," Brian said from the tiller, where he was nervously, proudly in training—so long as the sea remained gentle. Nor was his statement made without some small wistfulness. He stared asea, his hair like a cloud about his head and his flaxen eyebrows all but invisible in the sunlight.

"An it be true what Thorleif avowed," Bas said, "rejoice, Wulfhere. For else it's two of ye there'd be in this plane—which is now our abode for good or ill!"

"Blood of the gods! Bas—think ye *I* be here—I
109

mean. . . that there be two of *me* here?''

"Ha! An intolerable world then, two of ye, son of an Eirrish raiser of pigs!''

"Wulfhere old friend and drinker with Britons, much as hate's upon me to tell ye of it and spoil your insults, my father was after being of the descendants of High-king Niall the Great, one of the *ua-Neill* of Connacht. It was no pigs my father raised. Nor in truth was he a farmer at all.''

"Nonsense, by Thor's red beard! All the Eirrish raise pigs! Why, pork is surely the national dish and pigs' bladders the only toy of the young!''

Samaire's voice came in weary practicality, a whisper that forced them to fall silent in order to hear. "Truly there might be. . . another Samaire here, and another Cormac, and Brian, and you too, Bas?''

"Aye—but, Behl be praised, only one Thulsa Doom!''

"And only one Wulfhere,'' Cormac said, "Behl be thanked nigh equally, if Thorleif did indeed kill you—him. Who could abide two of ye, with your ever-itchy beard and your babbling?''

"Ye look thirsty, Wolf of Eirrin. Could I be aiding ye into the water that ye might quench your pigfarmer's thirst? Simple matter to hold ye by your heels—''

Samaire slapped her high-booted leg. "An ye two put not an end to your constant childness, it's a mother ye'll make me feel yet, the hapless dam of two bickersome boys!''

Wulfhere contritely ducked his head—in the manner, indeed, of a chastened boy. Cormac seemed not to notice her words. He'd gone all thoughtful, and gazed contemplatively at the skull-faced abonination sitting with back to mast. The Gael fingered the Moonbow on his chest.

"Thulsa Doom! It is my bidding ye obey, and naught else."

"Aye." There was only resignation in that word from lipless mouth.

"I want information of ye, monster!"

The red points in the eyesockets of Thulsa Doom's death's-head stared at Cormac mac Art. But they were without their usual fire of malice, for Thulsa Doom's mind was no longer his own.

"Ye'll provide information, an I demand it."

The mage's voice bore no semblance of happiness, though his hissing malevolence was also missing. "Aye. I will tell you what I can."

"Be there escape from this dimension of yours, a way back to—our own world?"

"I am trapped here. You are as well, as you came through with me though totally by accident. We cannot return."

That felt like a blow to the stomach, and Cormac heard gasps from the others. He tried, hopefully but with his voice bordering on the desultory. "And if we *order* ye to return us, blackheart?"

"I cannot. The slip-through, the 'gateway' I have so long used is destroyed. Never have I been so sorely held fast as ye held me, with swords, and with that man of Behl striving with his powers. I strove more mightily than ever I have before. Thus by accident I tore the slip-through, and brought through all with me—even these ships. And thus destroyed the link between this dimension and that other. I know. I strove to go back *there*, with you here. I could not; no means exists." The mage broke off and stared straight ahead.

"More," Samaire urged.

"Thulsa Doom!" the Gael snapped. "Heard ye

not Samaire?''

This time the wizard's words emerged bitterly, defiantly. "She does not wear the chain linked in the Beyond to this one!''

"*I* do. Speak. Add to what ye've said.''

"You cannot return," Thulsa Doom said at once, "because I cannot. Nor could I guarantee it if your coming through had *not* destroyed the means of transference, for it was all by accident and my desperate striving to break the hold of swords and the druid. Be assured that I brought you not here by design, Cormac mac Art who was my greatest enemy!''

Cormac's half-smile was grim. "For once, monster, I'm believing ye. Well then, we must make the most of it. This dimension does differ from ours?''

"Aye. It is the same, but some things have not happened here. Others have happened here that have not, will not in the other plane that was your home. There is a, a fork, a branching, in history. Both nature's forces and sorcery had do with that branching, long ago. Now there are two worlds, lying parallel and each invisible to the other. This one became my escape . . . for here I did not survive death, so long ago. Most things are the same. That would not have remained so, for—" the sorcerer broke off.

"For *what*, mage? Answer!''

"—for I would have taken possession of this world, and ruled it," Thulsa Doom said. "From Rome.''

"Rome!" Brian echoed.

"Aye.''

"In this world . . . Rome fell not? Rome still rules . . . even Britain?

112

"No no. All those things are the same; all major matters are the same. No—it was my plan, my hope, to rid your world of yourself, and this one—and then to rule this plane. Rome would be the best capital—for I would have replaced the leader of those who called themselves first 'Friends' and now are known as 'Christians.' Their chief priest or bishop is in Rome—from there he seeks to rule, but of course does not. *I* will—would have done. The Pope whose image I would wear would never die, would rule forever, and soon all would believe in his faith and his claim of direct descent from him chosen by their god."

"A lovely plan," Cormac mac Art said quietly. "An undying dead man. . . ruling a world devoted to the Dead God, Iosa Chriost!"

"That island that was there but not here," Brian said apprehensively, for he was more interested in the immediate and the personal than the inconceivable: unending world rule. "It is now . . . here? It is gone?"

Into the silence, Cormac said, "Answer questions from us all."

"It is not here," Thulsa Doom said. "It was never here."

"Nev—oh gods! Eirrin. . . *be it here?*"

"Aye. Eirrin exists. Britain exists. Norge and Dane-land exist. Rome left the shores of Britain some eighty years ago. Al-ric, king of the Visigoths, took and sacked Rome in the four-hundred and tenth year of the era of the Christians. It is the same. The August date was the same. Eirrin's kingdoms are the same."

All eyes aboard *Quester* were fixed on the mage now, all ears drinking in his dull-voiced reluctant replies as if they were ale and all were dying of thirst.

113

The sea rippled alongside the ship, and gurgled in its wake.

"Brian," Cormac said. "Is there. . . another Brian here?"

"No."

Brian gasped and jerked as though struck.

"He put to sea three years agone," the skullface said, "and has never been seen since. Indeed he never will, as he was slain on the coast of Alba by Picts—"

"Dead!" Brian said in a broken croak, and held up his hand before his face. It shook. He stared at that quivering hand, as though for assurance that he indeed lived.

"Then all ye need do," Bas reminded the youth, "is pretend a bit—and return to the bosom of an overjoyed family! Any errors ye make, in memory, can be laid to captivity or some sea battle."

"That," Brian said very quietly, "I have experienced."

They were silent, gazing upon the youth from Killevy up in Airgialla. All remembered how he'd had to do death on his best friend Ros, another youth whose mind was possessed by Thulsa Doom and who'd been striving to slay Bas. Cormac, whose mind bore scars, knew that act had etched one into Brian's brain, too, and Cormac felt both remorse and guilt, for it was in following him that Brian had come upon such horror and had manhood thrust upon him, ten or so years all at once.

"And Wulfhere?" Cormac asked.

"Aye—has Thorleif slain me here—my, uh, other self, I mean? Odin's god-like patience but this is a thorny matter to think on—even to try to talk on!"

The death's-head moved slightly to face the giant. "It is true. And aye, was Thorleif of Norge slew you, years past. There is no other Wulfhere here."

114

Wulfhere stared, then rose and stalked aft, to mutter to Brian that it was his turn at watch and tiller.

"And. . . myself?" Cormac was asking.

"Another Cormac mac Art exists in this plane," Thulsa Doom said, and it was as if the words were a palpable force that rocked Cormac where he sat, on a rowing bench. "No less scarred, no less skilled with weapons, no less deadly, *this* Cormac mac Art of Connacht. He is you; you are he."

After a time of silence while he thought on that, hardly with understanding, Cormac glanced at Samaire. He looked again at Thulsa Doom. "I would know whether—"

"Cormac!"

At her cry, Cormac broke off to look at Samaire.

"Ask no more about yourself. It is. . . eerie. Awful. Please."

After a moment, he nodded. "And yourself, dairlin girl. Are ye wanting to know about yourself?"

"I—I—" She bit her lip, looked at Thulsa Doom. "Aye!" she said, of a sudden. "I must know, and then it's no more questions I'll be asking. It is possible that here I am married yet to that prince who was my husband, in Osraigh. . . or that I died in childbirth. . . or. . . was slain by those Norse who captured me from the shores of Leinster. Such things are possible, wizard?"

"Aye, all such things are possible," Thulsa Doom said. "But—"

"Hold!" She thrust out a stopping hand. "Tell me only if there is another Samaire Ceannselaigh here, daughter of Leinster's dead king."

"Aye."

Again her teeth worried her lip. "And. . . my brother?"

115

"Feredach your brother rules Leinster, him who is called *an Dubh*—the Dark."

"My—other brother. Ceann of the Red Hair."

"He was slain by those Norse ye spoke of, on the soil of Eirrin near the coast, whilst he resisted his kidnaping—and yours. They carried you away, once they'd knocked away your sword and overpowered you—and threw him into the sea along the Leinsterish coast."

"Ceann!"

And even though Ceann mong Ruadh was alive in her own dimension, Samaire wept, mourning him, and commenced the keening in the manner of her people. Wulfhere turned, cast anxious looks about as if seeking escape. He'd had to give listen afore to the Eirrish mourn-keening; Samaire did it too well for his sensitive ears. Brian and Bas both looked as if they wanted to go to her; both looked at Cormac, with anxiousness on them.

The Gael said, "Weapon-companion!" and his voice was sharp.

Samaire stiffened and firmed her mouth. She stilled her laments for the Ceann of *this* dimension, a Ceann she had never known—and for that Ceann of the other plane, whom she'd never see again. And him waiting at Tara for their return with spoils to finance his plotting against his murderous brother!

"There is that which I must know," Cormac said, "despite Samaire's warning and my agreement. Thulsa Doom, blackhearted monster and *my slave*—answer. Am I welcome in this Eirrin, by the High-king on Tara Hill?"

The mage's single word was the most awful and shattering he had uttered; the ugliest word in any language. "No."

Then for a long while the ship scudded over the

116

plain of the sea, and there were no words spoken aboard her. Only the sun smiled; only the waves rippling past the hull chuckled. Samaire turned her back, and began to weep, though quietly. Cormac merely stared at the decking beneath his feet. Brian managed to look anguished and angry all at once.

At last Cormac mac Art began to speak, in a low, disconsolate voice.

"I'll not be asking if here I am *trenfher na Eirrain,* Champion of Eirrin, which I won by such great effort—in my own dimension from which ye've stolen me, scum of the ancient world! It's for Eirrin we're bound, and to Eirrin we go. Once again must I be someone else—and not my old 'Partha mac Othna' either, lest that name betray me. It's directly to one of the Doorways to the Tuatha de Danann I must take Thulsa Doom."

"Oh, Cormac!"

He nodded. "I know, dairlin girl—but it's unwelcome in my own land I've been, for a dozen years of my life. Blows to the spirit I've taken before, as well. I shall abide; I shall survive. As to yourself—" He looked about at his little group of friends; weapon-companions, all. "Ye others can and will go to Tara. Wulfhere, ye can be taking *Odin's Eye,* though it follows us with such docility. Though. . . once the High-king knows who ye be, Samaire, for your cousin Aine Cumalswife will recognize ye o'course, all will be well for ye. And for Bas, and Brian, aye and for Wulfhere, your friend from among the Danes who became friend of Eirrin by rescuing ye from the Norsemen, ye see!"

"In your company," she said. "Aye. Mayhap then you too will be welcome at Tara Hill, my love."

Cormac tightened his jaw and stiffened a bit, for she had not used those words to him afore, with others present. "Bas, of course, will. . . no mind. No matter. That be the way of it. It is what must be done."

And again there was silence, for all knew he was right, and firm on it. Nor did any dare ask the enslaved mage *where* that other Cormac, that Cormac of this dimension was, or what he did. It was Wulfhere who broke the somber quiet that overshadowed them like brooding thunderclouds.

"Ye've taken leave of your senses, son of— Eirrin."

Cormac swung to stare; all followed his gaze, looking at the giant Dane who stood astern with his fiery beard moving restlessly in the breeze.

"Blood-brother! I'll not be going to the hall of Eirrin's High-king, and I a Dane, in anyone's company! Likely I'd never leave alive—and that means I'd be taking twenty or forty of Eirrin with me into death! Oh no, Wolf. Nor this time will I be taking a fine ship in quest of a crew—whilst ye go alone with. . . *that*, seeking a Doorway ye may not find, to people who may not exist, who may or may not be ruled by a woman!"

"Wulfhere—"

"Call me blood-brother!" Wulfhere snapped. "I go with you. This time aye, I will suffer these feet to tread the soil of your land. It was in a filthy prison we met, you and I, and we broke free together, and we took ship together, and we sailed together after. I owe you my life—and you owe me yours, for it's more than once or even twice each of us had only just saved the other from ax or sword. But for you I'd have ridden a Valkyrie's horse long ago." Wulfhere stood solidly, stared and spoke stolidly. "*We* take Thulsa Doom to the Doorway, Cormac mac Art *an cliuin*—blood-brother!"

118

Cormac was obviously considering, though it was obvious there was nothing to be gained by raising argument. And true, in the decision he had announced, Cormac had felt much alone; egregiously alone. He knew loneliness, alone-ness well; he'd shared his life with it as other men with an ever-present dog. He could bear it. And. . . . he'd be passing glad for the company of his longtime comrade.

"It is a matter of which Doorway we seek, then," he said in a low voice, and they began to think and to discuss that problem, for Cathbadh had named them a choice of two locations.

The twin hills called the Breasts of Danu indeed resembled the mounded bosom of a woman reclining supine. They stretched long across the land but eighteen of the Roman *miles* northeast of the River Kenmare, which emptied into the sea down in the southwest of Eirrin. There they could go ashore, without danger of recognition.

The hill of Bri Leith was well north, sixty miles west of Tara Hill and south of Taillte. From Tara they must cross three rivers, the Boyne and the Deel and the Inny—and hills, and the bogs as well, or skirt them. It was Bas who then suggested that they could sail *Quester* down south of Eirrin, enter the Shannon and make their way up it to Lough Ree; thence up its length and onto the broad Shannon again, until they could make landing but a few miles east of Bri Leith and Long-ford.

Problems attended either choice. At last it was Cormac who decided. In manner most positive he stated what they would do. For gladness was on him to be positive about something, in this new life forced on him by a relentless enemy who hated him only for the man he'd been in a time incredibly long, long gone by.

"We will port at Balbriggan, but twenty or so miles from Tara. Ye others will go directly there, and to the home of your cousin Aine, Samaire. I and Wulfhere will skirt fair Tara, calling ourselves by other names—and taking Thulsa Doom to Long-ford, and the Doorway at *Slieve Bri Leith*."

Fast on the heels of his words came another voice. "Release me, Cormac mac Art, release me now, and I renounce all vengeance on ye—and these your friends."

Cormac stared at the death's head, and he was tempted.

"Join me! *Rule* this world!"

"Thulsa Doom, no man but would be a fool to place faith in any such promise from you. And ye'll not be ruling this world, mage. No. It's no release ye'll be having of me, whilst I live."

Brian saw a matter for laughter, and seized on it, for in all wakes the time comes for gaiety. "Sure and it's a sea of interesting looks ye three will be receiving, moving through our green Eirrin and one of ye with no face!"

Cormac showed him the pale reflection of a smile, and that seen dimly as in an old and filthy mirror of weathered bronze.

"No, Brian. For Thulsa Doom can be assuming any form he wishes—is it not true, mage?"

"Aye. The form of any person I have seen."

Cormac nodded. "Then it's a decent visage ye'll wear in Meath of Eirrin, monster, not that hideous shining skull! It's green your robe will be, and the symbols of Behl and Crom on ye—for I and Wulfhere will travel respectably, in company of what all will see as a druid!"

PART TWO

The Kingdom of Danu

Chapter Eight:
Into the Earth

"Eirrin," Wulfhere Skullsplitter said, "is *wet*. The weather's less damp asea."

"It's a healthy lot we of Eirrin are, meaning the weather agrees with us," Cormac told the grumbling Dane. He waved a hand. Misty grey-blue sky; green plain sweeping into deep woods with multicoloured leaves, green hill patching into brown; distant blue mountains.

"For sea-dogs," the Dane retorted, "mayhap Eirrin is healthful." He looked about. "Aye, and mountains ever in view, no matter which way one turns. This land has a million rivers, a million foul dark bogs that give off worse air than the grave, and two million mountains."

"Forget not the clouds ye've grumbled of," Cormac said, a bit wearily.

"Ah! The clouds—they rush about overhead driven by ever-changing air currents like ants from a kicked hill. And. . . it's ever *wet*."

"Misty," Cormac said.

"Wet."

Cormac mac Art compressed his lips. He knew it was not the weather or the scenery of Eirrin that had Wulfhere a-grumble so. Both men were weary. They'd been at the hill of Bri Leith for two days, and now they trudged, rather than strode. Worse, because of the autumn chill and the dampness and Wulfhere's nagging at Cormac about his native land—even unto the clouds overhead—they had been here two nights. Despair hovered over them like a vulture.

They had walked. And walked. Up the hill and down the hill. Around it and around it, wading through gorse and daggerbushes and furze. There was no sense in splitting up in their search for the Doorway to the Danans' subterrene demesne; Wulfhere would not find it. He could not. The Doorways, Cathbadh had said, would reveal themselves to him who wore the Sign of the Moonbow— and only to him. Only to Cormac, then. Otherwise the entrances were invisible, the protection of the Tuatha de Danann within the earth from those who had displaced them and lived on its surface. The two men must remain together. They roamed together, and Wulfhere grumbled aloud.

Cormac remained outwardly taciturn . . . and grumbled in his heart.

With them always came the apparent druid who

"Bas"; twice Wulfhere had, and then launched into a vicious hailstorm of curses. That had put thought on the Gael.

"An any should separate us," Cormac told Thulsa Doom, "it is my command that ye resume your own worse than ugly form at once. The robe and form of Cutha Atheldane, and the skull that is all we know of your face. Ye be understanding?"

"I understand."

"And ye'll obey, though we've separated and I not there to order or see?"

"Aye. I must."

And they trudged on.

"An island," Wulfhere said, "is a piece of land afloat but anchored on the bosom of the sea. Aye, and completely surrounded by the water."

Cormac said nothing. They trudged.

After a time he could not bear the silence that followed the Dane's remark, and he said, "Aye."

"Eirrin," Wulfhere said with pleasure, "with all its rivers and lochs and fens and thrice-damned bogs, and with its mountains all along the coast so that the whole land slopes inward to the center. . . Eirrin is water, completely surrounded by land."

"And Loch-linn of the Danes is perfection itself," Cormac said, hanging onto his temper only with effort. "Which is why ye left so long agone and never return. Come, blood-brother, it's only weary of this searching ye're after being. There's more grass under my two feet this instant than in all of Loch-linn. . . and more moisture in a lungful of the air of Britain than in all Eirrin's sweet air!"

Wulfhere only sighed, without reply. The other man was right; in this sort of situation, he'd have muttered darkly even about the paradisic Isle of Danu. He sighed anew. With all its anxious womenfolk. . . he should have remained there!

They walked slowly along the hillside, stumping,

one leg long and the other short, for it was easier than walking up and down, up and down. Though their movements were not quite listless, they were hardly energetic. Nor came this from lack of sleep. Though the nights were cold and heavied with the added chill of dampness and their limbs and backs complained at morningtide, both men slept well enough. The lives they'd led had hardly accustomed them to soft beds and the warmth of night-fires. If ever men could sleep anywhere, under any conditions, and indeed nigh at any time at will, the Wolf and the Splitter of Skulls were among their number.

Nor did their captive provide any problem. It was the growing feeling of fruitlessness that preyed on their minds.

Despair was a brooding shadow that hovered over them and their thoughts were dark with it. Surely they had trod every inch of this mocking hill, and of the greensward at its base. They had found no Doorway, not even a cave; there was no sign. They were weary of the search, and nervous that it was to come to naught.

Samaire, with Bas and Brian, had reluctantly parted their company and gone on to Tara. With Thulsa Doom in the likeness of Bas as he was now, the two weapon-men had struck westward—afoot. Neither was accustomed to horses, and Cormac hated that sort of transport that made a man's tailbones and thighs sore—and worse next day. Too, he stated a further reason for walking. What would they do with their mounts once they discovered the Doorway and entered the earth? The horses could not remain tethered. Nor could they be turned loose to roam free and doubtless cause consternation and damage for others. Nor, on this mission, was there a way to hire someone, even a boy, to accompany them and return the mounts once the Doorway was found. He'd likely become a flying gibbering idiot when his employers vanished. . . and might well be waiting with an army of angry, fearful men and stern druids when Cormac and Wulfhere emerged from below ground. If they emerged, after—how long a while within the earth?

And so they had walked, and waded, and forded, and slept out in damp chill, and now two days and two nights had passed here, and the third day still brought them nothing to lift sagging spirits. And so Cormac mac Art was morose, and Wulfhere grumbled about Eirrin and its clime.

Yester eve they had conferred. For two days, confident, excited, they had merely walked about, hither and thither, each expecting at any second to espy the object of their quest. When whim struck, one announced and both hastened to that place, only to experience a renewal of disappointment. Cormac felt no qualm about asking Thulsa Doom for the location of this Doorway. But Thulsa Doom did not know.

Last night they had decided to do what they should have done on arrival after their trek from the coast: put the quest on a systematic basis. Walk every inch of the hill. They would not admit defeat and leave this area until they had walked, one behind the other, around and around over every finger's breadth of the hill and its perimeter.

With them trudged the cause of this anguish and so much else that was unpleasant and evil, him whose death they sought, and him dead beforetimes. His green robe was a mockery that rustled as he walked. Nor, seemingly, did Thulsa Doom tire.

"An we find it now," Wulfhere said from behind the Gael, "we'll have to decide whether to rest ere we. . . go in. My belly's begun to growl."

"When has it not? When have ye not? Wulfhere!"
Cormac jerked and came to a halt so that the Dane
ran full into his back. "It. . . it be time to make that
decision," Cormac said, in a voice that was not
without a bit of quaver.

All weariness flowed from mac Art's limbs and
spirit as he stared at it: a wound had opened or
appeared, huge and gaping in the hillside. A dark
hole it was, twice the breadth of his shoulders though
several inches shorter than his height. But a moment
ago had been naught here but grass. Now gaped the
cave, closer to him than the length of his forearm. It
yawned darkly, a cavern into the hill but a few steps
above its base. Wide enow for two men to walk
abreast—two *short* men. And women. And the
animals the Tuatha de Danann had taken with them
from the face of Eirrin. . .

The diffused sunlight spilled into the cave for a
little way, then paled to grey. The grey became black.
There was no gauging the depth or length of this
tunnel into Eirrin's depths; there was only blackness.

"Cormac?"

Stepping a half-pace downward, Cormac turned to
look at Wulfhere. He swept an arm at the gaping hole
in the earth, large enough to be visible for many
many feet, much less these few.

Wulfhere turned his gaze that way. He frowned.
He turned the frown on his companion.

"See ye nothing, itch-beard?"

"The hill," the Dane said. "And grass. Cormac—
has the damp and our frustration got to ye, man?"

Cormac looked again. The cave was there. With a
glance at Wulfhere, he stepped forward. Within the
hole in the hill of Bri Leith, he turned to look again at
Wulfhere Hausakluifr, and him who appeared to be
Bas the Druid.

"Cormac!"

Wulfhere's eyes had gone wide. He hurled badly shaken glances this way and that. Cormac saw those eyes fall on him—and knew that Wulfhere saw him not, from a distance of less than a body length. Cormac mac Art remembered, and stepped forth. Waving aside the Dane's excited demands as to what had happened to him, he explained: Cathbadh had advised that the Doorways to the Danans would reveal themselves to him who wore the Moonbow.

"It is. . . there?"

"It is there, Wulfhere."

"The. . . Doorway."

"Aye. The Doorway to the Pople of Danu. We have found our goal." He looked again into the blackness that Wulfhere could not see. "Ye have but to tread in my tracks, and—"

"Cormac mac Art."

It was the voice of Bas; both men turned to look at him—or rather, his likeness.

"Forget this ill-advised adventure, Cormac mac Art. Ye know not what lies in that dark pit. Your own doom, perhaps. Think you a Gael will be welcomed by those the Gaels drove into this land's subterranean depths, into the cold and the dark? Take from me this Chain of Danu; free me, and neither Wulfhere, nor Eirrin, nor any born of Eirrin anywhere will suffer the slightest from me—aye, you and yours will be the chosen people! And too any others ye name, elsewhere. Riches will be yours, Cormac mac Art. . . no more exile, no more wandering. . . shall there be again one named Cormac mac Art who rules supreme in Eirrin?"

"Thulsa Doom! *Hush.* Say no more. Keep silent."

Knowing his commands were irresistible, Cormac turned from the mage at once. He found Wulfhere looking thoughtfully on him.

"Ye'd not be king over this land, blood-brother?"

"It's nothing that one says and no promises of his I'd believe, blood-brother."

Slowly, Wulfhere nodded. "It is tempting, though." The Dane was musing aloud.

"Oh aye. Aye, temptation is on me. Doubtless others have been tempted. I hold myself no good man, Wulfhere." Cormac held up his hands before his face, and there were scars on both. He examined the palms and dark long fingers. "It's much blood these hands have spilled, Wulfhere." The Gael's voice was inordinately quiet. "Widows have been created to weep because of the son of Art of Connacht. Had that Art not been slain, murdered with treachery done on him, none can say what might have been. But. . . to be given the choice now of allying myself with purest evil, or of striving to rid this world of it. . . no choice exists, Wulfhere. It's no bad man I am, either." Cormac gestured to the cave invisible to the other. "W enter, Wulfhere. Is it still with me ye go?"

Wulfhere was smiling. "Was you said the words, Cormac. I see no cave—but I can see where ye go, Wolf. And I follow."

At last the torches they'd brought would be put to use. Cormac entered the Doorway. Wulfhere followed. Aye, and now he could see: sunlit Eirrin behind, and the black darkness of the cave before. The huge Dane had to stoop even more than his friend, but this was no time to make complaint. With Thulsa Doom in the likeness of Bas of Tir Connail, they entered the cavern.

They walked between gloomy walls of earth and stone, on a floor of the same. It was bare and hardpacked and dustless beneath their feet. Uplifted torches surrounded them in a bright yellow glow that was engulfed by darkness but a few paces ahead. They advanced; the dark retreated, but was ever there, lurking, waiting, closing in behind them as they ranged downward into the earth.

Wulfhere glanced back, and his helmet clonked dully against a low ceil of solid stone. He saw only the darkness; they had followed the cavern downward, and its mouth had vanished.

"How can people live down here, in this blackness? Cormac. . . there *cannot* be people down here!"

Cormac said nothing. Doubts plucked at his confidence and his hopes, too, but he'd go on until uncertainty became certainty—one way or another. *An there be a crowned woman down here,* he mused, *sure it's Queen of the Dark she is!*

So, and so. Let it be that, then. If such there were, he'd be finding her. Behind him paced Thulsa Doom in silence; last came Wulfhere Hausakluifr. Cormac walked on, leading the others ever deeper into the earth. A silence surrounded them, and it seemed ominous, brooding, a menace. Waiting. Silence and darkness swallowed them. The air grew heavy with the odour of damp loam.

Their footsteps and the clink of chainmail were the only sounds, and close-pressing walls gave off echoes. Even their breathing seemed loud, echoic in this subterrene silence.

Cormac mac Art knew not how long they'd paced forward, ever downward, but his back had begun to complain of having been so long bowed. Many minutes, he knew; many, many minutes. He was sure that Wulfhere suffered even more, by reason of his great height. But the Dane did not complain. Cormac realized, and appreciated. Wulfhere Skullsplitter was

130

no child. He knew when not to jest or jape or make complaints.

Aye—and surely the ceiling's height is proof enow of the origin of this endless tunnel, added to the sorcerous invisibility of its mouth; this passage was constructed for people far shorter than I, than men of normal height. . . the Tuatha de Danann.

"Cormac!" Wulfhere's voice came in a rumblous whisper.

"Aye."

Cormac's voice, too, was cautiously low, for there was light ahead. They advanced toward the pallid grey glow. Now the walls ahead became visible, in a dim pearly light that seemed to have no source and yet was like. . . moonlight. It did not grow brighter as they approached, though they were soon able to see more clearly. The illumination was like that of earliest dawn just when the birds commence to sing, rather than the final blush at day's end. Toward that light the three walked—and what they became able to see directly ahead was a blank wall of stone.

Just as they reached that dead end of the passage they trekked, they saw that it was not; the tunnel split and went off at angles to left and right. In the broader space formed by the three openings in the earth, they paused, peering down each arm of the Y and looking at each other.

There came help then in the matter of choosing: from along the leftward passage came sound. It was that of weeping, in the naturally high voice of a woman or an adolescent.

After the exchange of another glance—and one directed at Thulsa Doom—they turned and entered the channel to the left.

Was it an omen of ill favour that the first sound they heard in this subterrene road to the tuatha de

Danann was of sobbing; that the first person they met here inside Eirrin was deep in sadness?

The passageway descended, angled—and they saw the weeper.

She was a girl or young woman, huddled on the cavern floor, close to the far wall with her legs drawn up and her head in her hands.

She was entirely naked but for a bracelet, which looked like bronze.

Deciding as he had about Sinshi that this nude little weeper was more girl than woman, Cormac paused, lifted a hand to halt the others. His buckler was on his arm and his sword in his sheath. They gazed on the girl, whose head was down while she wept with quaking shoulders and yet little sound as though she strove not to be heard; nevertheless she had neither seen nor heard their approach. In silence, the three trespassers of under-earth stared.

Never had Cormac mac Art seen anyone so pale.

An infant, mayhap; a toddler never out of the house. As this girl of the Danans had never been out of the earth. No sun had ever touched that skin, nor that of her parents or their parents before them, nor indeed any of her forebears, for some five centuries. They and their arcane art had somehow brought with them the light of their goddess, for this chamber was brighter, as though bathed in moonlight. But not sunlight. Aye, the Danans, for so pale was this one that she had to be of those people of sub-Eirrin, despite her great difference from those of the Isle of Daneira.

Though strange, the pearly colour of her hair, ever so faintly tinged with the palest slate blue, was far from distasteful. Cormac had seen ash-blonds afore, though hardly often, and he had seen too those whose hair went grey and even white ere they had lived long enough to gain the wrinkles of age; he thought such hair beautiful.

This Danan's hair was that hue all over her body, he saw, and she was superbly constructed—strangely no darker round her nipples than the inner shell of a mussel—and attractive by the standards of any people he knew, assuming they judged not beauty by the amount of flesh. Though true, he had not yet seen her face.

Like those of Daneira, this sobbing Danan was slight, lightly boned and extremely short; five feet, if that tall.

Cormac spoke quietly, with deliberate slowness and care for pronunciation.

"Whatever it is that puts sadness on ye, we'll not be adding to it."

Up came her head; wide went eyes more pale than ever Cormac had seen even among the Norse. Her sobs ended. Fine nostrils flared as with a little cry she drew back against a wall of rocky earth shored with both wood and stones. She stared, shrinking.

"We bring you absolutely no harm," Cormac said, uncomfortable in the role of gentleness; it was little practice he'd had. "D'ye understand my words?"

Silent and huge-eyed, weird-eyed, she nodded. Her head was longish, her face thin and with pronounced bone-structure. Like those of a rabbit though nigh without colour, her eyes swiftly shifted their skittish gaze from one to the other of the three men before her. Cormac knew that they were even stranger to her than she to them; they expected the unusual. On impulse, he squatted. Even at a distance of two lengths of his body, he towered over the girl on the floor against the wall, her legs and arms drawn up defensively.

"My name is Cormac mac Art. He of the red beard is Wulfhere. Wulfhere. This is. . . Thulsa. It's

133

from. . . above, that we've come. And in peace. . . oh."

He had forgotten. From between tunic and mailcoat he lifted the silver chain, with its pendent sign of the Moonbow.

The girl gasped, stared. Her head came forward a trifle to peer at the sigil. Her gaze shifted to the chest of Thulsa Doom. She blinked and tucked her lower lip betwixt her teeth.

"It is as friend of Danu and Her people I come, with my blood-brother and him who is my captive, bonded to me by the Chains of Danu." Cormac smiled. "We are not monster Gaels come to eat ye! Indeed, we come bearing some gifts, and begging a boon."

Still she said naught, but only stared.

"It's slowly I'm talking because it's apart our tongues have grown, your people's and mine, across the hundreds of years. Please do the same. It's of the Danans ye be?"

Long he waited for her reply; at last she said, in a tiny voice, "Aye. Cor. . . Cormac mac. . . your *hair!* And *his* hair. . . and so tall ye be, all three!"

Cormac showed her another smile, working very hard at being gentle and confidence-winning. "And to us ye be lovely small, child of Danu! I. . . it's on me to ask. . ." He paused. "See us as friends of yourself, g—will ye be telling us your name?"

She was staring past him with those positively unsettling eyes with less colour than the underside of a cloud. Abruptly realizing that it was not cold as he'd expected, so deep in the earth, he gave thought to the possibility that the Danans of sub-Eirrin wore no clothing. But her legs were drawn up and to one side, heels at her buttocks, thus concealing her privates in apparent modesty. Her arms remained

134

across breasts that he had already seen were firm and high and pointy of tip, like cones of snow.

He asked her again. Her gaze snapped to his face.

"Oh! I make apology—I was staring. . .the beard of. . .of. . ."

"Wulfhere," the Dane rumbled, and she jerked a little.

"Oh! And whât a voice! Your beard is beautiful, my lord Wulfhere. I—my name if Erris. Of the de Danann, aye. It's handmaid I am, to Queen Riora Feachtnachis of Moytura."

Queen Riora! This time Cormac's smile was broad and genuine.

Chapter Nine:
Battle Beneath the Earth

Cormac gazed smiling upon Erris the Danan, handmaiden to Riora, Queen of Moytura. His heart surged and he felt as if a breeze had arisen to blow warm air over him.

A queen ruled here, beneath and within Eirrin; a crownéd woman!

The queen of Moytura . . . Moytura: Magh Tuiredh, the site of the long, long ago battle in which the Danans had put defeat on the Fir Bholgs, the first rulers of Eirrin. As for the other names, Erris and Riora; well, the sounds were familiar, though Rory—Rudraighe—was a man's name. The naming of people had taken its own course here, he realized.

Cormac mac Art twisted about to share an elated look with Wulfhere.

Grinning, Wulfhere asked, ''And do the people of

Moytura wear no clothing?''

Immediately Erris of Moytura erupted anew into tears. Cormac resisted the desire to get up and strangle the Dane. . .

Rising, he pulled around the sizeable belt-pouch he wore, and fished within it while he approached Erris. He squatted before the small huddled form. His touch was gentle, and his hand on her shoulder looked like the shadows of night swallowing the wan glow of the moon. She looked up briefly, stricken and tear-stained; dropped her head to her hands again.

He felt foolish, proffering the necklace from the Doom-heim trove. Jewels they had brought, aye, hopefully to deal with a queen. But of clothing— none. All, every scrap of cloth, Samaire and the others had taken to Tara. Yet now he remembered that he had that to offer her which would cover her nakedness, though he hated with a man's instincts and urges to see it done. Naturally he and Wulfhere wore cloaks; they had wrapped themselves well in them, each night.

He cupped his palm under the disk of his mantle's brooch, drew forth the pin, and caught the disk in his palm. Setting them aside, he removed his cloak, placed it over her drawn-up form, to the chin. He tucked it around.

She stilled her sobs, looked up sniffing. For a long while she gazed into his eyes.

"You are kind," she said.

"Is it kindness to lend clothing to someone who has none? Here, here is the clasp to my cloak." He considered. "Ye have done wrong, Erris Rioranacht? ye were stripped and. . ." He looked about, and it came to him. This was not Moytura—not yet! "And cast out!" he blurted.

She nodded, her so-pale eyes watery and leaking tears down the cheeks of her thin face. Looking at him, she tugged the cloak up to cover all of her save her head—and her back, which was against the tunnel's wall. She told him.

Yes. She had been stripped, and cast forth—but not for wrongdoing. Because she was the queen's favourite.

Cormac frowned and a coldness grew around his heart.

Erris of Moytura spoke more, and all elation faded from him, and from Wulfhere, until it had ceased to exist and it was only distress they knew.

Riora of Moytura was daughter of Riora, queen. But a year ago the queen had died; her daughter was crowned. Riora, daughter of Riora, was queen of Danan Moytura.

But Queen Riora did not rule in Moytura.

Her cousin Cairluh had plotted with the mage, Tarmur Roag. Cairluh and Tarmur Roag had seized power in Moytura; *they* ruled.

Cormac clutched at a fleeting and unlikely hope. "Cairluh is not. . . a woman's name here, is it?"

Erris shook her head and cloudlike hair flew. She looked at him without smiling, and there was less colour in her eyes than in the nails of his fingers.

"Oh no," Erris said, but she did not smile at his suggestion.

Cormac sighed. "How is it then that the people of Moytura suffer a male cousin to rule in the place of her who is their rightful queen? Is your mistress so bad a ruler?"

"She is *not!*" Erris snapped with some anger and much vehemence, and then she softened and explained.

Tarmur Roag was a man of considerable power. A
138

simulacrum of Riora, created or called up by Tarmur Roag in the queen's precise likeness, ruled in her stead. She—or it, was controlled, of course, by Tarmur Roag and Cairluh.

"Hmm. And—what differences have come of it? Does it matter who rules Moytura?"

"Of course! My lady Riora is *Queen!*"

Cormac nodded. Yes, yes, of course, but rulers came and went. . .

"And Cairluh believes that with the power of Tarmur Roag we of Danu can rise up and overthrow. . . you who live above. The people are being stirred up to such a belief, and all—all, men and women and girls and boys—are being forced to train with weapons, to carry red death above along with the sorceries of Tarmur Roag!"

Cormac thought: *Aye, it matters who rules in Moytura within Eirrin!* For even though it was a ridiculous thought, a futile concept that these people could conquer his, there'd be much, much blood shed in the trying of it. And he knew that the sons of Eirrin would not stop this time until no Danan remained alive in all the land—on or in the isle called Emerald.

Clinks and a rustle announced the drawing close of Wulfhere. His voice was a hopeful croak. "The queen? What have the plotters done with your mistress?"

New tears scudded down the white cheeks of Erris as she replied. Riora, the real Queen Riora, languished in misery of mind and body in her own dungeon, an ensorceled and pain-fraught captive who was mocked and teased and preyed upon by the torturemaster. He had made brag he'd get a child on her ere he ruined her face and body forever.

With a long sigh, Cormac stared down, half-seeing. Gentle were the de Danann of the isle; not so these of Moytura of sub-Eirrin, whose queen's demesne included a dungeon and a master of the tortures administered there! He twisted partway about to stare at the face and robe of Bas the Druid.

Thulsa Doom.

So long as he lived, Cormac mac Art was in danger, and so was all Eirrin, for it was Cormac who had brought the monster here, and him evil incarnate and a hundred and eighty centuries old. And it was only a queen could end the mage's unnatural life that was not life at all but foul un-death. And Riora of Moytura was such a queen. . . and Riora of Moytura was dethroned and crownless.

Queen Riora is. . . presently *dethroned and crownless,* Cormac thought.

"Wulfhere. . . in order to end the menace of Thulsa Doom. . . I must attempt to restore their queen to her throne."

Standing beside the squatting Gael, Wulfhere said nothing. Cormac heard his great sigh. Then:

"Girl—Erris. *We,* Cormac and I, will aid ye and your queen. For no matter how many men it is that Cairluh and Tarmur. . . Ro have guarding her prison, we shall send them dripping gore to their goddess. Now—what of this Tarmur Ro? He is to be feared? He is impervious to this?" Wulfhere's ax hummed in the air.

"Tarmur Roag," she corrected.

"He—he is a. . . none is so powerful, not even Dithorba!"

Cormac said, "Dithorba?"

"Aye. Dithorba Loingsech, the queen's own adviser and himself a mage. But—"

It was Thulsa Doom who interrupted. "The two of ye cannot overcome this Tarmur Roag, Cormac mac Art. Release me now, O Cormac of the Gaels, and I swear never to bring harm upon ye or your land or any of its people, wherever they be, and all your friends, and to make you a king among men. . . *King Cormac*. . . more than a king!''

Cormac swung and stared with his lips held tight. ''I trust ye no farther than I could be throwing ye, skullface—uphill! Now be silent, and. . .'' He looked back at Erris. ''Erris, prepare yourself for a hideous sight, and remember that he is chained to me by Danu's own bonds.'' He slid an arm back and down and found her hand. It was not cold. ''Thulsa Doom: Be silent. And give over the likeness of Bas the Druid that ye dishonour—assume your own form, creature of death!''

The undying wizard obeyed. The robes and face of Bas swam, went all murky and tenuous, were gone. The gleaming head of death stared at them from above the dark robe of Cutha Atheldane.

With a gasping throaty cry Erris lunged up to press hard against Cormac's back. She clung there, and he felt her shudders. Wulfhere glanced at her back, and down. His eyes widened and he raised pale red brows. The Danish giant looked away—and then at her again, as if helplessly, to admire the young woman's naked back.

After glancing at him, Cormac said, ''Best ye back away, Erris, and swing that cloak about yourself properly.''

''He—he—''

''He has no face. He is a mage. He is in my control. I wear the Moonbow—and ye see it on him, too, downside up. Do as I bade ye.''

She released him reluctantly, looked at Wulfhere, glanced at Thulsa Doom, and then with the cloak held before her she squatted to catch up its brooch. Unblushingly she swung the cloak about her as he'd suggested, and pinned it above her left breast. The greyish blue mantle enveloped her completely, to the toes. Again she moved to stand close to Cormac.

"Erris. . . where be this Dithorba Loingsech? It's he should be as glad to be our ally as we his, I'm thinking."

She shook her head distressedly. "Tarmur Roag mocks his fellow mage by binding him with chains of silver—" Her head jerked up and her eyes were wide as new excitement and hope came upon her. "HERE, outside Moytura!"

A smile toyed with Cormac's lips; failed to manifest itself. "Any hands can remove the Chains of Danu, save those of the wearer of the inverted Moonbow—why have ye not released him?"

Her shiver was conveyed by the rippling of the encompassing cloak of blue-grey woollen. She licked her lips.

"I was just put forth from Moytura. Dithorba is guarded. I. . .I. . ." Erris looked down. "I was *too loyal* to my mistress. It is why I was stripped and thrust out here. . . for *them*. Those who guard Dithorba. Rough weapon men who are like blood-hungry beasts with Tarmur Roag's sorcerous bidding upon them. I was. . . I was to be their. . . 'Here, wench,' snarled those who thrust me forth, 'provide *entertainment* for the lonely watchers of Dithorba, that they may *recreate* themselves.' This was just before you came."

Cormac heard the emphasis on the word "you" without making any indication of reaction. Yet at her words of Danan weapon-men about, his and Wulfhere's hands had gone to sword-hilt and ax-helve as if at a signal. The Dane's crimson beard twitched, which meant he was smiling, somewhere within that flaming bush.

142

"And where is Dithorba, Erris. . . and his guards?"

She pointed past them. "Straight there. Along the other branch from. . . from the Door to Them."

Cormac mac Art saw to his shield-straps. "Say not 'them' with such a fearful heaviness on ye, Erris. . . Wulfhere and I, after all, *are* 'Them'!" He turned to look at his weapon companion of several years, grim and blood-splashed seagoing years as rievers. "Wulfhere?"

The giant hefted ax and buckler. Anticipation lit his cerulean eyes with bloody portents for the guards of Dithorba.

"How many guards be there?" Cormac asked Erris. She shook her head. "I know not. Less than ten methinks but no mere two or three—five, mayhap."

"Hmp," Wulfhere rumbled. "In that event, Cormac, why don't ye wait here? I'll be back from this encounter in a few heartbeats. . . "

Cormac gave him a look. "Stay ye well back, Erris," he said, and the two men set their feet in the direction she'd indicated; the other arm of the Y down the stem of which they had come from outside— Outside. At Cormac's beck, Thulsa Doom fell in behind them—and Erris stayed well back, indeed, staring at that hairless and gleaming skull.

They moved along the subterranean hallway with the cautious silence of great stalking cats. An occasional scuff of buskin on hardpacked earth or stone, and a faint clink of mail were the only hints of the advance of two weapon-men followed by a silent, faceless mage and a cloak-swathed young woman. All three men were forced to stoop as they went along that pearl-lit passage within the earth.

It came upon Cormac to wish he had asked whether the tunnel debouched into such a chamber or

143

"room" as the one in which they'd found Erris. Too late now. If not—fighting in this low-ceiled tunnel with oppressively close walls might well be to the advantage of the Danans. Cormac clamped his lips. He had not come here to fight the people of Danu!

If only surprise could be with him and Wulfhere. . .

They rounded a turning, and Cormac's eyes narrowed; aye, up ahead was an obvious widening and heightening on the other side of what resembled a doorway notched in the earth. Dithorba Loingsech was not bound in the tunnel itself, then, but within a larger chamber. *Good!* They approached more slowly now, careful not to jostle each other or to make the faintest sound.

At what might be called a doorway without a door, they paused. Within lay a chamber of stone that was nigh square, each wall perhaps thrice Cormac's length. Not a huge room, but big enough for the wielding of ax and sword and buckler, and the swift necessary movement of their feet.

In the far right corner was piled a cairn of stones, and there too was him they sought. The Moonbow of Danu hung upon his chest at the end of its silver chain, its points downward. This had to be Dithorba, who like Thulsa Doom was captive of the Chains of Danu. A very short and passing thin man he was, with a beard like dirty snow that was plaited on his chest; above, his pate was bald and gleaming. In addition to the Moonbow necklace, the queen's mage was chained to the wall itself—by shackles of silver. Pitifully, the old fellow wore naught but a loincloth.

Gael gave Dane a querying look; Dane nodded.

And the bigger man moved. Before Cormac could step forward, Wulfhere entered the chamber of stone. He sidestepped swiftly leftward so that there was room for his companion to enter and range

144

himself beside him—and it fell out that the guards were there, to the left of the entry.

Two men squatted, and the knuckle-bones in the hand of one struck the floor with a little clatter just as the newcomers came upon them. Four others stood about them. Instantly a dozen pale de Danann eyes fixed on Wulfhere the Splitter of Skulls, and every man showed shock.

A full half dozen there were, unnaturally pale, grim-faced men who were both armed and armoured. Their widened eyes changed swiftly; now they flared as unnaturally with the scarlet killing-lust. Cormac saw on the instant that Tarmur Roag was their master, and that the traitorous sorcerer of Moytura had made animals of these guards; they were mindless, fearless slayers.

The two dicers scrambled up and wrapped fists around pommels; six short pale men faced the two who had come so unexpectedly upon them. Surprise had been lost; Wulfhere had not immediately charged. Yet the men of Moytura hesitated, staring at men who to them were weird of hair and complexion—and gigantic of stature. Like their cousins of the Isle, none of these Danans was above five and half feet in height.

Corselets of scintillant, superbly wrought mail they wore, chain after the manner of Eirrin rather than the short coat of overlapping scales that armoured Wulfhere's massive frame from collarbones to upper thighs. The links were dark. Each Danan bore a sword rather than ax or spear, and their bucklers were ornately wrought, six-sided and inlaid and painted and enameled as though the makers had sought to make jewellery of the implements of war and red death. Shaped like crescent moons were their helmets, with outcurving wings that Cormac thought were surely silver, welded onto the sides of their round helms of iron.

As though frozen, the Danans stared. Cormac seized the moment.

"It's for Dithorba we've come," he said. "Stand ye back all, and live another day."

Wulfhere rotated his wrist so that his great ax swung in readiness. The face of mac Art twisted into a sinister and violent expression as he lifted his buckler. In his fist his sword was ready for the letting of Danan blood. A light that seemed to welcome battle blazed blue in his eyes like sword steel.

The Danans made reply in action rather than words. They came grimly, death-hounds of the land below-earth pitting their hatred-glaring selves against two tigers of the sea, men with hearts of wolves and thews of fire and steel, feeders of countless eaters of carrion; men to whom the death-song was sweeter than the love-croon of a maiden.

Wulfhere grinned and waited. Far greater men than these had been given pause by that smile that betokened joy in battle. Not so these sorcerously encouraged Danans; they came on.

Grim of mien, a man of the earth launched a sword-slash with a savagery that bespoke his unreasoning hate for these who challenged his charge—and his blind senseless obedience to the fell conditioning of Tarmur Roag. Only then did the redbearded giant heave up his weapon and with a tremendous swipe of that outsized ax destroy sword and beautiful mail, skin and bone, shoulder and chest so that the attacker was cloven to the pectoral and Wulfhere was forced to fight and worry his ax free. It came away drooling scarlet gore while his victim sank down with only a gasp to mark his passage from this world into the next.

The man beside and just back of him was shocked at the tigerishly lithe swiftness of the unbearded man with the dark skin. Then he knew shock again when that scarred intruder did not chop, but thrust, in a blurring forward motion of his entire right arm. Steel entered the Danan betwixt his collarbones and sank to the length of his own hand. That hand flexed in a spasm and his sword fell at Cormac's feet. The short man's body followed, twitching.

None cursed or made battle cry; the battle beneath the earth was fought in an awful silence but for the ring and scrape of arms.

The other diminutive sons of Danu came frothing on in a ravening onslaught so that Cormac and Wulfhere were forced to use all skill and swiftness against the close-bunched foe. Blue sparks flew from the edges of shield and hacking blades and the terrible clangour of war arose.

A mighty sword-sweep missed the Gael only because he blurred backward a half-pace. Then forward; Danan blade rang off stone wall with an ear-splitting screech that sent a thousand bright sparks aflying. At the same time, Cormac's point whisked forth like a striking blue-grey serpent and vanished into the eye whose socket it widened. Another sword came rushing at his side; before he could shift up his buckler Wulfhere's ax-blade came whining to shorten the deadly sliver of death by a halfscore inches. Ten inches of Danan iron clanged and clattered off wall and floor of yieldless stone—and three inches of Gaelic steel destroyed Danan chainmail and opened its wearer's stomach nigh to his backbone. A dark hand of incredible skill and strength gave the sword a quick twist and jerked it forth so swiftly that it was clear and rushing elsewhere ere the spate of blood followed.

147

In the narrow chamber walled all about with closely pressing, echoic stone beneath its low ceil, the clangour of striving weapons was nigh onto deafening.

At the doorway stood robed man and cloaked woman, watching; Erris had forgot her fear to press against the undying wizard while she stared at a sight she had never before witnessed. So too stared Dithorba, moveless in his bonds amid the pile of loose stones.

A hideously grimacing head rolled over the floor of hardened earth, sheared from Danan shoulders by the bite of Wulfhere's ax. At the same time, an ugly grunt was wrenched from Cormac by the impact of the edge of a Danan blade on his sword-arm. His fingers quivered, threatening to drop his own brand.

But an inch lower and he'd have lost the arm or been struck to the bone at least; only the linked steel sleeve of his mailcoat saved him from that horror. With the battle-fever on him he felt no pain, only the blow. Promised nevertheless a bothersome arm later and a huge tender bruise, he snarled blasphemous curses and drove his buckler forward with such vicious force that it not only struck the attacker full in the face but snapped the man's neck.

The last Danan died instantly, to fall without a mark on him.

Chapter Ten:
The Wizard of Moytura

The deadly steel-hued eyes of Cormac mac Art were wild and glittering as he snapped his head this way and that, seeking the next foeman. There was none. It was over that swiftly, in a mad flurry of hand-to-hand ferocity that left six diminutive men of under-earth lying amid a spreading welter of blood whilst the victors had scarce begun to pant.

Wulfhere lowered his red-smeared ax and glared at his comrade. Blood dripped from his arm; it was not from his veins.

"Is that *all,* Wolf? I've not even raised a sweat!"

"Blood-mad demon from the demesne of Hel!" the Gael accused, and grinned an ugly wolfish grimace. "What is it ye want? It's six men we've just been after hacking our way through with steel, and ye're after bemoaning the lack of their number!

There—that one moves still; be a kind man and swiften his pace into Danu's arms that he suffers less."

Wulfhere first frowned in puzzlement at the seeming verbal attack. Then he began to grin, and his ax slit an agonized man's throat with surgical precision. Cormac was meanwhile looking across the corpses to the rear of the chamber of earth and stone.

"It's Cormac son of Art I am, a Gael from the land above. I and this redbeard are come to release ye, man. . . ye'll aid us in the freeing of your queen?"

The old man blinked, and one foot shifted amid the loose stones surrounding him like a premature burial cairn. He gazed on Cormac, and there was anguish in his eyes. He spoke not.

Cormac mac Art frowned, looking up from his squat; he was carefully wiping his swordblade on the skirt of a dead man's tunic.

"Can ye not speak? Can ye move your head, then?"

The old man nodded.

"Ah." Cormac rose and sheathed his sword. "It's sorcery done upon ye, is it?" He turned. "Wulfhere, we—"

"Cormac! FALL!"

The Dane's shout rose high and loud with a definite note of desperation. Cormac knew the tone, and saw the horrified face, and he knew this urgency signal they had each used in past. It told him that he was sore menaced from behind, could not meet the menace, and must betake himself out of the way instanter. He responded with swift obedience to exigence. Cormac did not fall; he dived to the unyielding floor with a clash of buckler and a twist of his head that allowed helm and hair to absorb the impact.

Prone, he sensed more than heard the overhead whiz of some unknown missile. He was already scrambling around to bring up sword and shield to meet whatever malign force might have materialized between himself and the Danan mage. Aye, materialized, for the experiences with Thulsa Doom had conditioned him to accept the awful reality of sorcerous attacks.

It was Wulfhere and the others who were behind him now, and from that direction he heard something hard smack the stone wall near the entry; the thrown object was not metal. On his back he faced—no one. Nothing. There was only the pile of grey and grey-brown stones, twinkling with flecks of quartz and feldspar, around the bare thin shanks of Dithorba.

Frowning, his mind weighted with the darkness of confusion, Cormac twisted again. *Was* Dithorba helpless—had the Danan hurled something? But he was chained. . . Asprawl and raised partway on one elbow, the Gael stared while Wulfhere stooped. The big man straightened, hefting the fist-sized chunk of rock he had picked up.

"This *leaped* from the pile and rushed at your back, Cor—Cormac! Another!"

Cormac mac Art lay on his back, legs extended toward the cairn, his neck twisted so that he faced Wulfhere. At the Dane's words his nape crawled. There was no time to give thought to the eerieness, though; again danger threatened imminently. Even as he started to turn his face again in Dithorba's direction, his left arm moved in a rush. Weapon-man's reflexes sent his buckler sweeping up in protection, however blindly. Luck or the gods of Eirrin guided his arm. Instinctively he swung it up and in before his sprawled body, ere he could see what he was doing.

There was a grating chunking impact on his shield, a smallish round targe, and his arm shivered. He groaned then in pain, for onto his leg dropped the flying stone he had providentially deflected with his buckler. Several pounds in weight, the rock fell on him below the hem of his mailcoat's short skirt. Leather leggings afforded protection, there, but the blow was forceful and he felt it to the bone.

Staring eyes told him that Dithorba remained helpless. There was no one else there. No one had hurled the stone. Yet it had come flying. Twice then, stones had hurled themselves at him.

While he was starting to rise, another chunk of granite sprang at him from the jumbled pile about Dithorba Loingsech. With a feeling of horror Cormac saw the inanimate thing detach itself from the others, become animate. Agleam with twinkling quartz, it came skimming at him, low so as to catch him in face or neck.

Cormac hurled himself down and aside. He rolled. Suddenly the most important goal of his life was getting himself off the rough floor of stone and earth and into a vertical position.

It had come again.

Dark sorcery stalked him.

Again, Donn, the Dark One, dread lord of the dead, roamed the world, and again his keen eyes had fallen on Cormac mac Art. Again it was not man or beast attacking him, but the mephitic manifestation of the malign power of some wrathful wizard; the uncanny horrors of sorcery; the death that affrighted and confounded even as it came seeking, like a loosed arrow that could not be met with sword and ax or even intelligence-born tactic, but could only be feared and avoided. And yet it was worse than any humming arrow, for such at least was the product of human hands as was the bow that loosed it and even the power that drove it.

Here there was naught to attack, no place to hide and no hand or body at which to direct slaying steel.

But what or who was the source of this attack?

The Moonbow of Danu the Goddess still flashed dully on his breast, and its reversed mate hung still just below the collarbones of Thulsa Doom. Not from that master of frightsome illusions and the walking dead this unnatural assault, then; it was another who struck, and him invisible or directing from afar.

A huge stone shaped like a mollusc of singular size came whizzing, and Cormac dodged convulsively.

"Wulfhere! To your shield-side and along the wall to Dithorba! Erris—keep ye back, girl, for ye've no defense against this assault of rock! Thulsa Doom, move not so much as a fing—*uh!*"

So intent was mac Art on his directions for the circumvention of the indefensible onslaught that he was caught by it; a knobby stone just bigger than Wulfhere's fist slammed into his right bicep. Sleeve of linked steel rings saved him from shredded skin and broken bone, but his hand flexed and his sword dropped to clatter. Cormac staggered, getting his feet back and out of the way of his own dropped glaive. With his pain-filled eyes on the source of the silent, hair-raising attack, he bent for the sword.

He paused while he reconsidered. Then he retrieved his sword—and sheathed it. Still in a crouch, staring at the cairn as though it were some snarling beast or Donn-sent demon, he backed two paces. He caught up a sword of one of the fallen Danans. As his fingers worked, shifting and shifting the pommel for the feel and balance of this brand shorter than his own, he glanced over at Wulfhere.

As Cormac had bade, the Dane was moving warily along the wall, advancing toward the corner; thence he would move across the chamber's rear wall to the corner in which Dithorba was bound.

Cormac's nape prickled; a chunk of granitic rock lifted without a sound from its piled fellows and went end-over-end at the huger target of the redbearded giant.

"HO!" Wulfhere cried. "Practice does a man good!"

With an almost preposterously expert sweep of his ax, the giant struck the rushing missile away—over an arm's length from his body.

Another followed close behind, rushing low. Cormac did not wait to see its effect; Wulfhere was prepared. sweating, though from neither heat nor exertion, mac Art rushed toward Dithorba. But the invisible attacker was not distracted. A rock came spinning his way, but a pair of inches above the ground, to catch his shin. He danced, saw another chunk of stone rush off at Wulfhere while still another lofted itself at him, and in dodging he fell.

"Leave this place!" Dithorba's voice was dry, crackly with age. "Ye cannot free me, so long as I wear the Moonbow points down; Tarmur Roag will put death on both of ye giants. Leave me; this is only death for ye both!"

"Why made ye no reply be-*uh*-fore!" Wulfhere demanded with some petulance, briefly interrupting himself to fend away a platter-size stone. It scraped across his buckler with an ear-scratching noise.

"Go!" Dithorba Loingsech cried. "I held my silence in hopes Tarmur would not know of your presence and the deaths of the guards he set to watch over me. He knows. More weapon-men will come.

Go, go, ye cannot free me; ye cannot fight stones hurled by a powerful mage far from here!"

"Augh!" Wulfhere crashed against the wall. Precisely in his armoured stomach a skull-sized stone had struck the Dane, and he slid weakly down the rocky wall with a screeching of steel scales.

"All we need do is pluck that necklace from round your neck, Dithorba Loingsech!" Cormac snarled, and like a vicious animal he used shield to bash away a flying shape of rock that twinkled as if set with a score of diamonds.

"And these chains? Be not foolish, dark man— your comrade is already down and more guards are doubtless on their way!"

Steel will cut silver chain very nicely, Cormac thought, but he said nothing.

Three grey stones leapt up from the dwindled pile; they hurtled at him in a flurry, separating naturally.

With his targe he smashed away the largest, though he heard stout wood crack; in stooping to meet that crotch-aimed lump of rock he bent under the second, which he heard hum past his ear. The third, aimed at his body, struck his helmet with a belling crash and a shower of shivered stone.

His head ringing both at ears and within, Cormac fell and did not rise.

"Wolf!" the Dane called in concern. He was getting himself grunting to his feet with the aid of wall and ax-helve. And two sorcery-driven stones rushed at him.

Cormac's blue-grey mantle fluttered and bare white legs flashed. Across the floor strewn with stones and corpses and slippery with blood raced Erris of Moytura in a lunatic dash—and in seconds she had reached the shackled mage. As her hands rose to his necklace he swiftly bent his head; the slave snatched away the chain and the Sign of the Moonbow. She hurled it to the floor of hardpacked earth.

Immediately Dithorba went rigid and his eyes closed.

A big flattened rock, just elevating to begin its assault on Wulfhere, clattered back onto the other stones remaining about Dithorba's ankles. Nor did more stones move.

Totally heedless of her nudity, made the whiter by the slate-hued cloak of Cormac mac Art, Erris squatted beside the fallen Gael. He was up on one forearm, twitching his head, staring dully down. His helmet was dented, though no blood seeped from beneath its rim.

"An we. . . free Riora, Erris. . . it's you. . . who's made it possible."

"Oh please, please Cormac mac Art—be all right, get up get up oh please. . ."

A great burly form loomed over her, squatted beside her. "What's this? Be ye tired from this little fray, battle-brother? What ails ye?"

Cormac looked at him. "I have a headache."

Wulfhere laughed gustily. Cormac detected the trace of hysteria that denoted relief on the Dane's part. The man was unequipped to cope with an injury to someone he loved, and the men of his chill land were too sure of their masculinity to avoid stating love for another man. Nevertheless Wulfhere's way was to lard on bluff jests as cover for nervous concern that made him most woefully uncomfortable.

Work remained to be done, and Cormac willed himself to move. His pushing himself was accompanied by twinges in right upper arm and left thigh. His head seemed to tighten within a deep grey band and he staggered in a long moment of vertigo. Leaning on the Dane, he bent to retrieve the Danan sword he'd dropped. He frowned against the throbbing in his head as he straightened. Cormac turned to Dithorba.

"See that ye move not, Dithorba Loingsech," he said, and he went to the old man and caught his thin arm in a vising grip.

Dithorba shrank and closed his eyes; the other man wielded sword. With five careful strokes of the Danan blade, Cormac freed the queen's adviser of his four chains. He gazed a moment at the sword; held it up for Wulfhere's eyes. The Danan blade was both bent and badly notched.

"Hmp! Ruined, by Odin's eye! My ax would have cut through thicker links of silver than those without taking note—much less bending!"

"Iron," Cormac said quietly. "All their swords are of iron, not steel." He went to one knee beside a corpse, moved to another. "Iron! All their helms, their armour. . . not steel, Wulfhere, but iron."

While he spoke and moved among the bodies, Erris moved to Dithorba. With more respect than self-consciousness, she removed Cormac's cloak and swept it around the spindly old man. Naked, she stood with head deferentially bowed. Dithorba but nodded. He stood looking from one to the other of the strangers, rubbing his arms. Despite their being held immobile by Cormac while he struck through the chains, each stroke had brought a painful wrench. The shackles remained, though but one link of silver chain dangled from each.

Danan and Gaelic eyes met.

"Ye've come from above," the dry, brittle old voice said. "A Gael, with that hair and skin and those eyes. We've not forgot what ye look like."

Cormac nodded.

"But ye come not as enemy." Dithorba glanced at

157

Wulfhere. "And. . . you. A giant with hair the colour of the pain-rock that yields iron. Two from above—and not as enemies, but to set me free." The old man shook his head and the plaited white beard stirred on his chest. Erris was a slave, and he took no note of her while she fussed with the cloak's clasp.

"Wulfhere—Erris has better use for his tunic than the man lying yonder with no wound on him," Cormac said. "Dithorba Loingsech: my name is Cormac mac Art. Wulfhere the Dane is my battle-brother. . . my blood brother, though our mothers knew each other not. It is to release ye we've come here. It's help we can provide each other, you and we."

Dithorba glanced at Erris, who was gazing with longing on the man of her people who lay dead among the others, him with neither wound nor blood on him, save at his nostrils. Reluctantly, Wulfhere went to that corpse.

Dithorba said, "To rescue me, and aid each other. Why?"

"Together," Cormac said, meeting the old man's light-eyed gaze levelly, "we must try to free your queen." Cormac swung his right arm vigorously, against a stiffening of the bruised bicep.

Dithorba stared for a time into the slitted eyes of the dark, scarred man. He nodded, briefly. "Aye—I'd set my life to that end. But. . . why yourself?"

Turning, Cormac extended a pointing finger at the tall, dark-robed figure in the doorway. "There stands a mage of much power and evil, and as ye well know this holds him mine." He touched the Moonbow on his chest. "It is because of him I must have. . . audience with Riora of Moytura, after she is enthroned with her crown upon her."

"I must be hearing more of this matter. . . that creature has no face!"

"Ye've said Tarmur Roag knows of our presence here, and was he hurled those stones though he be not here to see us."

"I wore this chain," Dithorba said, picking it up. "He saw ye through my eyes—whether I held them open or closed. But—"

"Ye spoke of his sending weapon-men," Cormác reminded. "Mayhap we'd best be getting ourselves elsewhere for talking."

Dithorba's eyes widened and he blinked. "Aye! There's been so much, so fast. . . it had actually fled my mind. Aye—armed men will be here in minutes!" And with those words, Dithorba Loingsech vanished.

Chapter Eleven:
The Dungeon of Moytura

Wulfhere Skull-splitter rose from a denuded corpse. He held a tunic of some thin, shining cloth of a pearly opaline hue. "Here, girl, ye can don this or make covering of it—though I seem to have slipped with my dagger, and made a slit or two in places." Then as he turned his grin faded and he blinked. "Where— Cormac! What's happened to him we loosed?"

"He. . . disappeared," Cormac said dully.

This time Erris's concern was for covering herself, not the vanished mage or the manner of its accomplishment. She went naked to Wulfhere, took the tunic with a tiny word of thanks, and stepped past him. Though she'd been naked when they found her and but a few minutes agone denuded herself anew to clothe the queen's adviser, she now kept her back turned while she slipped the soft, thin fabric of the tunic over her head.

"Thor's beautiful red beard," Wulfhere said, "but I'd love to be asea again, facing only such trifles as gales, whirlpools, a few boatloads of ravening Frisians and Norse, and a simple sea-monster or three!"

Cormac looked at the other man with complete empathy.

Erris came to the side of the Dane, and looked up; the man towered a foot and a half above her. "Again I make thanks to you for my clothing, my lord Wulfhere—though your *accidental* slip of the dagger bares both my legs to the waist!"

Before either man could comment, Dithorba was among them again.

Exclamations greeted his reappearance; none was fully coherent. The loinclothed man in Cormac's cloak lifted bony hands for silence.

"I have been to my own chamber in the palace. It has been searched, and is empty. They have not found my secret room, though, and I took not even time to clothe myself. Erris! Come—we must show them how Dithorba travels!"

Erris drew back, though Cormac saw that there was more nervousness on her than fear. Dithorba stretched forth a hand; slowly one of hers reached out to take it. Bony, wrinkled old fingers gripped smooth young ones no less white. There was no warning, no fading; the two Danans merely vanished. Cormac and Wulfhere jerked at the popping sound, as of two palms slapping together.

The two weapon-men looked at each other.

And Dithorba was back. He stretched forth a hand. "Cormac mac Art. Come."

"What. . . what have ye done, man? Where are ye after being?"

161

"I've told you. My secret room in the palace is far from here. There Erris is safe and not unhappy that her handsome thighs are bared; there we can talk and plan. Come."

"Ye. . . ye have the ability to. . . to move yourself, by. . . some cantrip?"

Dithorba shrugged bony shoulders on which Cormac's cloak hung like a sail on a windless day. "Time grows short. I can take with me but one at a time. No, no spells or cantrips. I have. . . such ability to travel. I merely will myself to be elsewhere; someplace I have been and can see in my mind. And I am there. It's my life you're after saving, son of the Gaels; I cannot do harm on you! Come."

Cormac looked at Wulfhere. The giant's mighty chest heaved a great sigh.

"Methinks it's either that we trust him, battle-brother, or remain here and see how many of Tarmur Roag's Danans we can slay ere they give us our deaths."

"I see which of ye counsels well," Dithorba said, and Wulfhere grinned.

Cormac did not essay to answer the unanswerable. He took the Danan's small, dry old hand.

He knew an instant of complete mental dissociation, as though his brain were aswirl amid blinding sulphurous mists that would swallow it and choke him to death. . . and then his legs were jarred badly, as though he'd taken a downward step when he'd surmised himself on level ground. He straightened, feeling the spinning of his brain, the tingling that ran up his legs. As if coming from the dark into the light, he became aware—and was looking at Erris.

"A law should be passed to force ye to wear a tunic such, slitted to your waist," he told her inanely, and was instantly aware of it, for his brain had not yet

162

been his own. He looked about.

He was elsewhere.

Dithorba had brought him hence from the chamber outside Moytura as swiftly and simply as that, and he was none the worse for the instantaneous transfer. They were in another room of stone, this one decorated and with a floor of handsome, well-fitted stones, smoothly polished. The walls were hung with draperies in rust-red bordered with silver; the cloth was the same fine, scintillant stuff of which Erris's tunic was made—and indeed, Dithorba's breechclout as well. Shelves and niches and an alcove had been fashioned into the stone itself; in them rested utensils and clothing, various closed pots and caskets of assorted sizes. There squatted a stone table; there a bench onto which were bound red pillows, there another, its pillows of blue. Light illuminated the room, without apparent source. Nor was Dithorba present—

But he was, and with Thulsa Doom.

"The giant bade me bring this one first—he's nigh attacked!" Dithorba said, and was not there.

Without patience or peace of mind Cormac waited, and then here was Dithorba once more, with Wulfhere Hausakluifr. The Dane grunted; his legs bent and he nearly fell. Cormac saw that the shorter Dithorba had miscalculated for them both; Wulfhere had been conveyed here at a level different from the Danan and like Cormac had. . . *arrived* off balance.

"We must not talk loudly, though as ye see, this chamber has no door. It is most privately mine; to my knowledge none other in Moytura possesses my ability to mind-travel. Yet we can be heard, for my apartment is just beyond that wall and through that one is a guardpost. Too, none can be sure of Tarmur Roag's power; a man who either raised a lamia or

163

created the queen's exact likeness, even unto the voice and mannerisms, is not one to wager lives against. Finally. . . even stone walls can be broke through, should we be heard."

In seconds the wizard had clothed himself in a robe of the same cloth as the draperies that mitigated the cold grey roughness of stone walls. Cormac was able to assume that lichens existed here within the earth; the robe's purple must have resulted from the action of stale urine on such growths. The rust colour of the drapes, he supposed, came from just that: rust, or the paint-stone from which came iron. The sleeves of Dithorba's robe, which fell past his ankles, were round, open, and three-quarters the length of his arms. Wulfhere paid him no mind, but was staring unashamedly though shamelessly at Erris. She appeared not to notice, which Cormac mac Art assumed was a pose.

Behind a drape Dithorba opened a wooden door; from within that little chamber he drew forth a leathern bag. It sloshed; Erris lost Wulfhere's attention. Soon the three men were appreciatively wetting their throats with ale, at which Erris turned up her nose. Under other circumstances so might Cormac have done; the stuff was hardly of the best and he feared to ask what served as grain, beneath the earth where no sun shone.

"I ask again, son of Gaels. Why came you two here?"

"A wizard stalks this world, all the world, like a plotting spider," Cormac said. He pointed at the long dark robe surmounted by the head of death itself. "Thulsa Doom. Anciently dead he is and raiser of the dead; master of illusion and enemy of all men; a servant of the serpent god he is, time out of mind." And he told Dithorba of the wizard who was dead

164

and yet not dead, and how they believed he could be slain for good and all. "Only the Chains of Danu hold him at bay now, or he'd be snarling like an animal—and worse."

"Well I know the efficacy of the silver chain and Moonbow!"

While Cormac had spoken, Wulfhere laid buckler and ax and helmet on the long table of stone. Leaning against it, he combed hair and beard with his fingers and kept the corner of his eye occupied with the watching of Erris.

"My blade sliced that tunic not enough," he muttered, when she handed him another cup of ale. Most valuable that cup; the Danans must have found a vein of precious metal and mined it well, for the cup, like the chains and the trim of draperies and of Dithorba's robe, was of silver.

She gave the big man a look that was part archness and part defiance, and turned away—though, he noted, with a swift movement that made her sideslashed skirts fly. Abruptly that little face was smiling back at him over her shoulder.

"Ye be so clever, my lord—without knowing that handmaidens of the queen accustomedly wear only these bracelets and a girdle suspending two long strips of cloth!"

"It's danger you've brought to Moytura then," Dithorba said, "Cormac mac Art of the Gaels."

"As ye've said, your goddess protects us and Moytura through her silver chains and Sign, wizard of under-earth. Now tell me of your queen."

Dithorba did. Riora Feachtnachis she was called, the very young ruler of the Danans within Eirrin; Riora the Fair, righteous One. The story of the treachery done on her and her intimates and advisers, and of their imprisonment, was as Erris had told it.

Simulacrum or Riora-mimicking lamia wore the coral crown and sat the throne of Moytura. Through her or rather it Cairluh ruled; he in turn was dominated by Tarmur Roag. The queen was endungeoned, watched over and tormented by one named Elatha the Whip. About her were her handmaidens and others, as well as her ministers and the commander of her guard. Others had been slain.

Cormac thought on it. It occurred to him that he need not worry about gaining entrance to the dungeon; surely this man could convey him there by his own unique means!

"And Tarmur Roag is powerful. What powers else have ye, Dithorba Loingsech?"

"With a few little abilities learned in time," the Moyturan said quietly, "ye've seen most of my powers, Cormac mac Art. Much can be accomplished by a clever, thinking man who can disappear and reappear where he will—unless he is fed a drug, and taken in his sleep as I was. Oh, I am not without other abilities, but Tarmur Roag is my superior. If only I possessed the martial skills of your extraordinary self, Cormac of the Gaels, Elatha the Whip were no deterrent to the freedom of my lady Queen!"

Cormac showed the Danan his ghost of a smile. It little resembled pleasantry or mirth, but few others living had seen more. "Ye need not seek to persuade me; ye know my purpose and the necessity of its doing. Ye have my size and skills, Dithorba, so long as ye can take me anywhere at all, and that faster than the curvet of a trout! Anywhere at all—such as into the queen's dungeon."

"Cormac!" Wulfhere was distracted even from Erris.

Cormac turned on his friend a mild look, then returned his slit-eyed gaze to Dithorba. "Be there a bit of food hereabouts, Lord Dithorba?''

The old man looked most sorrowful indeed. "Not a morsel.'' He sighed. "The queen's own advisor—reduced to thievery!'' And he vanished.

"Ouch!'' Wulfhere grunted. "Erris! I did but fondle what normally ye wear bare—where's he gone now, Wolf?''

"To someone's kitchen or storehouse, there to snatch provender for us, poor man,'' the Gael said. "Do ye have animals in Moytura, Erris?''

She frowned. "Animals. . . oh! I've heard of such—no. They live on that which we cannot grow here, Cormac mac Art. Wulfhere—please! Many kinds of mollusc we have, for we have cultured them and coaxed them over the years to. . . modify, so I'm taught. And fish aplenty too, of many varieties. And lichens, and oh! marvelous mushrooms of more than one variety. Ye—ye've seen. . . animals? Legend has it such were here, once, but could not survive. Beasts that walk like. . . like us?''

"On four legs. But whence comes the cloth for your clothing, for these drapes?''

"The mif and the great spiders,'' she said, and when questioned she explained that the mif was a great worm that throve here within the earth, and of its dried slime excellent cloth was made, along of course with the filaments spun by spiders Cormac did not care to see.

"Ugh,'' Wulfhere said succinctly and with fervour.

"An ye like not our cloth,'' Erris said, low-voiced, "keep your enormous hands away from this I wear, then.''

"Mayhap we can find time and place to remove it together,'' Wulfhere said, "later.''

Cormac sighed, turning away—and Dithorba was there, bearing food stolen from someone's very cookfire, for the pot was hot and issuing a most savoury aroma.

Thrice he left them, and thrice he returned laden, and none asked questions. They ate and drank then, four of them; Thulsa Doom required no nourishment.

The visitors learned that nay, not all rooms in Moytura were carved from living rock as was this one; stone was cut and used in building, and there was a mortaring paste they had made, too, to hold together blocks of stone in this land of no baking sun, no softening rain, no freezing snow or ice. In a great pool and in the two rivers that ran near there were creatures of sea and fresh water, and some were of a sort never seen above. Their hides were much used; as mining was constant and iron and silver plentiful, frames were easily made for the stretching of hides of walrus and water-creatures even bigger. Every scrap of cloth otherwise came from spiders and mifhe; the large snow-hued worms fed on the gigantic mushrooms that throve here within the earth. The queen's adviser, the handmaiden, and the two weapon-men from above dined well on dishes of various fish and molluscs and mushrooms, and when Wulfhere made brag on one dish, he was advised that it was comprised of mushrooms, a mussel they called ab, snails and two kinds of lichen. Whereupon the Dane deemed himself sufficiently well fed to confine his grinding teeth to fish and a mushroom dish.

And what of the pearly light that bathed sunless Moytura?

Dithorba, who was indeed possessor of few necromantic and thaumaturgic powers or knowledge, could not tell them. It had been devised, or brought by the first settlers from the land above, long and long agone. It was Danu's light. She shed her silvery moonish glow on her own that they might not have to dwell in darkness but were ever in this soft twilight, and no more Dithorba Loingsech knew.

Nor did he know what was meant by steel. None such was there in all Moytura, a land sprawling, large as Meath above, among natural caverns and chambers and those created by men, beneath and within a seabound land anchored to the ocean's floor. Too, the working of iron was no ancient skill with them, and it became plain, now, how long ago the Gaels had bested the People of Danu, for all their magickal powers.

For it was the Gaels had brought iron to Eirrin, whose people—the Tuatha de Danann—were workers and users only of bronze; the tin they needed for their plentiful copper came from Britain. Since then the Gaels had learned to modify their iron unto the making of steel, while those of Moytura had progressed only so far as iron. All was wrought, and impregnated with tiny bits of slag. Apparently bars of wrought iron were not here packed with charcoal in containers of clay, so that with sufficient heat it became steel. Nor did Cormac or Wulfhere advise Dithorba of the process.

"Steel," Gael said to Dane, "cuts iron."

"And these men are small," Wulfhere said, with a hand beneath the table of stone; despite her protestations, Erris had taken seat beside him. "Umm. Fair odds for me here would be about a half-score to my one, then."

Cormac gave him a look. Seeing that the man was serious, mac Art rose and roamed the room, high-bending his legs, swinging and cranking his arms, now and again bending suddenly or dropping into a squat. He had just eaten well, and would not ask for possible danger and the necessity of all skill

169

and agility until he was certain his body was ready.

It was. His skull had been unbroken by the blow; ale and food had done away with his headache, and a pair of bruises were little to him who had fought with far worse wounds and debilities.

"The direct way would seem best, Dithorba. Will you be taking me to the dungeon?"

"Loki's wiles," Wulfhere swore, "what a request!" Then he added, to Dithorba, "And return instanter for me."

"He will not," Cormac said, while Dithorba fetched a robe to take to his queen, "unless there's sorest need. Despite the Chains of Danu, Wulfhere—remain ye here . . . with Erris." Seeing the Dane's grin, Cormac added, "—and Thulsa Doom."

Dithorba came, carrying a robe. Helmeted, cracked shield on arm, sword girt at his left hip, Cormac extended a hand. Dithorba took it; the others saw the two men become not-there, and there was a slapping sound in the ears of Wulfhere and Erris and Thulsa Doom. Again Cormac was experiencing the unpleasant dissociative sensation, the dizzying spinning of his brain. Again he staggered and again temporary bewilderment was on him, as of his just having wakened.

He blinked, came alert, swiftly cleared his head while his hand left the Danan's and went to the pommel of his sword. There was reality and security and comfort there, in the familiar heat-hardened wood with the cool spots that were insets of bronze and silver, tooled and chiseled and all designed and well shaped for enwrapping fingers.

Hand on hilt, Cormac mac Art looked about.

Here was eldritch gloom. No penetration was effected by the strange light of the moon that was Danu's property and manifestation. Illumination there was, aye, and of a sort familiar to mac Art. This light was the pallid, ever-restless yellow of torches set in iron cressets or peg holes drilled into walls of forbidding and gloomy stone. Here no drapes hung to soften or add colour to these rocky walls. There was only the stone, living stone, a mottled grey that was darker higher up, from the greasy smoke of torches and oil lamps and braziers. Iron poles braced the walls and there were shelves formed of the outsized tap-roots of great trees, for these provided wood for the Danans and Cormac now understood why mighty trees died unaccountably on the surface of Eirrin. His eyes swept cell-like divisions, stone and hide and wood, with great doors on iron hinges.

To his nostrils came the odours of smoke and sweat, and too there lingered the acrid stenches of excrement and of urine. He knew they were of human origin. And he knew that much of the sweat had poured forth in fear and pain.

Chains gleamed dark and sinister, dark-splotched tables squatted malignantly about the floor. His gaze paused at a large brazier of black iron, set on iron legs above a firepit. From the pot thrust several dark stems of iron, each equipped with wooden grips. *To facilitate wielding when the irons are hot,* he mused grimly. The coals beneath the brazier were still golden and the air seemed to quiver above them. Cormac's lips tightened. He'd seen torture-irons before.

Too, in that grim sprawling chamber beneath the earth, there were moans.

Cormac looked about him, at the human alluvia thrown up by the changing tide of fortune that had swept Riora Feachtnachis from her throne.

Some of the sounds and misery emanated from within closed cells into whose darkness he could not

171

see—though fleetingly he bethought him how better if Dithorba had transported them into one of them. Instead, they were in the wood-columned, stone-columned, sprawling main chamber of the dungeon. That barn-large chamber was peopled.

There stood a well-built man rising threescore years, with a dark spot just below his ribs that was either a burn or a bruise; a huge splotch of yellow and purple flowered ugly on his right upper arm, the mark of a violent blow of another day; from his nipple stood a sliver of wood blackened at the end by burning and atremble with his uneasy breathing; his so-pale beard was shortened and darkened on one side, singed; his arms were drawn back around a column and secured to the same chain of iron that ringed his naked midsection and the column, which was a mortared pile of square-cut stones whose edges cut into the prisoner's arms. A few feet to his right a young woman lay huddled—insofar as was possible for her, with her bare left leg lifted high and chained to a great nail standing darkly from a column to the ceiling; her weight was balanced on naked buttock, which was both befilthed and marked by a whip.

Elatha the Whip, Dithorba said, Cormac thought with his teeth pressed tight; the lord of this demesne of dim ugliness was sinisterly called "the Whip," torturemaster. Closeby another woman, and her in her middle years, stood slumped against the stone wall against which she was held, partway erect, by chains fastened to large-headed iron pegs driven into the wall—or morelike thrust ere they had cooled into drilled holes, so that the pegs sealed themselves there; the tatters of clothing that hung on her made this prisoner a more piteous sight than had she been naked. To her had been done that which was unspeakable, and Cormac's jaw quivered with the

172

grinding of his teeth. Staring in helpless fascination upon the loathsome demonstrations of the work of Elatha the Whip, Cormac turned. . .

Standing against another wall, shackled there so that she was agonizingly spreadeagled, stood a moaning maiden who was young and shapely; though she wore a sort of breechclout of filthy once-white, Cormac saw that it was neither tied nor bound by brooch but that wooden slivers pinned the mocking scrap of cloth to her hips; one lovely apple-firm breast was fire-blackened and a terrible bruise marked her swollen cheek. Near her a young man was chained, with slivers of wood thrusting from beneath his toenails and whip-stripes dark and ugly across his muscular stomach. But a few feet from them was a sort of machine, a device for constant torment. It was of simple construction, for nothing complicated was necessary to the creation of human misery.

Up into the bottom of a long table constructed of strips of wood had been driven scores of slim iron nails, so that a tiny portion of the tip-end of each protruded upward; on that toothily ugly table of torture lay a naked man, and him not young. Stiff and straight he was bound there, and he had been beaten severely across bare and flaccid buttocks. Beside that sombre table of anguish stood another Danan, and him unbound.

This was the largest man Cormac had seen among the Danans, powerfully built with muscle-knotted arms and legs and chest; even his height was a thumb's length greater than that of most of these people of Danu. On one burly thigh a dagger was sheathed. At his left hip hung a short slim sword. He wore only a leathern covering for his loins; something like walrus hide it was, while great thick leather bracers encased each thick wrist. His ankles and feet were encased in buskins of leather that was dark with sweat and smoke—and bearing darker splotches that mac Art knew were from the flying spatters of the blood of others. Scarless and of a sternly hostile mien, this man held a whip longer than Cormac's body.

The big man was staring at Cormac and Dithorba.

"Elatha!" Dithorba said, in an emotional whispering burst.

Elatha the Whip but stared at the two who had appeared in his demesne within the rock of under-earth. His whip trailed from his hand like a menacing black serpent ready to leap with cold determination to bring pain and scars.

"Bastard," Cormac snarled, "sired by a pus-demon and whelped of a fly-swarming sow!" And his sword came sliding up from its sheath.

Elatha said nothing. His lips twitched; perhaps that was a tiny passionless smile. His arm shifted; his long whip trembled along the stone floor behind it. He snapped it back then and, striding two paces forward as he brought it whistling forward, the torturemaster sent his leathern serpent of torment rushing at Cormac mac Art.

The Gael seemed only to twitch, fading rapidly aside while instinctively jerking up his shield to save his face from an incredibly aimed lash. With a great drumming sound the whip struck his buckler, and its tip came snapping over to send a slash of fire into his forearm.

Pain was a shock; so too was realization of the Danan's skill and the vicious deadliness of his whip. Blood dripped where its tip had bit, for that long whip ended in a knot about a V-shaped plug of iron.

"Get ye back, Dithorba! He'll slash out your eyes!"

Dithorba back-paced; Elatha the Whip said nothing but only smiled. A seemingly gentle twitch of his wrist sent his whip scurrying snakelike across the floor to him. Cormac started forward. The whip snapped back, again came racing forward. With the same leftward sidestep and the same swift jerking up of his buckler Cormac again saved his face—and again his forearm was opened to let his blood fall to increase the number of dark spots that covered the floor of the hell-chamber. He bit his lip against groaning out his pain.

Blood of the gods! He durst not rush this demon of a whipmaster; the devil had absolute control over his serpentine weapon and knew precisely how to protect himself against sword-charge by the taller man; either Cormac remained at bay or charged into maiming lashes, or backed—to be followed and cut open—or used brain as he seldom had to in what he saw as simple one-to-one encounters.

Already Elatha's lash was snaking back to him in response to a flick of his thick wrist. Cormac pondered, poised and trembling like a hound with the nervousness of the hunt on him. From their slitted sockets his sword-grey eyes glittered as he stared at the Danan whipmaster.

The two were some ten feet apart. Cormac knew he dared make no rushing Wulfhereish charge, despite his inclination to do; he'd be cut open or worse ere he reached Elatha. The torturer would but have to retreat a bit then, to place the same distance between them. . . having gained greater advantage by the infliction of a wound. Silently he stood, daring, mocking; *come to me*, his grim little smile taunted, *try it!*

Cormac held his ground, his eyes flicking this way and that. His brain pondered, worked, propounded ridiculous hopes and suggestions. He was helpless to attack; he must hold on the defensive, though he was hardly accustomed to it.

Again Elatha attacked. Swiftly he backed a pace, again strode lunging forward with his sweeping lash, so that the force and strength of his wrestler's body backed and drove the long whip.

Twice had Cormac dodged leftward; to the right he moved this time, and in a cat-like pounce. The jingle of mail was followed by the great loud cracking sound of a whip's snapping empty air. Elatha's eyes had swerved to follow the Gael with his pale glance, but he'd been unable to change the direction of his powerful whip-stroke.

For the first time, he spoke. His voice was as emotionless as the eyes of a serpent.

"Ye be fast."

Cormac said nothing. Having gained the tiniest of psychological advantage, he would now adopt the menacing silence that had been Elatha's.

After a moment of silence, Elatha's face moved in a soundless snarl and he cut again. Once more Cormac waited until the torturemaster's brawny arm came over, and then he moved. This time he did not dodge, but ran. He could not bear the inactivity of remaining only a defender. Several paces rightward he rushed, and then he charged the torturemaster of Moytura's dungeon.

He was within four feet when the swift sideward jerk of Elatha's wrist brought his whip leaping over like a striking reptile. It curled around his attacker's buskined right ankle. The whip wrapped but once, for it had not been hard-directed, in Elatha's desperation.

Cormac stumbled, windmilling arms laden with buckler and brand. His charger was broken. Elatha

176

jerked; the whip came free without yanking Cormac's legs from under him. As the Gael regained his balance, Elatha paced swiftly backward. His arm was already snapping his length of leather to himself, and behind.

The whip rushed out. It slapped loudly on leather and wrapped four times about Cormac's right leg. Then came the bite of its iron fang, and leather legging split just above the Gael's knee. A gust of air leaped from his lungs, with the sound of voice in it. He strove to prepare himself for what must come next; there was no time. The moment the whip began its encircling, Elatha's bicep leaped and he yanked.

Cormac was jerked to the floor with a crash and a grunt.

Grinning openly, Elatha the Whip transferred his stock to his left hand and spun to wrap the lash once about himself. He was brought thus that much closer—while he drew his short sword of dark iron.

Trapped a-wallow on the floor with his leg caught and held tautly extended, Cormac used all his strength and will.

He flopped onto his back; he sent his buckler racing up to meet a downrushing blade of iron that resembled in its shortness those of the Roman legions who'd lately roamed the world they had claimed to own. Iron blade crashed down on ironbound shield of hardened wood while Cormac's own blade flicked out like a sliver of blued lightning. With a terrible impact like that of hammer on forge, Elatha's sword struck the metal rim of the other man's shield. A stone had cracked the wood of that buckler; now sword driven by powerful muscles actually ate into its rim, iron into iron. Despite his braced, cording muscles Cormac's buckler was driven down nearly to his body; the sword of Elatha was no less notched than the shield-rim.

The sword of the Gael meanwhile rushed through the whip that stood taut betwixt his leg and Elatha's waist. Its point missed the Danan's flesh by less than the breadth of three fingers.

Great shock showed itself on the face of Elatha the Whip, who Cormac was to learn had never felt pain or known any semblance of defeat or fear; the man was accustomed to plying his whip and the other dread tools of his trade on unarmed victims, and them usually with dark despair already on them. His whip was worse than halved; his sword had failed to find flesh and was both notched and bent; the arm that wielded it was beset by a thousand needles from that terrible impact.

The burly Danan spun away, and his face bore no longer an expression of mockery or triumph.

At the same time Cormac rolled and stood. His leg complained, for blood darkened the leather there where the severed whip dangled. He faced now a man armed with a short whip and a short sword, and it notched, and Cormac mac Art was no longer at the disadvantage.

The Gael was made overconfident thereby.

Elatha was hardly in despair or helpless. A master of whip-wielding needed no more than the yard or so of good leather strap he clutched, and he proved it. Gone was the deadly iron fang at the end of his lash, but it struck the wrist of Cormac's sword arm so forcefully that it wrapped twice just below the leather bracer and snapped the meaty base of his thumb with its very tip.

The Gael's arm twitched with a jerk; Elatha yanked; Cormac's sword flew from his open-flexing fingers to ring skidding across the floor of stone and stone-hard earth.

Elatha was smiling openly and far from prettily. His short sword leaped beneath his foe's buckler and its point grated hard against Cormac's ribs. Only the Gael's armour of steel chain saved him from death then, or from the wound that would have been the next to last. Still he grunted and was staggered by the blow he felt and the grating pressure on a rib. In truth, iron point slipped between linked chain and pierced through padded tunic to touch the skin over the rib. The blade widened back to the point; a circle of steel held it; the rib did not give.

Even while his arm was whipping around in a half-circle and his empty sword-hand grasping the short length of whip between himself and the Danan, Cormac's smallish round shield rushed up and around to slam its ironbound rim into Elatha's upper arm.

Another man grunted in pain and another hand flexed open. A second sword clanged to the floor. And another man jerked the whip. Elatha, struck hard in right shoulder and yanked by left arm, was jerked leftward and overbalanced. He staggered sidewise and only now remembered to release the whip-stock.

It returned to him instantly; Cormac slammed it thudding into the other man's right cheek and then his gut and then into the center of his leather breechclout. Blood started from Elatha's cheek and mouth from split skin and a broken molar. At the same time Elatha started to double over, with both hands leaping to his crotch.

A mailclad forearm crashed into the torture-master's mouth and his eyes rolled loosely. Elatha went to his knees, leaning backward now; Elatha toppled sidewise and lay groaning through shredded lips.

Panting, working his stinging right wrist, Cormac

mac Art retrieved and sheathed his sword.

Elatha's brand he caught up and crashed violently against a pillar of stone so that the blade bent a quarter way in on itself. Hurling it from him, the Gael turned to the torture table.

"Elatha. . . bested and down!" Dithorba said from behind Cormac, in an elated whisper that bespoke his nearness to disbelief.

"Who be this man?" Cormac asked, having discarded his buckler to pluck at the table-bound man's cords with both hands.

"Lughan Senlac, my. . . my fellow adviser to the queen. Will ye not save time by merely cutting him free, defeater of Elatha?"

A groan escaped the oldster bound facedown on the table, his soft buttocks darkly marked by Elatha's whip.

"Lord Lughan," Cormac muttered, "I loosen these knots rather than slice them, for the reason that Elatha the Whipless will soon replace ye on this table."

After a moment of silence, Lughan gasped his reply. "Be not concerned. . . with haste. A tiny space of time more on this. . . restful bed will not finish me. To the end ye state. . . I can wait!"

Chapter Twelve:
The Guardian

The prisoners of Cairluh and Tarmur Roag were free of bonds and cells in Moytura's dungeon; their former torturer lay groaning and sweating on his own fanged table. His weight, his greater development of chest and belly and thighs pressed the ends of the scores of upward driven nails into his flesh more deeply than they had bitten Lughan Senlac. There were no guards in the dungeon; prisoners were weak and helpless, and Elatha was proud and jealous of his reign.

Cormac mac Art held the shortened whip he had taken from him who had wielded it to such agony, even to the deaths of some. For Cormac and Dithorba had found two in the cells who need not be freed; they had died of whippings that had torn them open and ruptured internal organs.

"Dithorba and I have business elsewhere. Here lies him who put sore torment and indecent horror on ye all. Who will take this whip?" He stretched out his hand, the whip lying across it like a napping serpent.

It was the young man who stepped forward, he who bore the marks of that same strap of leather across his muscled belly and who limped from the wooden splinters that had been forced under his toenails. Dithorba had identified him as an officer in the household staff of Queen Riora, by name Tathill; the young woman bound near him was his sweetheart. Perhaps he would bear no physical scars of this imprisonment; she would, all her life.

"I will wield that black eel on the creature who made it sting so well," he said quietly and with strain, "and yield it up to whomever wants it else."

"I," a weak voice said.

Cormac gazed not with shock but with sadness on the speaker, the older woman in rags, with the marks on her of obscene torments and mockery. Surely, the Gael thought, such as she would not have dreamed of vindictive whip-wielding before she'd been brought to this grey domain of pain and degradation. It hurt him only that he had not put his cloak on again, that he might clothe her in it. Elatha's foul breechclout he would not offer her. Guards or other keepers would be outside bound doors, though obviously no sound of the battle here had reached their ears. At their dicing most likely, Cormac thought, and turned to look after Dithorba. The old mage was walking back into the dimmer area of the dungeon, his robe flapping and the one he'd brought for his queen hanging over his arm. He paused at the doorway of a wooden enclosure, and looked within. Cormac saw the man stagger as if struck, and heard his gasp.

And he heard the weak girlish voice: "Stay back!"

Cormac had taken a perverse pleasure in leaving the freeing of two men until last; they were the strapping, handsome Commander Balan of the Royal Guard and Torna, long Riora's tutor and now most favored adviser. Now the Gael turned from the still bound pair and strode back past the torture table and light. Dithorba stood in dimness.

The chamber into which he stared was a square some ten feet on a side; a chamber of royal size for the imprisonment of Moytura's royalty.

The slim young queen was within. She wore only a spiked girdle and collar of iron, both drawn tightly and held by cinch-pins. Her straw-coloured hair was dragged back and bound to the cruel girdle behind, so that her neck was constantly strained. Riora of Moytura was bound astride a great stone wheel, like a millwheel, that abraded her inner thighs and displayed her lewdly. Aye, and she'd been marked by Elatha's whip. The dragging back of her tresses strained her face so that her brows were unnaturally arched and her cheekbones threatened to thrust through taut skin.

Tinted only by the faintest of tawny hue, her eyes swiveled from Dithorba at Cormac's arrival. She stared at him.

When the Gael started forward, Dithorba stayed him.

"Lady Queen, a Gael from Eiru above, Cormac mac Art his name. He and a companion saved Erris from becoming a toygirl to a squad of six rapacious guards set over me, and slew them all. He freed me, and has just defeated Elatha though he bears wounds of the long fangwhip. All this, lady Queen, in quest of your freedom. The sounds my lady queen now hears are of Elatha's own whip on his own foul body."

183

"Talk and talk," the Gael said. "Why stand we here?" Again he started forward.

"Stand ye back!" the queen bade him, and she winced at the pain the exertion put on her. Her hands were behind her back, her legs bracing the upright millwheel, to which ropes bound her. She softened the command: "—friend of Danu and Moytura—and Riora."

"Your pardon for the questioning of a weapon-man, lady queen. . . but why must we stay from yourself?"

"This I have. . . borne," she said in the voice of strain forced upon her by the back-drawn hair. "I can. . . longer. For ye both, though, there's death within this chamber. . . I am bound not only as ye see. . . but by the sorcery of Tarmur Roag as well. Aye, and guarded. . . Cor-mac Mackart. There is a. . . Guardian."

Cormac stepped close to the doorway to peer within the large chamber. He saw three walls of stone and one of wood; a chipped bowl of fired clay and a dented iron cup; a length of chain. Another hung from a nail in the wooden wall, as did a short flail with three tails of plaited leather. . . or rather the hide of some great denizen of the waters, as was all leather of Moytura. Two crumpled bits of cloth lay forlornly on the floor. He saw naught else, not even a pile of stones.

"I see naught of menace or Guardian."

"I am queen, Cormac. . . I am not. . . questioned."

He gazed on this naked, whip-marked, painfully bound young woman with wonder and respect. An she could talk so in these straits, she was queen indeed!

"Ye cannot free me, Cormac. He who comes
184

through that door, save for Elatha, will instantly die. Tarmur Roag. . . demonstrated. It's he must be captured and forced to release me; I'll have no champion such as your huge self slain so, for naught and to no avail.''

Cormac was hardly huge. He realized, though, that in Moytura he was. Standing beside Dithorba, he made a child of the man, both in height and physique. A thought of hope came on him.

"Dithorba! Can ye be mind-hurling me to her side, man?''

The succinct reply shattered the Gael's excitement: "No.''

Cormac's face stiffened. After a moment, he asked, "Then. . .dare ye carry me to her, by your sorcerous means?''

"No!'' the queen cried.

"In this matter, lady Queen, your commands are second to mine. It is possible for too much nobility to be on a person, even a monarch.''

Both Riora and Dithorba stared at this tall, darkskinned stranger to their land who dared speak so to a queen. Cormac kept his gaze expectantly on Dithorba, who realized the Gael still awaited his answer.

"I dare, Cormac mac Art.''

"No, Dithorba! I forbid it!''

Cormac saw to himself. Blood oozed no longer from his twice-punctured left arm. His buckler remained serviceable—hopefully. His right wrist bore only a pair of barring lines, with neither wound nor stiffness on him there. The wound to his leg was only to the superficial meat, not into muscle, nor had it had time to stiffen. His Saxon knife was in its sheath and his sword was ready for the drawing on the instant.

185

Deliberately he drew Dithorba away from the doorway, out of sight of the piteously imprisoned queen.

"We go in," he said quietly. "The moment we alight, release my hand, and return ye here." When Dithorba nodded, Cormac turned and shouted to those others they'd released. "Free Balan and Torna! Take up chains and Elatha's dagger; whatever armament there be, and remain ye there—sentries may come."

The last was an afterthought, added in hopes their weakness might be forgot in renewed fear that he knew led in some to renewed strength. Such surely would be the case at least with Balan and the young man who was showing his energy in the flogging of Elatha.

Cormac took Dithorba's hand. "In."

He said it too loudly; from her prison came Queen Riora's weak shout: "No! It's your death!"

Cormac felt Dithorba's hand quiver and he gripped it the tighter. *"My* command, Dithorba my friend," he said softly, "In—and leave me."

The familiar unpleasant sensations came immediately, and then Cormac was jolted, stumbling. Even so his hand fled Dithorba's and leaped to the hilt of his sword. On this third occasion of his transport by means of another man's mind, the Gael's brain and eyes cleared more swiftly.

His staring eyes saw that Dithorba had already left him, and was peering into the chamber from beyond the doorway. Their sorcerous means of transport had triggered no attack, for they had not passed through the door. Cormac stood in a crouch, feral-eyed and with sword and shield at ready. His slitted eyes swiveled to the side; he saw naught but Riora the Fair and Righteous.

186

Awkwardly he caught her hair in his shield-hand, betwixt head and binding; his sword sliced swiftly through the rope that had forced her head up and back. It was allowed to assume a natural position. Her eyes focused—and she cried out. Dithorba's call of alarm crowded close on hers.

Her Guardian had appeared in the queen's prison chamber.

Cormac had hardly expected to face here a foe of his own height and apparent build, nor had he ever seen a man so helmed and armoured.

No skin of the Guardian was visible. His scalemail coat fell from neck to knees; beneath it he wore leggings of good mail that vanished into short boots. Mailed gloves covered the hands that clutched sword and six-sided shield; faced with bronze it was and on it a death's head had been picked out in awl-punched dots filled with black enamel. But once had Cormac seen such an eye-covering helm, on an arrogant Roman commander. From that visored helmet depended a camail of mail, which was connected in front to the nosepiece of the helmet so as to conceal the tall figure's entire face.

Cormac faced a grim and silent foe covered all in iron.

With some nervousness on him though without sinking heart, the Gael remembered to crab-step from the bound queen of Moytura. She must not receive a chance slash.

"It's your queen this be, man. Elatha is—no more. I am come here to set her free, and if ye insist I'll be doing it through yourself. Sheathe sword and stand ye back to serve your queen, for she *will* be free."

The ironclad Guardian said nothing. Cormac could not see so much as eyes, to read their expression. Stance and ready-lifted buckler, with the upraising of

187

the broad long sword in mailed hand, were indication
enow of his reply and intent.

The man of iron paced forward, not toward Riora
but at Cormac.

"Ye'll be dying then, for all your armour,"
Cormac said, and moved but the tips of his fingers,
ensuring his grip on shaped hilt.

He would let the other strike first, move while he
took the stroke on his shield, and attack instantly and
viciously. No such traitor as this, and him stupid
besides, deserved to draw breath.

The Guardian's arm came around in a blur.
Cormac's shield caught the sword-edge and his arm
turned to let the sword slide on, thus allowing the
attacker's momentum to continue—while the Gael
moved rightward and drove his blade forward. The
impact of sword on shield was tremendous, a jolting
surprise to mac Art's arm and mind, as was the fact
that the other's bronze-faced buckler moved so
rapidly. Yet it did not quite catch his rushing thrust;
rather than plunging as he'd intended into an
armoured side, Cormac's blade screamed through
iron links and completely transpierced his foe's
shield-arm, near the shoulder.

Cormac yanked his blade forth. It was well for him
that he did not assume the fray to be over then, but
remained mindful of the other's long brand and his
shield.

He had already seen; no blood marked the blade of
mac Art.

Nor did his opponent seem to take note of his
wound; he backswung and Cormac had to skip while
thrusting back his shield to avoid the prodigiously
powerful slash at his neck. Again the iron sword
crashed on the Gael's shield with a sound to torture
the head, eardrums, and again the terrific impact

shook his arm and rattled the teeth in his head.

He moved two rushing paces on, for a few snatched moments to relieve his shield-arm. . . and to try to hurl from his brain the numbing influence of shock.

Again he looked at the blade of his sword; he could not believe what he had seen—or rather not seen. It was true. The steel shone bloodlessly. Nor did any so much as ooze from his ironclad foe's arm, which should have been pouring scarlet, if not spurting with his heartbeats.

Still without so much as a grunt or a curse, he who had been set to prevent the queen's rescue struck again.

This slash came high, and Cormac at the last instant chose not to meet it with his buckler. Nor did he counterattack with his usual thrust; he ducked low and chopped deeply into the Guardian's left thigh.

That titan in iron chain staggered—and back came his arm, in a hardly interrupted backswing.

This time Cormac *dived* away, and again he saw with hair-raising incomprehension that his blade was unblooded. His antagonist swung to follow; again he staggered a little on a leg that nevertheless held him erect—and bled not.

Mac Art did not wait but struck hard, side-armed and with all his strength. The Guardian's shield dropped swiftly into line so that Cormac's blade chopped half through it. The wood held. The iron man was cleaving; Cormac lunged desperately forward to be within that sweep—and to crash his buckler into his foeman. Into the junction of arm and torso it smashed, so that iron shield-rim slammed both chest and arm and the boss centered between them drove into the hollow just above the silent attacker's armpit.

The Guardian's slashing glaive struck naught but air though his mailed arm rapped Cormac's back. The Gael bore on, to hurl backward a foe who should have been down and half bled.

The Danan staggered back with a harsh jangle of overlapping iron scales that covered him from nose to toes and fingers. His left thigh, shorn half through, gave. He began to topple. Bracing himself, Cormac jerked his sword arm with a rapid up and down movement. With a screech of steel on wood and bronze, the blade came free. Panting, Cormac watched his silent foe crash backward to the floor.

Under such circumstances a man either yielded or died. Cormac stepped swiftly forward.

"Yield ye! Drop the sword or it's no hand I'll be leaving ye to wield it again against a friend of your queen!"

A mailed leg and booted foot kicked at him. Cormac had been right. The Guardian was stupid, without sense in him to leave off when he was defeated. Up rushed a mailed fist to drive Danan sword at Cormac mac Art in a vicious slash.

Though surprised, Cormac was not astounded; he had been prepared to make movements in response to such insanity. He backpaced two swift steps, tarried but an instant poised on the balls of both feet, while he watched the big iron sword swish. It swept by in a blurred semicircle of dark blue-grey before his body. The strength of its wielding carried it on; Cormac rocked himself forward again, knees bending deeply.

He carried out his threat. His slash sent his fallen opponent's sword flying. Its hilt was still grasped in mailed fist.

And the Danan's hard-swung shield slammed into Cormac's hip as though the Guardian had sustained no terrible wound to his upper arm.

Cormac was swept violently aside; had the rim rather than cloven face of that six-sided buckler struck him so, bone would have cracked. Nor had Cormac mac Art ever known a man who fought ever again after sustaining a cracked hip. In pain he ran to remain vertical, and slammed into the wall. That scraping clang rose simultaneous with the clatter across the room; sword in mailed, severed hand had rebounded from the opposite wall to ring on the floor. Cormac too rebounded, gritting his teeth against the pain in his right hip.

Jerking his head and willing himself to ignore pain and dark incomprehension, Cormac swung about to renew assault on a foe seemingly impervious to wounds.

He was in the act of striking still again at the armour-covered figure stretched on the floor when he saw that which jolted his brain and made him shiver. From the stump of his severed wrist, the Guardian poured forth no blood.

"Blood of the Gods," Cormac snarled, with no thought on him for the singular inappropriateness of his favourite oath.

His brain staggering, the Gael aborted his ruined sword stroke. Sudden intense heat prickled over his body and sweat seemed to leap from every pore. In that instant he went pure professional, for so he'd been and was still, though in the paid employ of none. His brain moved to another level; became icy cold; functioned at high speed.

"Dithorba! In and pick up his sword—cut free your queen!"

Already his foe had taken advantage of Cormac's brief moments of confusion to thrust himself to his feet, using both his shield-hand *and his right stump* to lever up. The hexagon of split wood and bronze was a golden blur as he swung it violently, rapidly back and forth. He advanced on Cormac the while, and the Gael was forced to back from that rushing wall that would hurl sword from his hand—or smash his arm.

To his right Dithorba appeared, near the fallen sword. Still the mailed hand clung to the hilt, and the queen's adviser could not shake it loose. As dry old fingers worried at linked iron chain, Cormac backed from a shield swept back and forth so rapidly it was but a blurred wall.

Suddenly the helmeted head turned its armour-swathed face toward Dithorba.

The old man had given up attempts to free the sword of the severed hand, and was carrying the grisly linked objects toward the upright stone wheel astride which his queen was bound. Still keeping Cormac at bay with the rushing buckler, the Guardian started toward Dithorba.

Though the shield-created wall continued to daunt him, Cormac knew the invisible eyes of its wielder could not be on him.

He lunged forward, diving to the floor. He rolled onto his back and slashed upward. Solid steel crashed on iron chain with terrible force, and thin rings of iron yielded. Bearing hand and wrist and half of forearm, the hexagonal Danan shield flew across the chamber and crashed to the floor just at the feet of Dithorba Loingsech.

There was no blood.

And the Guardian moved on toward the wide-eyed Dithorba.

"A creature of Tarmur Roag's!" Dithorba called out, in a voice that rose with both fear and the excitement of incredible discovery. "Cormac! There is no hand in this mail-glove!"

Cormac started to cry out for Dithorba to vanish;

instead he took faster action. He rolled again and chopped into the leg of his uncanny foe, just at the point where mail disappeared into boot.

The bearer of that awful wound but twitched at the blow, meanwhile continuing the step. The unbleeding leg swung; came forward, down; it buckled on impact with the floor. The Guardian teetered, leaned, fell sidewise. Again he crashed to the floor.

He did not lie still. Still he fought. The woundless leg swept out and its mailed shank just grazed Dithorba's lower leg. With a groan of pain, he staggered. Then the armoured warrior began to rise.

"In Crom's name—this is insanity!"

Cormac's shout still rang when frustration swelled within him and his eyes went shiny. Rage took him. Lunging across the downed, faceless creature, the Gael brought a tremendous stroke rushing down. Steel blade slid again through iron rings and so hard had he struck that the sword rang off the floor beneath the Guardian's leg. Just below the hip, that leg leaped free of its moorings—bloodlessly.

The stump of the other leg slammed into Cormac's ankle.

With a groan, he staggered and fell to one knee. His heart seemed to have descended into his ankle; it pounded there. With an animal viciousness twisting his features, the enraged Gael struck away the leg that had kicked him.

Laboriously, the legless trunk began pushing itself up on the stump of its right wrist; its shield meanwhile came streaking at mac Art. Aye, *its* shield, for he knew this could be no man, but some unnatural *thing,* a fell product of Tarmur Roag's wizardry. The Danan buckler rushed at him; easily Cormac cut the supporting arm from beneath the thing. It fell back, armour and shield crashing.

A shudder rushed through Cormac mac Art. Without rising he chopped, chopped again. Armless now, the unbleeding trunk writhed. Cormac's sword bit into the armoured midsection, smashed the chest. On the point then of chopping at the neck covered by shining metal camail, the seething, shaking Gael shortened his stroke. With fine precision, the last inch of his steel tore away the camail.

The veil of chain had covered nothing.

The helmet rested on nothing. There was no face, no head.

With horripilation a maddening writhing along his arms, Cormac knew that there were no arms and legs either; nothing. There was only an animated suit of armour, huge by DAnan standards, that had come nigh to putting the blindness of death on him.

He rose shakily, staring down at what had been his foe; the trunk of an armour coat, surrounded by lopped-off pieces of man that had come from no man; pieces of armour in the shapes of human limbs.

After a long moment he gave his head a swift hard jerk. Blinking, he turned to the nude young woman bound astride what appeared to be a millstone. He sheathed his glaive, which was unblooded despite all its awful work. Drawing his dagger, he swiftly freed Riora. She sagged forward. Trying to hold her away from the hard cold steel of his armour, he caught her and eased her from the wheel of her torture.

The Queen of Moytura clung, trembling as she stared down at the trunk protion of the thing that had been set to guard her against rescue.

Legless, armless, headless, empty. . . the armour continued to twitch and writhe.

Chapter Thirteen:
The Queen of Moytura

Riora of Moytura, queen, was slim as a willow tree
and yet with soft and rather voluptuous womanly
turnings to her form. White was her skin, almost
transparent, and little more colour tinged the hair
that fell to the dimples above her backside. Though
she was slim and pale and short like all her people,
she had no look of frailty about her. Her quivers were
understandable, as she held on to the big stranger to
her land, who had dared disobey her and had as a
result destroyed her ghastly guardian and set her free.
Though he was armoured and aware that his carapace
of steel rings could tear and bruise her skin with even
his slightest movements, Cormac could not think of
her as fragile. He stood, though, rather stiffly,
unable to think of aught but her nakedness and
the harshness and danger to her of his armour.

"You are brave," she murmured. "You disobeyed me and came into this horrid cell, with no idea of what you might be facing."

Cormac could think of nothing to say. Unaccustomed words came; good words. He spoke them.

"I had seen you," he muttered, with gruff galantry. He would tell her later of the urgency on him for her freedom. At present she was overdue for the kindness of flattery.

"He. . . it hurt you, I saw it. You fought on. You destroyed it." She arched her back to look up into his face. "Your brows. . . your black hair. . . so *fascinating!* Am I—are we so, to you, Cormac of the Gaels?"

"Aye." He gazed down into her wan, angular face and saw that she was both pretty and interested in him as more than saviour and curiosity among her pale people. It came on him that there was no more colour in Riora's eyes than in an inch of water held in two cupped palms.

"L—Lady Queen. . ."

It was Dithorba's voice; neither of them glanced his way.

"Dithorba has a robe for you, Queen of Moytura," Cormac said.

"I have been. . .naked so long. It seems forever . . . Elatha . . . that foul spider has daily thrown me down on this floor and. . . used me." She glanced down. "Aye, I am naked, and queen, and you are clad in iron that is cold and hard—and it grates." She sighed. "And there are things to be done." Again she looked up into his scarred face. Her hands pressed his arms, disregarding the chain that indented her skin. "The Queen of Moytura is indebted to you, Cormac mac Art na Gaedhel. Moytura is indebted to you. And. . . my name is

196

indebted to you, Cormac mac Art ńa Gaedhel. Moytura is indebted to your. And. . . my name is Riora. I, Riora, am indebted to you, Cormac, and I thank you."

While Cormac floundered for words, she released his arms and looked at the other man.

"Thank you, Dithorba," she said, putting out an arm. "The robe, to make me more a queen and less a woman. Ah—and it's *mine*, too!" She smiled, astonishing Cormac who would not have thought her capable, so soon after being released from a stern imprisonment that had been fraught with torture. "Ah, Dithorba, into the queen's chamber to bring herself her very own robe! How can one trust a man with such abilities? Why—you could be in my very bedchamber at any time."

Dithorba's face was stricken. Had Cormac any doubts about the old man's love for his young queen, they were dissipated now. Riora saw it too, and immediately her smile vanished. Taking the robe to hold against her, she reached forth with her other hand to squeeze her adviser's bony shoulder.

"Only a jest, my friend. If not before, after this day Dithorba is first among all Moyturans!" Then she turned her head to look at Cormac over her shoulder and from under eyelashes that were more pale than any he'd ever seen. "First, of course. . . with Cormac mac Art of the Gaels, friend of Danu and Moytura—and Riora!"

While she turned away to don the robe, Cormac and Dithorba kept their eyes fixed as if by honourable pact on each other.

"Hump!" the queen's voice came brightly. "Neither of you watching? Queen Riora is slipping!"

Both men looked at her with wan smiles.

The robe was a pale blue, that of the sky she had never seen, sewn with a complicatedly twisting design in silver thread, at bosom and down to the girdle, which Cormac now saw was of gold thread and jewelled as well. The silver pattern was repeated at the end of each three-quarter length sleeve and at the gown's hem, which fell just past her ankles. Strangely, the Gael saw that clothed and with her body outlined and hinted at here and there, she was more fetching than had she been in her shameful nakedness. Now her stance was different, her shoulders back, and her eyes too had changed; the girlish woman had become a queen.

"You said that Elatha was being beaten, Cormac—and you told. . .the Guardian that he was no more. Which is the case?"

"Unless they've beaten him to death, Elatha lives, bound to his own toothy table."

An expression of pleasure appeared on her face—and then her features stiffened. Suddenly her face was bereft of all warmth and much of its beauty. She moved forward, toward the doorway behind Cormac; he stepped aside. As the Queen of Moytura passed him, she deftly plucked his dagger from its sheath without interrupting her stride.

Aye, five feet one and not a spare ounce of flesh on her save that of womanhood, Riora Feachtnachis was regal.

Cormac looked at the wheel, glanced around at the walls, at the thing on the floor. He looked at Dithorba.

"It's all of us ye must be taking from here, Dithorba, one by one. And we'd best start now, for who knows what guards may come, or someone bearing food?"

As Dithorba nodded, both of them heard outside the dungeon's main chamber the sound of respectful greetings to the queen. And Cormac, to whom her eyes and words had shown more than gratitude but greetings to the queen. And Cormac, to whom her eyes and words had shown more than gratitude but indeed the promise of more, the desire for more, thought that which would not have made happy the woman in her:

A crownéd woman! A crownéd woman!

Then he and Dithorba left that chamber of torture and preternatural horror. Just without the doorway and in the main dungeon again, they paused. Both men stared in silence; they watched while Queen Riora, with viciousness and obvious gusto, killed the bound Elatha. She used Cormac's dagger, and she did not hurry her ugly work.

With Cormac's Saxon knife dripping in her hand, she turned to see his frown. Around her stood her people, in silence that may have been shock or approval.

"You look disapproving, my champion," Riora Feachtnachis said. "Would you have dealt differently with a monster who has tortured me and forced his body on me twice daily for a week?"

Cormac paced toward her, aware of the silent stares of her advisers, her handmaids, her Guard commander and the captain; the queen's closest aids to brain and body.

"He deserved worse, lady Queen. But when it is necessary that I do death, it's swiftly I deal it."

For just a moment she stared, her face working. Then with one hand lifting her skirts, the queen ran to him in manner hardly regal. Clothed now and with her hands wiped, she was heedless of his armour; Riora hugged him.

"You are *good*, Cormac, *trenfher*," she breathed, calling him "champion" once more. "Good, a good man. Moytura needs such, Cormac mac Art; Moytura needs you—Moytura's queen needs you!"

199

Over her head Cormac noted the cold glare of Commander Balan. Uncomfortably he said, "We must depart this place, lady Queen. All are released; now Dithorba must transfer us to his quarters, where await your loyal Erris and my friend, Wulfhere." He pondered; could she end Thulsa Doom's existence *now*, though her fair head bore no crown?

"You will come at once, my trenfher?" She did not let go the man who stood so tall over her.

"An he agrees, Balan and I will wait until all others are gone—lest our arms be needed here."

Riora met his eyes, nodded, and released him. She turned to Dithorba. Cormac saw that she knew the old man's abilities; she stretched forth her hand to him. Seconds later, queen and mage vanished.

"One wishes you had not bent Elatha's sword, Cormac mac Art," Balan said.

He was a large man, far from unhandsome, strongly built and with uncommonly short hair. He was in perhaps the third decade of his life. Both bruises and the marks of hot irons darkened areas of his ribs and chest, and his beard was singed. The man seemed unconcerned by his nudity; his body was good.

Cormac recognized his statement as a challenge, nor had he any desire on him for conflict with the commander of the royal bodyguard. "It's truth ye speak, Balan. I should not have done. Will ye be straightening the blade, or shall I?"

"I will," Balan said dourly, and, using his foot and the table of torment on which lay Elatha's bloody body, he did.

The others stood by, nude or nearly, injured and weakened and some with scars on them they'd be bearing to the end of life. They were a pitiful group of tortured nobles and highplaced slaves, all accustomed to the good life around the throne, and Cormac mac Art was far from comfortable among accustomed to the good life around the throne, and Cormac mac Art was far from comfortable among them. That poor girl who was Captain Tathill's sweetheart; could they withstand what had been done to them here? Could he bear the awful marks and scars she'd wear; could the very young woman stand the knowledge that he found her far less beautiful than she had been?

"Who will bleed for those who have bled and will bleed in years to come?" Cormac mac Art muttered, stroking the hilt of his sword with his fingertips. "Elatha, a tool, is not vengeance enow."

Before any could ask what he'd said so quietly and grimly, Dithorba was back—and with him Queen Riora.

"Cormac! Wulfhere and Thulsa are *gone!*"

Cormac felt as if he'd taken a blow to the belly. Then worms seemed to crawl within him. He fingered the Moonbow on his chest. He was concerned about Wulfhere, aye, and if the man were dead blood would flow like a river. But. . . Thulsa Doom in the hands of others was worse, aye, and enough to put fright in strong heart. For if some fool were to remove the Chain of Danu from that vengeance-driven monster and end Cormac's control over him. . .

He remembered to ask about loyal little Erris, unmentioned by Dithorba. Riora answered in a dull voice, turning partway from all eyes; Erris was there, in the secret room that now had a gaping hole smashed through one wall; she was there still, though without head or breasts.

"So we're found out, and your enemies have my friend and my prisoner, and are my enemies," Cormac snapped. "They will shortly come here, for they know too that Dithorba is free, and surely his powers are known to your cousin and the mage. Dithorba! Where lies a place of safety for us all?" He glanced about at the pitiful little group of people become his responsibility. "A safe place with food," he added, for it was obvious the prisoners had been fed but whimsically.

"Lughan. . . is dead," the older woman said, rising from the naked body.

Riora came to the Gael, who had spoken so swiftly and decisively while Balan and her advisers remained as if in shock. Cormac noted again how Balan watched, frowning, and he saw the man's Danan-pale knuckles go even whiter around the short sword that had been Elatha's.

Balan has an eye for the queen, and mayhap there's been aught between them, for sure and she's a passionate woman, Cormac thought, and he'd not be forgetting.

It was Torna who spoke, the only one among them who bore some fat. "The rear room of the Inn of Red Rory! Ye know it, Dithorba."

"O'course. But. . . if he be not loyal?"

Balan shrugged, stepping forward with some dignity despite his nakedness. "Cite me our choices," he said, and all were aware of the sword in the naked man's hand.

It was at Cormac Dithorba glanced; the Gael kept his eyes on Balan. Dithorba devised his meaning, and he too looked at the Guard commander for decision.

"My lord Torna first," Balan said, "as he must seek to make. . . arrangements, with Red Rory."

Dithorba took the hand of the queen's chief adviser. They disappeared. The queen continued to press herself to Cormac, all heedless of his chainmail—and Balan. Cormac was most aware of that man, and of the others as well. Dithorba was soon back, alone; all seemed well at Red Rory's.

"Lady Queen? Will yourself come now?"

"Take Balan," she said, and turned only partway

202

from Cormac, from whom she took not his hands. "See that Commander Balan is clothed and armed immediately. Balan: have thoughts of raising a force of men for us."

Balan had opened his mouth to speak; meeting his queen's eyes and hearing her last words, he nodded and said naught. His gaze raked Cormac as he took Dithorba's hand, and then they were gone. Cormac had not put his hands on the blue-gowned Riora, while hers had not left him.

Again Dithorba returned; this time he took young Captain Tathill. Six females remained, and Riora and Cormac. Instantly Tathill was gone, she stretched herself long to seek Cormac's lips with her own, all heedless of the watching girls and woman. He saw that the woman of middle age was aware of his discomfort. She gave him a small understanding smile across the top of her monarch's head.

When Dithorba returned once more, the discomfited mac Art wrapped powerful fingers around the queen's azure-sleeved arm, and let her feel their strength. "Take the queen now, Dithorba."

"No!"

Riora's voice was loud and peremptory. Regaining her composure swiftly, she turned and coolly bade Dithorba take the others first. Her arm remained around the Gael, on the side of him away from Dithorba and her women. He wondered if she felt safe with him but had doubts about the Inn of Red Rory and was thus a wise ruler aware of her own value, or. . . if she wanted merely to continue possessively holding him she had called her champion.

Embarrassed and looking as if in some pain, Cormac shot Dithorba a look. The old man would not meet his gaze; he was less capable of making demurrers to his lady queen than the tall, rangy man she presently clung to. And with her free and no emergency on them, Cormac dared not countermand her or attempt even to argue. A sensible reason for her tarrying here was too obvious.

Dithorba took Tathill's sweetheart, who was definitely in need of bed and blankets and whatever these people had of poultices and potions. Five remained; four were young and well-formed. The usurpers and Elatha the Whip had obviously been more than pleased to imprison the queen's fetching handmaidens with her.

As they were taken unnaturally elsewhere, Riora pressed to Cormac and her lips were warm and soft and partway open, seeking and moving on his mouth. Her hands found his, drew them inward to her breasts. In seconds the links of his mail were marking his knuckles, for she pushed herself in forcefully as if her goal were the crushing of her bosom. Her breathing heightening, Riora had no care for the presence and eyes of her girls; Cormac had, but he was soon made to forget.

He responded helplessly to Riora's insistent lips, her urgency. . . aye, and Cormac mac Art responded to the flattery, to the fact that this warm body crushed so urgently to his was that of a ruler of men. . . other men. His pulse began to be a drum in his temples.

"Ah! Alone but not alone—I want you, Cormac mac Art! You must remain here, remain in Moytura with *me!*"

Cormac sought words and sought not to be stiff. "Much. . . remains to be done, lady Queen, ere the crown is restored to yourself. The future is far from now and it's injury ye do yourself by this behavior before your. . . intimates."

"Intimates! I have no intimates—my lessers!" She thrust herself back from him, though with both hands still on his arms. Her faintly tawny eyes flashed and seemed to flame. "You dare much, Cormac the Gael!"

His face worked. How to tell any woman, much less a queen, that she put much discomfort on him, that he was embarrassed for her? And this was a dangerous woman as well, passionate and swift to change her mood. His melancholy troubled look was not mirrored in her features, which drew and writhed with emotion. Was it anger? Was she acting? He did not know. He could not know; he knew this woman not at all. Certainly she could be cruel as a cat: witness Elatha's slow, agonized death.

Though he'd never have expected such a feeling of himself, he was glad that he wore mail and that Dithorba had brought the gown for her to clothe her nakedness.

He was still seeking words when he heard the noises.

Far away behind her, chains rattled. That scrape and creak was of a great door's being opened. Now he could detect the murmurous undertone of several voices, male. Aye, and those tiny clinks; he knew the sound of weighted scabbards sliding and thumping against mail under the impetus of the wearers' steps.

Cormac's arms rose and his wrists turned so that his hands moved over and in close on both her forearms. Riora mistook his intent, apparently not having heard the coming of men, though he was not sure whether her eyes shone or glittered. He forced her hands from him.

"Men come," he whispered, looking past her into darkness, that part of the dungeon that was a corridor leading to steps and the great door for sealing in prisoners. "They descend steps—hear ye, Queen Riora? Armed men approach, nor can they be other than minions of your cousin Cairluh. Get ye behind me. Ye have my dagger still?"

She heard them then, and in a rustling whisper of skirts Riora hurried to the iron-toothed table whereon lay the bloody corpse of Elatha. Swiftly she returned, bearing Cormac's knife. It was marked with blood. The sound of muttering men drew closer and Cormac could see on the wall well up ahead the dance of yellow light; torches borne by striding men.

"Elatha!" a voice called, but the shouter was too far up the passage to be seen.

Coming instantly after that call, Dithorba's appearance a few feet away brought a jerking response from Cormac mac Art.

"Give me the dagger, lady Queen—Dithorba! Men come. Take her and hasten back for me, man!"

Riora clung to both dagger and Cormac while Dithorba looked confused. The Gael's hand leaped out to grasp her slim wrist. Riora gasped, and his dagger clinked to the floor. Immediately he *flung* the queen of Moytura to Dithorba, and Cormac was quietly talking the while.

"Take her hence. Return ye to the chamber of her late punishment, Dithorba!"

Snatching up the knife he'd taken long ago from a Saxon who had no further use for it, Cormac mac Art wheeled. Crouching, he ran with a cat-footed lack of sound into the depths of the dungeon. Behind him he heard a squeaking sound from a human throat and knew Riora's protest had been continued into a room elsewhere in Moytura.

Just as he was rushing at the doorway to that which had been Riora's prison chamber, mac Art remembered her warning that the entry was guarded by some wizard-sent murder.

Too late now to stop, he instead drove himself forward with a renewed burst of momentum. He sprang through the doorway and as far into the chamber as he could hurl himself. He was drawing steel even while he turned.

There was no attack, no menace. Here was the great stone wheel on which Riora Feachtnachis had been bound; here lay his former foe, the untenanted suit of armour he had chopped to bits. Without, he heard the clamor of excited exclamations of consternation and rage; the Danan soldiery had found the broad area that was empty of all but the corpse of him who had presided over it.

Within the chamber was no menace; perhaps the slayer at the door had died with the destruction of the Guardian, or the removal of the prisoner. Cormac's dagger was in its sheath and now he scabbarded his sword. Stepping quickly back around the mill-wheel, he squatted. Mayhap someone would come and but glance in, then rush back to report the place empty; astonished by that fact, he might miss the man squatting in the shadows behind the wheel standing in its frame of stone and wood. If not, the Gael should be able to hold the chamber, provided he could reach the door and remain just within.

"The queen!" he heard a yell, and after an instant of silence he heard the steady jingle and clink of mail on running men. A Danan weapon-man appeared at the entry.

"Dung and darkness! She's not here! Danu's eyes—*what's this*?"

With another crowding close behind, the Danan in silver-winged helm and scalemail of dark iron entered. He squatted to examine the remains of the Guardian.

"It—it be just *armour*, Din, empty armour! and

hacked as if—"

He broke off, having raised his head to find himself looking directly into the deepset eyes of Cormac mac Art. The Danan's own glims grew wider when the man behind the torture device stood and was revealed to be impossibly dark of skin; by Danan standards, he was no less than a giant.

"The queen is gone from here, traitor. It's soon back on the throne she'll be, and best ye begin to run, now."

Both Danan weapon-men were frozen in staring silence. Then, "You. . . you. . . what *are* you?"

"Him who conquered Elatha *and* that toy there at your feet, a monstrosity set by Tarmur Roag to guard the queen."

The man in the doorway jerked his head back in the direction of the torturemaster's grisly corpse. "You. . . you did that to Elatha?"

Cormac hesitated only for a moment. "Aye, and it's shame on me for letting the beast die so quickly. An ye'd seen the condition of the queen's maidens, of her high advisers and Commander Balan—ye's serve no longer bloody-handed men who conscioned such and who employed such a spider as Elatha."

The two exchanged a look. "Uh—but you. . . never have I seen such skin. And—be all your hair. . . *black?* It is not possible! Who—*what are ye?*"

"An elemental, called up by Tarmur Roag," Cormac said, who had previously called himself Partha mac Othna, and Curoi mac Dairi, aye and even Kull, to an equally mazed Briton one night on a dark strand. "But even I could not hold with what he has caused to be done, and. . . I rebelled. It's to no one I belong now, though I'm after pledging loyalty and aid to the queen—*your* queen."

The two men continued to hesitate, eyeing him.

Believe him or no, it was plain that neither relished a passage at arms with this over-tall stranger with the dark skin and hair they knew to be impossible. Yet neither wished to lose face—or life, by means of sorcery?—by calling for the help of their companions. No challenge had been issued, either by the Danans or the "elemental"; all three swords remained sheathed, though two wan hands and one dark gripped their three several hilts.

One of them decided to stave off the decision a bit longer. "Where—where is. . . Riora Feachtnachis?"

"*I* call her Riora, little man. It is of your *queen* ye speak? Dithorba! Behind the wheel!"

The robed Danan had appeared, well within the chamber and facing the weapon-men.

"It's Dithorba Loingsech! Swiftly Dungan—seize him!"

Dithorba whirled; the man named Dungan shot out a hand to catch at his robe; Cormac swung around the millwheel. Dungan released Dithorba and reached for his sword. While Cormac's right hand stretched toward the mage, his shield drove forward as if bow-shot. Dungan's arm came up just in time to parry the unorthodox attack with his own buckler, shield against shield. There was a great crash and Dungan's shield-arm slammed back into his face. At the same time, Cormac caught Dithorba's hand. Ten fingers linked and pressed.

Ere the man called Din could blink, his companion was down with blood on his mouth and both the big dark man with the scars and the queen's mage had vanished from the chamber.

It was a strange and motley group that gathered in the back room of the inn of highly trusted Red Rory. Motley too was the manner of their clothing, which included bedsheets. The innkeeper's own wife was tending the hurts of the former prisoners, aided by the older woman. Balan was gone when Cormac arrived, sent by his queen to find loyal men and bring a report of the activities of the usurpers.

The Gael was not long in that crowded room ere he was certain the queen had bade her girls be silent. They stared, large-eyed, while he bent and wriggled his way out of his mailcoat. His assortment of small wounds complained. Ale there was; food, a well-fed man in an apron told them, was coming; there could not be much bustle, so as not to arouse the attention of the patrons in the inn's main room. Riora was in a corner, talking quietly with Torna. While she paused to shoot Cormac a hot-eyed look, Dithorba hurried to join that conference.

Cormac did not. He drank off a draught of ale, but glanced at Riora, and approached the aproned man. The Gael carried his pouch, slid from his weapon-belt.

"Ye be Red Rory?"

"Aye," the fellow said though there was no sign of red in his cloud-pale hair and no ruddiness on his face. "And you are the hero of us all, he who—"

"Aye, all ye've been told—none of which I could have come close to accomplishing without Dithorba Loingsech, true hero of Moytura. And see that ye remember, Red Rory: your queen is a strong and heroic woman! It's a physician that's needed here, man, and here's what ye'll be needing to do to avoid suspicions of other guests: go to the kitchen, cry out, emerge with your hand wrapped in much cloth, and send for one with knowledge of wounds and the potions for them."

Red Rory smiled. "A clever hero as well," he said. "None of us had thought of such a ruse. Indeed, we all feared calling for skilled help, that someone might be

210

suspicious of his coming."

"There are those here who have need of it. My name is Cormac; call me that, not hero. Need there is for the placing of Captain Tathill and his dairlin' into a room of themselves, very alone. As for me—none others must see me."

Rory nodded. "That I know, having seen yourself now, Cormac!"

"In minutes, Rory, I'll be dropping for need of sleep. Food can wait until I wake; a little more ale I'd be appreciating. First this day I did much walking, and that on a hillside—seeking the Doorway to Moytura, ye see. Then another and I were forced to do death on the six set by the usurpers to watch over Dithorba. Next it was Elatha, and then a *thing* created or raised up by Tarmur Roag to hold the queen. It's hours and hours I've been on these feet and at hard exertions, Red Rory, and I will be needed here. That must be later—I'm nigh onto collapsing. Ye've a brewing room below—can I reach it without being seen?"

"Aye, Cormac Trenfher, but—"

"It's there, in marvelous privacy, I'll be sleeping, Red Rory. And violence may be done on that person who wakens me out of time!"

Within the hour a physician arrived; both Tathill and his young woman had been smuggled out to secret and private lodgings—and Red Rory had dared lie to his queen about the whereabouts of her trenfher; her champion. In truth that one had stretched his bruised length—and what a length it was!—on the floor of the brewing room back of the inn's kitchen. He was snoring.

The physician, as he was departing, was led there by Rory.

While he was seeing to the supine man's wounds, the snoring was interrupted, lids rose, and eyes like

211

sword-steel stared into Danan glims.

"Durlugh the physician," Rory said quickly, and a bit fearfully.

Cormac said nothing; his eyes closed; he was snoring again ere Durlugh had finished his work. In several places was the champion's body smeared and poulticed, and Durlugh and Rory departed. Nor was there brewing the next day, for in the world above that was his own, the sun came and went and was just coming again when Cormac mac Art awoke.

It was then he discovered that he'd been found by the Queen of Moytura, and she had a wakening surprise for him. It was herself.

Chapter Fourteen:
Tarmur Roag

"What kind of ceremony?"

"All are there," Dithorba said. "Cairluh, Tarmur Roag, the simulacrum of Riora, the priests of Danu, and the people have been bade to come into the great Square of the Moon before the temple. Too, the filays and seanachies are present."

Cormac straightened. He was clothed only in his breechclout which he wore tight. He had been exercising, he told Dithorba, testing legs and arms, flexibility and reflexes, after yesterday's exertions and the hurts put upon him. His left forearm had been wrapped again and again with the lightweight Moyturan cloth, that his buckler would not chafe the two wounds left there by the fanged tip of Elatha's whip. Elsewhere his skin was colourful with bruises.

He repeated the other man's last two words, his eyes

narrowing until they were invisible. "Poets and chroniclers?"

"Aye. You know their function here?"

"The same as among my people; they keep alive the time-that-was for the Now and the time-to-come. They are our. . . our history. And Moytura's too?"

"Aye," Dithorba said with a nod. "The same, Cormac. Tarmur and Cairluh plan something of moment, then. An announcement, methinks. The false Riora is going to make a speech to the people, assembled before the temple, that her words may have Danu's blessing."

Cormac considered, started to scratch his left forearm, realized what he was about, and left off. "They know of my presence here, and that you and Riora are free. They have Wulfhere and Thulsa Doom—oh, saw ye them, Dithorba?"

"No, Cormac."

"So, Tarmur Roag and Cairluh have decided to take some swift action. Prompted by my presence and yours and the queen's freedom? Aye. . . mayhap the false Riora is about to announce marriage with Cairluh, or abdicate, in favour of her dear cousin?"

"It is as Torna and I believe."

"Balan?"

Dithorba shook his nigh-hairless head. "Commander Balan was for the barracks of the Queen's Guard. There I dare not go—nor have we seen or heard from him."

Cormac nodded, thinking. He rubbed the bruise on his right upper arm, staring reflectively at nothing. "Dithorba. . . ye know where your queen is."

Dithorba put on an innocent face as he looked around. "Why nay, Cormac. I see her not."

Smiling, the Gael said, "It were better thus. Now—do you bring Torna here whilst I get clothes on

214

me, be ye so kind."

With a nod, Dithorba departed the brewing room; he used his feet.

A brewing room, Cormac thought. *The planning place for the restoration of a queen—by a foreigner! Danu, Danu, it's a whimsical lady ye be, moon-goddess! A brewing room, behind an inn. . . and what a queen!*

He turned to the heavy framework that supported ale vats and mugs; it was of a size to speak well for Red Rory's business. Cormac walked around it, to where his clothing lay entangled with a blue gown. He looked down at Riora. She blinked lazily up at him.

"Ye heard?"

"Nay. I. . . think I was unconscious for a time," she said. "Oh, *Cormac!* You are absolutely—"

"Later, little girl. There's business afoot. Best ye rise and come see to the business of your kingdom."

"You call the Queen of Moytura 'little girl'?"

Cormac smiled; she'd but jested, and he'd missed her point and now called her by name—the queen! She levered herself into a sitting position, reached for him; he backed away.

"Dithorba was just here," he told her. "Give listen."

And as he dressed and then grunted into forty pounds of linked-steel coat that had so long been a daily part of his attire, he told her what Dithorba had just reported, and their surmise. Swiftly he sketched a plan; a concept—a hope. She considered that with an expression both stricken and yet hopeful. Rising, she drew her soiled blue robe over her head and smoothed it as best she could.

They had just emerged from behind the vats when Dithorba returned with the senior adviser, Torna. Cormac began speaking at once.

"It's the queen's advisers ye two be, and it's her champion I seem to be, now. Now methinks the swiftest action is called for."

Torna nodded. "If we be right, Cormac mac Art, in but minutes Cairluh will have been proclaimed king by the false queen."

Cormac looked at Riora. "We have a bargain, lady Queen?"

"We have, Cormac. Once you have accomplished my reinstatement, I shall perform the strange task you have requested."

"Your pardon, lady Queen. . . but will ye just be speaking it aloud for the ears of these your ministers?"

She blinked in surprise, arched an eyebrow—and repeated their bargain, and her strange and grisly promise to mac Art.

"Dithorba," Cormac said, "take me to the temple, to the very side of the creature calling herself Riora."

"It's on the Crescent Balcony she is, Cormac. There too are guards."

Cormac signified that he understood and was ready, and they joined hands, and were gone. The moment they were there, on the outer balcony of the Temple of Danu, Cormac was speaking.

"Dithorba, time races and we catch it now or miss it forever. Fetch the queen here man, and instantly! Then it's to the barracks ye must go, and—"

But Dithorba had winked out amid a little sound like the clap of hands.

A far louder one succeeded it; a resounding cry form many, many Danan throats. The Gael looked out on the strange city that was subterranean Moytura, and down on thronging thousands of the People of Danu. Their light-eyed faces were turned up at him, and many uplifted hands were pointing.

His knees in the partial crouch of a weapon-man's readiness, he turned his head to his left. There, others stared at him; two. A handsome young man in a robe white as foam of the wave, with a large collar of silver on him, a carcanet from throat to mid-chest. It flashed with jewels. His robe was girt with a doubled cord of woven cloth-of-silver, and his fair hair was lustrous, clean and long-combed. At his side, bejeweled, in an ornately ornamented and purfled robe of the same marmoreal white, on her pale locks a chaplet of silver and coral chased with gold, stood. . . Riora.

Nay. Not Riora. Some Thing called from an unnatural elsewhere by Tarmur Roag! A lamia, mayhap. And mayhap Dithorba was more than right, in giving me this new dagger!

Ready to act, he becautioned himself to look behind him; along the white-colonnaded balcony.

No wizard was there; doubtless Tarmur Roag thought it wise to remain out of sight of the people whilst his plans were put forward by Cairluh and. . . the simulacrum. Cormac instead saw three Danan weapon-men in fine armour polished to high sheen, and with bronze on their wrists rather than bracers of leather. As their eyes met Cormac's, all three reached for their swordhilts.

So too did Cormac mac Art—and turned, and plunged toward her who was Riora's exact likeness and him the Gael assumed was the queen's plotting cousin, Cairluh.

"It is *done*, Cairluh!" mac Art said, biting out the words, and he drove his sword into the white-robed woman with such force that the point brast through her back and tented her garment before tearing through it.

Cairluh stared in horror; so too did the people below. It was the total and all of Cormac's plan; that

217

he come here with all swiftness and, pausing for naught, seek to slay the thing in Riora's likeness.

A chorus of screams and roars of rage swelled up from the people gathered below, as their eyes reported the stabbing to death of their queen by a towering man with dark skin never got of Danan parentage.

They were still shrieking when she they thought their queen was transformed before their thrice-shocked gazes.

The skin of that lovely Riora-face became a liquid, melting and oozing, running. A frightful howling sound issued from her lips even as they changed. Then Cormac, Cairluh, three frozen weapon-men and thousands of duped Moyturans saw the queen become a ravening snarling demonic *thing* that was shaggy with red hair. The snowy robe fell from the metamorphosing body. Red too were the tufts of hair on the fox-like ears, though black was the hideous snarling animal's face and the taloned claw-hands of the creature.

The crown of Moytura clattered to the floor of the balcony.

Dithorba was right, Cormac thought, and he transferred his swordhilt to his shield-hand. *Iron and steel will not slay a demon, a lamia.*

Far from dead the thing was, and as it pounced, Cormac drew the dagger Dithorba had foresightedly given him and in the same motion plunged it into the heart of the monster. A single curving claw sought to tear open his arm; it left instead a deep groove in his bracer of good cow's hide.

With another snarl that lofted into a shriek, the thing gouted blood around the silver dagger. Staggering sidewise, it struck the parapet that ran around the Crescent Balcony, and fell over.

Below, the people cried out anew, and not this time

218

in rage. Citizens nigh trampled one the other in their efforts to hie themselves well back from the tumbling monster. It struck the green-and-white stones of the Square of the Moon with a loud and sickening thump and a great plosion of blood.

Then all who could see stared, as the slain demon-thing that had worn the likeness of their queen melted again—into a shiny putrescence that gave off the stench of a thousand dead fish.

Aye, Cormac thought, *silver slays the demonic!*

No cries rose now from the populace. There were only murmurs. Again many eyes rose to the balcony. A new silence fell, followed by more excited muttering and isolated shouts; at the side of the demon-slaying stranger had appeared two well recognized figures: Dithorba Loingsech and the Queen of Moytura.

Below, the last trace of the demon vanished.

Stooping, Dithorba picked up the Coral Crown of Moytura, and placed it on the head of his queen.

Yet no cheering bedlam arose; the people were too shocked and confused to react so. Had not they seen their queen afore; had not they seen that she had been a foul slavering *thing*? Now—was this their Riora? And the giant at her side with un-Danan skin. . . what or who was he, and from whence? Was not that the Sign of the Moonbow on his chest? The queen was lifting her arms to them. . .

The silence deepened. Into it Riora called, "I am Riora, Queen of the Moyturans, Chosen of Danu. And this my champion, Moytura's champion, Danu's champion—Cormac mac Art!" And in a natural tone she said, "Your voice is stronger, Cormac—tell them."

He did. The Gael bellowed out a few sentences, speaking slowly, pronouncing carefully and knowing that to them he spoke with a frightful strange accent. It was the content of his words that held import: he identified her at his side as the real queen, and accused Cairluh and Tarmur Roag of having done treachery on her.

No proof was necessary. Cairluh provided it. He turned and fled, holding high the skirt of his regal robe to facilitate the churning of his surprisingly muscular legs.

Again Riora lifted high her hands to her people; a queen crowned and in a soiled blue gown. And this time the cheers rose. After a moment of smiling on them, she turned to the three weapon-men who'd been coming at Cormac and who now stood frozen, as horrified again and again as those in the square below.

"In your hands I see swords," she said, "and on you I see the clothing of the Queen's Guards. *I* am that queen. Sheathe your weapons!"

The trio did. One fell to his knees; his companions swiftly emulated him.

"Basest treachery was done on me," the queen said. "And you were tricked—you thought that. . . creature was I?"

All three kneeling men assured her that they had; from the anguished eyes of one tears rolled.

"Then into the temple, Queen's Guardsmen, and take Tarmur Roag, traitor to all Moytura—traitor to Danu!"

The three guardsmen rose, bowed, and drew their iron swords. Cormac's hand hovered at his hilt while he watched those men in crescent-shaped helmets for any hint of movement toward Riora. There was none; their pained expressions remained. One man spoke.

"Lady Queen. . . below are the Lord Cairluh, and Tarmur Roag, the filays and seanachies and other guardsmen. There were a score of us for the. . . the ceremony; seventeen are in the temple."

220

"All dupes, as you were? Cormac asked.

The men's expressions showed that they did not know. Some of the men below with the usurpers might well have been tricked into believing the lamia was the queen. Yet some were almost certainly knowing tools of the plotters, loyal to Cairluh and Tarmur Roag because of threats or promises or both.

Cormac strode past Riora to the head of the stairway leading down into the temple.

The Temple of Danu of Moytura was laid out in the shape of a crescent; a moonbow. Nor was it huge, as the Gael had already surmised from the balcony's length. The arms of the crescent flowed out away from him on either side. The roof was supported by four colonnades that marched along the arms of the crescent; columns of pale stone blocks banded around by bronze. Within the innermost lines of columns, between them and the outer walls, hung deeply purple drapes or curtains, trimmed in silver. He assumed a sort of gallery or passageway lay behind, betwixt hangings and walls.

The altar rose at the far end, in the center of the string of the moonbow. From Cormac's vantage, the statue of the goddess appeared to be of excellently detailed workmanship, and all of silver. Plated to iron surely, he supposed, or to stone. The temple floor was of smooth and refulgently green marble or a similar stone of that unusual hue. On it stood men, and they stared up at him.

Five were priests. Just under a score wore the helms and armour of the Queen's Guards. The central figure was a plump man whose grey beard was plaited, like Dithorba's. On the chest of his shimmering silver robe hung a Moonbow sigil; a Chain of Danu that was like the one Cormac wore. Beside him stood Cairluh. The traitorous cousin even so swiftly had doffed his snowy robe to reveal himself in a coat of fine scalemail, and sword-armed. Around the two plotters, for Cormac assumed him in the robe of silver to be Tarmur Roag, were ranked others he took to be filays and seanachies; poets and chroniclers or historians. Thus in Eirrin was history of centuries passed down, without written words.

A movement at his side drew Cormac's attention.

Both Riora and Dithorba had come up beside him. There too were the three weapon-men, with nervousness and some anguish visible in their faces. Along half the length of the temple and up the steps, the queen's usurping cousin and he who had effected his schemes—or laid them—stared at their queen and the dark, tall man beside her.

With a fine sense of royalty and drama, Queen Riora lifted an arm and extended an accusing finger at the silver-robed sorcerer.

"You have failed, foul wizard! And you, Cairluh, murderous cousin! This man has slain Elatha, and brought me forth from the prison where I was tortured, with my girls and Torna and Balan and others. Lughan has been murdered, by Elatha the Whip! Now this same man, Cormac mac Art, slew the monster who wore my face and body—and the people *saw* that transformation; they *know* of your treachery and of the foul thing that bore my face! They *saw* it melt and ooze away to naught, that thing you put upon my throne—the throne of Moytura!"

Cormac was watching carefully. He saw horror on the faces of four priests; saw the fifth smile thinly. The poets and historians stared too in shock, and backed from Tarmur Roag and Cairluh—all but one, him in the blue tunic and beige leggings. As for the weapon-men. . .it was hard to be certain, but Cormac thought that two looked shocked, horrified.. Two of

222

seventeen!

If he was right about those two, then they were the only fighting men loyal to their queen, with himself and these three beside her. *Six of us. . . against sixteen with Cairluh. . . and Tarmur Roag with his dark powers!*

It was not possible. Had one of those with him been Wulfhere. . . had these men beside their queen been of his own people, or Danes. . . but they were not.

It was not possible. Two could put defeat on six, when the two were Wulfhere Skull-splitter and Cormac the Wolf; six could not defeat sixteen, when as allies mac Art had only the small men of Moytura. And besides, there was Tarmur Roag, and Dithorba had more than merely admitted that the man in the silver robe possessed powers transcending his own.

And then, horribly, there were four, not six. Suddenly men below drew shining blades of dark iron, and sheathed them anew in the two Cormac had rightly taken to be without knowledge of the treachery and deception. They fell, almost in silence.

Tarmur Roag smiled.

"That foreigner from among those who drove our ancestors from Eiru will aid ye no more, Riora! Let him and those three beside you come down among us, that we may *see* who rules Moytura!"

While the queen stood stricken silent, Cormac drew steel and brandished the blade in a shining arc above his head.

"It's the Sign of the Moonbow I wear, given me by the People of Danu driven from Moytura by *your* ancestors, Tarmur Roag. . . for favouring rule by a male! Six guards ye set to hold Dithorba; they lie dead and here he stands. Elatha the Whip daily raped the *Queen* of all Moytura—and Elatha lies dead. Who of those little sniveling cowards and traitors about ye will

223

ye send to take me, Tarmur Roag—who will come to his *doom*?''

Cormac mac Art was striving as much to persuade and fire himself as he was engaging in the standard challenging rhetoric and braggadocio of weapon-men throughout the world. And he felt his own spirits surge, the blood seeming to warm in his veins, even while he sought to cut the confidence from beneath those traitorous guardsmen below as the scythe went through the grain-field.

Cormac descended two steps and stood in a posture of arrogance and confidence.

Below, sixteen men stood with naked iron in their hands.

Tarmur Roag's arm rose and the silvery sleeve slid away from a white wrist as he pointed at the Gael.

''TAKE him! To him who cuts down that foreigner goes command of the guardsmen. . . the King's Guard!''

The guardsmen hesitated, exchanged glances. Suddenly one started forward, grinning. Command! Then another followed—and then all of them, none wishing to be left behind and all hoping to put death on the foreigner or to be there when it was done and thus hold favour with the next commander.

While he stood on the steps and glared down at them like a snarling wolf at bay, sixteen armed men began converging on Cormac mac Art.

It was then that the thunderous booming sound exploded from the other end of the temple and filled the large chamber with rolling echoes. On the temple floor, many men turned to stare at the tall brazen doors on either side of the altar.

''Balan!'' Dithorba muttered, and Cormac knew there was more hope than certainty with the old man. Again someone hammered on that faraway door.

The voice of Cormac mac Art roared out, with all the volume he could put into it. "Ye unarmed poets and chroniclers of Moytura—draw aside that none may put wound or death on Moytura's finest!" Then he swung halfway around. "Dithorba—use your power, man! *Open that door!*"

Frozen in indecision, Dithorba jerked, blinked. He smiled—and vanished.

Cormac saw him reappear at the other end of the temple, saw the mage forge swiftly forward to grasp the bars on the great door. No eyes were on him—until Tarmur Roag looked back over his shoulder.

"Kill that man!" he bawled, pointing.

"Kill Tarmur Roag!" Cormac shouted, and without looking to see whether the three loyal Danans were with him, he charged down the steps.

Now men were shouting, and Dithorba's cry came but thinly: "Take away your weight from the door!"

The three rearmost of the traitorous guardsmen had wheeled and made for him. One, seeing that so many were hardly necessary to cut down a single old man, swung back to join his fellows against the big dark maniac coming like a charging bear down the steps. At that a second of those making for Dithorba paused, biting his lip; surely two of them were unnecessary for this piddling task, and if it might be his sword that slew the foreigner who opposed his masters. . . He too turned back. He joined the mass of men who waited, crouching, swords up, for the charge of Cormac mac Art.

One man continued toward Dithorba, who was pitting all his strength against the massive bar across the door. Again it shook and boomed with assault from the other side. Now two others rushed after Dithorba's nemesis; unarmed both: poets or chroniclers. At the sound of the slap-slap of their sandals

225

behind him, the weapon-man looked back. He was forced to pause, to turn with upraised buckler and ready sword.

"Would you do death on Reyan, foremost among poets of Moytura?" one of his pursuers demanded.

While the guardsman hesitated, full of the high respect for the poet of all men on and within Eirrin, the bar rose—and crashed down outside its iron rest. Dithorba tried to skip away but was bowled over by the inwardly rushing door. Into the temple boiled Balan at the head of a score or so swarming guardsmen of unquestionable allegiance and intent.

Balan paused. His eager followers brought themselves to a halt at the lifting of his shield, though they glared about like leashed hounds with the scent of blood in their nostrils; twenty men in scalemail armour, shields whose faces were etched in silver with the moonbow of their goddess, and from whose helms projected crescents of silver; men exactly like those with Tarmur Roag and Cairluh. Their pale eyes roamed the interior of the temple.

They saw the poets and chroniclers of Moytura, who had drawn to one side; they saw a mass of their fellow Queen's Guardsmen in number about equal to their own; they saw beyond them the semicircular stairs with Cormac but two steps from the temple floor, brought to pause by their advent; above them they saw three others, partway descended, swords naked; and at the top of the flight was their queen.

"Balan!" Cormac shouted into the sudden silence. "Behind me is the real Riora; Tarmur's creature is slain! As for these—every guardsman ye see belongs to Tarmur and Cairluh, and they're just after murdering two of their own number!"

Balan hesitated only a moment. Then he pointed with his sword to the traitors.

226

"Yield!"

Tarmur's voice bellowed out a moment after: "Slay!"

So it was to be, and battle was joined in the very Temple of the Moon. The Queen's Guardsmen were pitted against the Queen's Guardsmen. Her commander led one band; her treacherous cousin and the sorcerer the other. The groups closed with arching blades crashing through hastily interposed shields in a storm of ringing iron. The two forces were soon indistinguishably intermingled.

Into that milling mass of sword-wielding men Tarmur Roag durst not unleash his sorcerous powers. Instead, wheeling, he hurled it at the stranger who had brought on this thwarting of his plans and their execution. But a few minutes agone he had been scant seconds from the rule of Moytura; now all his plans were endangered, aye, and his life as well.

Tarmur Roag gestured.

A spear of dullest, shadowy black streaked at mac Art.

He both dodged and struck out at it with his buckler. A sensation as of ice assailed his shield-arm as he scrambled aside, nearly falling from the bottom step. His slitted eyes saw that his buckler had been holed through and through, as though by an awl in the hands of resistless god.

His nape prickling and his arm still atingle, the Gael sought to avoid further such magickal attacks by rushing the two Moyturans who had not whirled to meet Balan's men but remained to brace the tall man with the dark skin. Their faces were set as in granite and their eyes were ice. He saw that they were *controlled* men, fighting animals, like those who'd guarded Dithorba.

There was a *whoosh* overhead as another long spear

of darkness rushed from the mage. Behind Cormac, gurgles sounded, and then the crashes of falling men. He need not turn to know that the three guardsmen had paid a bitter price for being so slow to follow him to the defense of their queen.

He advanced on two of their fellows, traitors both. They separated.

Death came and pressed him close and he hacked and smote, running a shield and bending an iron blade with his own sword of silver-flashing steel. That man recovered swiftly and hewed without troubling over his blade, which now formed a definite curve.

Spitting a sulphurous oath, the Gael swept his battered, boled shield in a whizzing blurring defensive arc before him; it turned the bent blade and swept away the other man's so that the fellow was wrenched halfway around. Cormac drove his own sword forward in a terrible disemboweling thrust that sheared through iron scalemail and brought an ugly croak from its victim. His eyes glared at the dark man—who gave his blade a wrenching twist and yanked it free. Blood followed; dropped sword clanged on the smoothness of stone floor; its owner sank beside his blade.

Cormac had not waited to see that man fall. Instead he strode past and swung his blooded blade at the other man. The Moyturan fended it off with his hexagonal shield, which lost half its silver decor thereby.

Over his shoulder Cormac's eyes recorded iron ranks at clash and stamp; blood spattered as Balan's and Tarmur's men battled with edge of blade and point of sword. Battle-lust ruled the Temple of the Moon and Danu could but watch as her own people fought among themselves. Sharp-edged brands of dark iron flashed and glittered in blue-grey streaks, and sword-hacked men fell vomiting scarlet.

The center of the temple of the goddess became a sea, a writhing storm-swept sea, of shining mail and blood.

A hard-driven slash chopped a wedge from Cormac's weakened buckler in a blow that jolted his arm to the collarbone. His blade streaked his arm with Moyturan blood as he slashed in return. The other man grunted when his carapace of iron scales gave way at the waist to sharp steel sliver driven by steel-sheathed muscles. Cormac's sword chewed deep. The man was staggered by the blow but stood blinking, not realizing that his own blood washed forth after Cormac had twisted free his blade.

The Gael started past him; the Moyturan hacked.

"Crom's name, man, know ye not ye're *dead*?"

Cormac slammed his shield into the rushing sword. There was the booming grating crash and screech of metal on metal, and the guardsman staggered again. His darker antagonist drove forward, using his shield as an advancing wall heading a body block that would have staggered a horse.

The charge smote the wounded guardsman like a thunderbolt. He was dashed to the floor. Crimson surged from his side while steel-spring muscles carried the Gael past him.

Red chaos ruled the temple, which was become a clangourous maelstrom of surging, hacking men.

Crumpled Moyturans of both sides lay in their glistening blood while their souls raced off to join Donn, Lord of the Dead of Eirrin. Cormac saw the air alive with swords that flashed blue and sprinkled crimson drops. Staggering from woundy blows, men yet strove to fight on; some for queen and throne, others because they were the controlled tools of a wizard with not a care for them, body or soul.

The Gael saw Balan hurl an attacker from him with a mighty twisting heave of his six-sided shield and, while he roared out his constant cry of "Riora and Danu!," sent his point leaping out to gird into the breast of another. An iron blade battered down on his helm; Balan trembled, staggered, cursed—and swept his smeared glaive around in a whistling half-circle that sliced away a sword-arm.

Cormac's grin was wolfish and ugly. Balan of Moytura not only knew how to use body and blade and buckler, the man reveled in it! His command, the Gael mused, was the result of no woman's favouritism or political appointment!

But as Cormac looked about, the ugly little smile gave way to a frown.

Where was Tarmur Roag?

The frown became a snarling scowl; the mage had skirted the mass of men, while none dared so much as glance aside from points and iron edges that sought and chewed like the fangs of ravening wolves. Aye, the plump traitor was ghosting betwixt the pillars on the far side of the great hall. He headed for the purple drapes that obscured the wall.

Fleeing for some hidden door, Cormac thought, and he rushed after the Moyturan wizard.

The Gael must leap high; a man came staggering back from the ringing combat to crash to the floor at his feet like a felled tree. Cold eyes blazing, Cormac raced on. On his shield-side howling devils crashed their flashing blades through bucklers and flesh; to his right, across fifteen feet of gleaming green floor, the steps rose. A glance told him that the queen stood still there, with Dithorba now at her side.

It's danger she's in, Cormac thought, *should one of the traitors see her and bethink himself of charging the steps. A sword at her breast and all fighting*

230

ceases—and Balan and the rest of us are butchered!

But nay, he reminded himself; Dithorba was there, and could whisk her out of the danger of any traitorous attack in a twinkling.

Cormac reached the edge of the main floor; plunged past the colonnade of bronze-bound pillars. Ahead of him, Tarmur Roag reached for the violet hangings. The edge of Cormac's eye remarked a guardsman racing toward the mage, but he knew not whether that man was Balan's or Tarmur's.

With a freezing cry ripping from his throat, the Gael charged Tarmur Roag with all the speed of his powerful legs.

Having begun his action, the treacherous wizard completed it: he ripped away the heavy curtain ere he responded to Cormac's shout.

Behind the drape lay the wall, with two feet of space between. There stood a night-dark robe surmounted by a noisome death's head; around its neck gleamed a slim chain of silver and on the robe's breast flashed the sigil of Danu, moon-points down. The undying wizard was otherwise unbound. Beside him stood a redbearded giant who looked nigh naked without ax or scalemail corselet or round Danish helm; in chains he was, and with a gag covering his mouth. Cormac saw that iron links secured Wulfhere's wrists to his ankles, but without play enough to allow the Dane to get his fingers at his gag.

That scene Cormac mac Art saw all in the flash of a moment. There was no time for a sigh of relief at seeing Wulfhere alive and Thulsa Doom still immobilized by the Sign of the Moonbow; Tarmur Roag turned at the Gael's shout and his pallid gaze fell on the dark man who raced at him with naked sword in hand.

At sight of him who had done such violence to his

231

plans, the Moyturan wizard's eyes seemed to spark yellow, as with leaping flames of hate. He gestured viciously, as if he were hurling some missile.

Was instinct saved mac Art; piratic weapon-man's instinct caused him to lunge sideward. Materialized from nothingness, from the air itself and the arcane power of Tarmur Roag, a long shadow-spear drove at and past him.

In that desperate dodgery Cormac lost his footing. He fell, armour crashing and grating on the floor of glaucous stone.

Tarmur Roag whirled and with both hands whipped the Chain of Danu from around the neck of Thulsa Doom. He tossed it away, and plucked a dagger from a sheath up the sleeve of his silvery robe. Instantly the eyesockets of the skull blazed the red of witch-fire on a foggy night. The will of the undying wizard had been returned to him—and with it returned his sheerest malevolence and lust for vengeance.

Cormac rose in time to see two things: the charging Moyturan weapon-man had swerved to attack him, not the wizard—and Wulfhere's chains did not prevent him from lifting his hands as high as Tarmur Roag's neck. The Dane grasped the mage by the throat with a suddenness and violence that jarred the dagger from Tarmur Roag's hand.

The guardsman came on for Cormac. *It's no time I have for this interfering idiot,* the Gael thought, angered at the delay. He took one step forward while he launched a sword-cut with such irresistible strength and savagery that it met his attacker's stroke and sheared through his blade as though it had been cheese.

Half the traitor's blade flew through the air to ring clanging and skirling on the floor. The other half completed its chop, though weakly; Cormac's raging blow had nigh broken the man's arm along with his sword. Now, just as viciously, Cormac kicked him up under the hem of his mailcoat, bashed him in the head with his buckler as the retching fellow started to fall, making sick noises. Then the Gael's sword came whizzing back to cleave into the other's face at the nose. The gory corpse sprawled and Cormac had to set a foot against it to free his blade of the Moyturan's skull.

Tarmur Roag's face had taken on colour for the first time in his life. It went red, then began to blacken. His eyes bulged and his tongue quivered out. His heels cleared the floor as Wulfhere lifted, and a great shudder went through the Moyturan mage. Then, as Thulsa Doom marshaled his senses and started past, the Dane swung that ugly corpse so as to stagger the ancient wreaker of evil.

Tarmur Roag's body fell limply. Thulsa Doom rose from his knees and turned blazing red eye-pits on the giant. In the wizard's bony hand was Tarmur's dagger.

"*Wulfhere!* Pig of a blood-bearded barbarian. . . for you I can spare a moment!"

A long sword of shining steel whizzed down in a blurring streak of silver. The dagger drove at Wulfhere—and was carried away with the arm that wielded it. No blood splashed as Thulsa Doom groaned and turned his awful faceless head toward his attacker.

With a second wild sweep that narrowly missed the Dane's swelling chest, Cormac's sword lifted the skull of Thulsa Doom from his shoulders. The flying death's head struck a pillar, rebounded to the floor with a loud cracking sound, and rolled.

"HAIL THE QUEEN! RIORA REIGNS!"

Cormac recognized the bellowing voice; it was

233

Balan, triumphant. He and his remaining men had defeated their erstwhile fellow guardsmen. And Tarmur Road lay dead. And the undying wizard was beheaded.

But he was not dead.

The headless, one-armed robe turned, stopped when its front was turned toward the yellow-white object that gleamed on the floor fifteen feet away.

Then Thulsa Doom started for his head.

Cormac was already striking away the chains that linked Wulfhere's feet to the wall. On one knee then to sever the lenght that connected the Dane's ankles, Cormac saw the horror that brought silence on all else who witnessed: the tall, headless robe bent, clutched up the skull, and set it upon the center of its shoulders. Instantly it adhered and was fast.

A ringing peal of satanic laughter burst from the death's head mouth and echoed from the temple's stone walls.

Then Thulsa Doom ran, with astonishing speed, toward the steps at whose top stood the Queen of Moytura.

Bellowing *"Dithorba!"* Cormac leaped after the undying wizard. Behind him, chains clinked as Wulfhere started to follow.

Dithorba had said he possessed but few talents beyond that of his strange travel-by-mind. At last he demonstrated; his was the Danu-given power of Cathbadh. A wall of flame leaped up a few feet in front of the running Thulsa Doom. Cormac saw that the fire rose not so high as those of the mage of Danu's Isle, and was pale blue rather than yellow and orange. Nevertheless the fire-wall served its purpose. The skull-surmounted robe skidded to a stop and back-paced hurriedly.

"Attack!" Balan's voice cried, and frozen Queen's

Guardsmen were mobilized. . . though only Balan and six others were on their feet.

Snarling, Thulsa Doom seemed to waver, to shimmer. . . and became a plaintively wailing Erris of Moytura.

Cormac was running, and his broad sweeping cut was already begun. Again he lopped off the head of the undying wizard. It rolled on the floor, a piteous sight to shake strong men: the head of a pretty young woman whose eyes and mouth gaped and whose lovely pale hair flew.

And then Erris's head was a rattling, hairless, fleshless skull; the true head of Thulsa Doom.

Once again the robed body went for its severed head. . . but Wulfhere, charging past Cormac like an enraged bear, seized the headless body. Both fell, to roll wrestling, desperately seeking crippling holds. Cries rose as the robe vanished, and the flamehaired giant appeared to be wrestling with a huge growling shaggy bear. . .

And then Wulfhere fought a lashing, writhing serpent. . .

And then a woman, her with orange-red hair and green eyes, in leathern armour and tall, tall boots that rose up under her tunic, a woman who cried out, "Wulfhere, No! Wulfhere—"

Shaking like a wind-blown aspen, Cormac tore his pouch from his belt. Ruthlessly he spilled onto the temple floor the gifts he'd brought for a queen: garnets and emeralds, a great twinkling sapphire and two sunny amethysts, a necklace of coral and stones found only in Europe. The treasure of Doom-heim twinkled and sparkled on the stone floor. It was the sack Cormac mac Art needed, now.

A few steps he took, and caught up the death's head of Thulsa Doom, and popped it into the leathern bag.

As he drew its strings, the wall of blue flame died without leaving so much as a smoke-smudge on the temple floor.

The Queen of Moytura descended the steps while Cormac mac Art strode toward them. Behind her came Dithorba. He carried a hammer, brought from the Inn of Red Rory.

A few feet away, Wulfhere rolled grunting and cursing on thē floor. Wide-eyed guardsmen saw with fearful horror that he seemed to be wrestling with the same man who approached their queen.

With a proud queen's sense of drama and her dignity—and an awareness of Cormac's height—Riora Feachtnachis halted at the bottom step but one. Thus her eyes were slightly above the level of Cormac's. He extended the leathern bag, puffed bulgy with the skull it contained. He rested it on the step at her feet.

"Lady Queen," he said, "our bargain."

The man with whom Wulfhere wrestled shrieked in anguish and horrid knowledge; the final death of the Undead wizard was imminent.

"Lady Queen," Dithorba said, and he handed her a hammer all of iron.

Her light eyes met Cormac's directly.

"Strike!" he urged, almost shouting.

"Not so fast, Cormac, Champion," Riora said. "There is another matter we must discuss, first."

Cormac stared at her. He spoke quietly, his teeth tightly together: "We have a bargain, Riora. My part was to return yourself to the throne. That I have done. Your part is merely to strike this bag with that hammer, to smash the skull of Thulsa Doom."

"Oh, Cormac," she murmured, but he gazed implacably. Riora's face firmed. She lifted her chin haughtily, and Riora spoke for all to hear. "The

Queen of the Moyturans will grant the boon you ask, Champion of Moytura, Savior of Moytura. . . in return for that which Moytura has not—a consort and husband for its queen, and one worthy of her and her people. Yourself, Cormac mac Art!''

Chapter Fifteen:
The Throne of Moytura

"Lady Queen," Dithorba said, with reproach and accusation in his voice. "You gave your word; both Torna and I were present! It is as Cormac has stated!"

Her face stiffened still more; her jawline was as if chiseled from stone. Her mouth, insofar as her sensuous lips were capable, assumed a straight line.

Her head lowered slowly, until her eyes met Cormac's. As a reminder, she tapped the head of the hammer into her palm. "Stay with me, Cormac mac Art, Trenfher na Moytura!"

From behind the grimly staring mac Art, Balan's voice roared out and echoed from wall to wall of Danu's temple: "NO man of the GAELS may rule the Tuatha de Danann! There may be no such consort of our queen!"

Riora's light eyes went cold and hard as diamonds as

she stared over Cormac's head. She lifted an arm; she pointed. "Cormac my darling, my champion—*slay* that traitor!"

Cormac backed from the steps and moved to one side. The pouch of leather lay at Riora's feet; still Wulfhere strove to hold the headless Thulsa Doom and still the latter struggled to break free of the huge man. Cormac turned to gaze into Balan's eyes, and the Danan commander stared no less levelly. Cormac looked again at Riora, who stood with chin high and eyes cold. He waited until she looked again at him.

"I will *not*," he told her.

After a long moment, Riora cried in a voice almost pitiful, "Who rules in Moytura?"

"The queen," Balan called, "and no other—and never one who is not of the de Danann!"

Cormac's voice was a mere mutter, which only Riora and Dithorba heard. "A girl, who knows not how to behave herself as a woman, much less a queen. . .and who does dishonour on herself and her people by breaking her word. . .and insisting on the impossible."

Riora swung her eyes and then her head this way and that, as if seeking approval or aid; any sort of reinforcement for her unreasonable and egocentric willfulness. She saw none. All stared, and on the faces of some were worried frowns—nervousness and worry both for herself and her people.

"But. . .it is my will! It is what I *want!* Can never a queen have what *she* wants? Must she belong to her people and the old men who advise her?"

There was no reply.

"Wulfhere," Cormac said, "release Thulsa Doom."

Wulfhere still struggled, for though two Danan guardsmen had stabbed his opponent, they sought not to pin Thulsa Doom and so he was unaffected, woundless and strong as ever once their iron blades left his robed body.

"Wha—"

"Release him, Wulfhere!"

Wulfhere objected, and did not understand, and did as his friend demanded.

The headless body rose. It seemed to look this way and that, though without eyes or even a skull to set them in. It rose—and advanced on Riora. The queen cowered against Dithorba, then reached out piteously to Cormac. He put a symbolic additional pace between them and stared coldly at her.

Thulsa Doom approached.

Dithorba could not bear it; again a wall of weak blue fire rose before the stalking horror.

This time Thulsa Doom only paused. Then he, it, walked through the fire. His robe caught at the hem and the yellow flame licked up. The undying wizard reached the foot of the steps—and reached for Riora Feachtnachis.

With a little cry, the fearful queen squatted and brought the iron hammer smashing down onto the leathern pouch Cormac had left at her feet. The hammer struck the bulge of the skull within; all heard it crack and saw the bulge flatten.

Instantly the headless body twitched into gruesome shuffling movement. The unspeakable ancient abomination that was Thulsa Doom lurched into uncontrolled and uncontrollable movement; spastic jerks and twitches took possession of the robe that was his sole manifestation. The queen struck again. The long dark robe convulsed and staggered, shuddered and lurched even as the yellow flames rose up its shifting folds.

Then the flames roared up unnaturally, formed a

plume of fierce yellow-white. Straight up that jerking figure they rose in a plume, and—vanished. That which had been Thulsa Doom had turned to ash, like dust that settled to the temple floor as after a windstorm during a drought.

Men murmured; their queen crouched, staring, shivering.

Only then did Cormac return to her.

From beneath her hammer he drew his belt pouch. The bag was limp. He opened its drawstrings, widened the mouth, and upended it. The small quantity of fine, almost transparent dust that sifted down may have been all that remained of that fearsome skull. . . or it may merely have been dust, in the bag aforetime. Nothing more emerged save those few grains of dust. Cormac held only an unornamented leathern sack; the pouch that had contained the dread skull of Thulsa Doom was empty.

After eighteen thousand years, a hundred and eighty centuries, Thulsa Doom was dead; permanently dead. Evil incarnate had left the world.

Cormac stared at the woman who crouched on the steps in a manner far less than regal. She looked like an awed, fear-filled girl whose eyes begged for understanding and comfort.

"It is done, Riora. The throne is yours. Tarmur Roag is dead. Your cousin is wounded and your prisoner—and from what I've seen of ye, better for him he'd lost his head to Balan's sword rather than a mere few fingers."

She stared. Her lips moved. No sound emerged.

"It is done," he repeated. "Wulfhere and I must return to our own. All the world owes ye a debt, though I'll not be thanking ye for doing that to which ye were forced."

She found her voice. The hammer clanked on the

steps as her hand moved out to clutch his arm. "Cormac. . . stay. Be King of Moytura—King of the Danann."

"I will not. I cannot."

Her voice lowered and her fingertips stroked the skin of his forearm. "Stay anyhow, then. No crown need be on you. Tarry with me."

Cormac looked around. Poets, chroniclers, priests —ah!

"Balan! Yon man in the yellow tunic—he wants arresting and questioning. And. . . all the priests save him." He pointed.

Balan turned; his men, so long frozen, came alive. The man in the tunic of primrose hue betrayed himself by falling to his knees and swearing that Tarmur Roag had forced him. The priest Cormac had singled out glanced about and, as if evading some dread plague, stepped away from his cohorts. They glared their malignance at him and at the Gael.

"He in the yellow tunic, and those four," Cormac said, "I noted well, earlier. No shock or surprise seemed upon them at news of the treachery done here, or of the queen's imprisonment."

Balan nodded. "Many will want questioning," he said.

"Many will DIE!" Riora cried, rising, quivering.

Cormac looked at her, and his face was inscrutable—unless it was sadness it showed, and perhaps a trace of pity.

"Odin's beauteous red beard, it's days I've been prisoner, and not enough food given me to nourish a titmouse! Be there food in Moytura?—and ale?"

Cormac smiled slightly at Wulfhere, and he nodded. "We will remain, and eat and sleep and share ale with ye of Moytura. . . our brothers beneath the earth." *And on the morrow,* he mused, *we will hie ourselves rom this place of an unworthy ruler.*

The queen turned bright eyes on him, but Cormac's expression when he looked upon her was unreadable. Then he turned from her to stride half the temple's length and to pick up that which Tarmur Roag had slung to the floor; the Chain of Danu that had so long held Thulsa Doom.

The little band of people who made their way from temple to royal palace learned that they'd hardly be going hungry; a celebratory feast had been ordered long hours before and was in preparation. No matter that it had been for traitors who expected to celebrate their victory in usurping rule in Moytura; there was victual and ale aplenty for the truly victorious. And the menace of Thulsa Doom was ended.

Eighty guardsmen were found locked in an old barracks. Balan made an assumption about their loyalty, based on the fact that the plotters had mured them up. Of none others save the six who'd fought at his side in the temple—and the three wounded others now attended by the queen's own physician—could he be sure. Hence the eighty became at once the Palace Guard, and officers were set to arranging their shifts. None knew how many others might have been privy to the plot of Cairluh and Tarmur Roag—and in sympathy with it. Peoples had been so stupid before as to throw over one distasteful ruler only to install the equally bad, or worse, and of a surety would do so again.

As for Cairluh, Balan insisted that the queen's cousin—who was also Balan's, Cormac learned—Cairluh receive either medical treatment or instant execution as a mercy; the queen was for sending her plotting cousin at once to the dungeon she'd so recently quitted, and him with wounds untreated.

Cormac heard her shout at her Commander of Guardsmen, the Lord Balan. Balan never raised his voice. Dithorba and Torna joined their entreaties to his, speaking much of what was seemly. They prevailed.

Cormac and Wulfhere were given sumptuous quarters, a room for each, and with every inch of stone covered and disguised; the Moyturans saw enough of bare rock. The Gael soon learned that his room abutted and adjoined the royal apartment. Onto an overly soft bed he tossed the Chain of Danu that Thulsa Doom had worn. He stood gazing at it, fingering his own Moonbow.

While Wulfhere was served by ale-bearing young women, Cormac went seeking Balan. He obtained privacy with the commander, despite the fact that the latter was passing busy. His queen was bathing and seeing to herself; her advisers and aides saw to the business of the queendom.

"It's a brace of questions I'd ask of ye, Lord Balan."

"We are weapon-men together; call me Balan. You who saved us all—ask."

"Ye love the queen? No—I mean: Ye love Riora?"

Balan's face went rigid. "I would kill you for her, brother weapon-man."

"There'll be no need. It's among our own Wulfhere and I will be returning, on the morrow, however ye reckon day and night in this kingdom of twilight. And Balan: It's no love I have on me for Riora."

"Nor do you understand my loving her."

Cormac shrugged. "It is no business of mine to say, Balan. Have—have ye been lovers?"

"Nor is that for you to ask, Cormac mac Art."

"True. I have asked. I have some. . .semblance of a plan, Balan. Her feeling for me is infatuation, no

244

ore. I would know of yourself."

"We have been lovers. We have spoken love. We have even spoken of marriage. She is. . . a difficult woman."

"Umm. Moytura could—your pardon, Balan—Moytura could be the worse for her in uncontrolled rule, and far better with you as her lover, or more. Ah. Your face has turned to stone. I'll saying no more."

Nor did he. But the Gael held much inner converse with himself, and was still at his thoughts when Wulfhere had downed six huge cups and was disporting himself in his chamber with a maid more than willing. And still the sombre mac Art turned thoughts in his mind; he was still pondering when a door opened behind him. He turned.

She was beautiful. The gown and jewels and chaplet crown on her were beautiful, and her face with its reddened lips and darkened brows and lashes and eyelids to break the Danan pallor and set it off to her advantage; Riora the Fair and Righteous knew how to enhance the natural sensuous loveliness that was hers.

"I would have the Champion of Moytura escort me to the feast, Cormac."

He considered. Aye, he would do that, and he did. He was aware of many eyes on him, more than a few of which held troubled gazes. And the queen and courtiers and their two guests banqueted, and quaffed ale. The Gael and the Dane were plied with questions about the outer world, so that they were able to ask but few of their own. Cormac did learn why his head had bothered him since he'd set foot here, and why too the goddess-flame Dithorba had raised, just as Cathbadh on the isle, had burned blue rather than brightly. The air of Moytura was not good, and fire was a great danger in this world without plants, though underground rivers found the sea and air from the sea found all parts of Moytura. It was thus simple for Cormac to prevail upon Dithorba for a strong sleeping potion, though the mage counseled more ale

Considerably later, Cormac mac Art opened a door from his chamber into a sumptuous and sprawling one that was darkened by the drawing of heavy drapes against the perpetual light of Danu. There awaited a sensuous woman for her champion, and he joined her. Once he had done what he intended with Dithorba's potion, stupor replaced desire in the eyes of Riora and her quickened breathing relaxed more and more. Then the queen was asleep.

Cormac returned to his own room, dressed, and went along the hall to the chamber given over to his Danish friend. Abed with no less than two Moyturans, Wulfhere protested violently—and grumbling, rose and dressed himself. Aye, the smiling young women with him knew where they might find the lord Balan.

Balan stared at the two men in much surprise; both were dressed, and armoured, and with their weapons by them.

"She sleeps," Cormac said, without preamble. "And no, we did not, she and I. Wulfhere and I leave tonight, Balan—now. Nor do I wish to leave behind in Moytura an enemy, and for naught, and him a weapon-man with high skill and bravery on him."

"I am not so petty, Cormac mac Art."

Aye, the Gael thought, *it is why yourself should be king of Moytura—and not Riora.*

"For saving us all from torture and the slow death—and the de Danann from misrule by Tarmur Roag through Cairluh, Cormac mac Art of the Gaels, we and even Danu herself owe you debt."

"Balan: you are better than a good man. You have a queen now whom you are too good a man to serve. It's no thanks I deserve for setting Riora again on the rone."

"Be careful, my friend. I love her." Balan looked own. "Danu help me—for what you say is true. For e her rule will be a life of joy and misery, each ving way to the other. For Moytura, she is onsiderably the lesser of two evils. I cannot be her usband. No man can control a queen, and I'll not be y wife's *subject!*"

"Balan: attend me, and hold rein on yourself hilst ye hear my words. She sleeps. . . deeply, for I sked Dithorba for a sleeping potion and gave it her. asy man," Cormac cautioned, as Balan showed action. "The more fool yourself, Balan, an ye are ot by her side when she wakes—on the morrow and ery morrow after."

"I like not your drugging her, but I'll not dispute ose words."

Cormac was smiling. "Go there. Ye'll be finding at she has a gift of me, Balan. . . a certain necklace f silver. Lovers may wish to wear a sign, an identical iece of jewellery," he went on, lifting from his reast the sign of the Moonbow he'd so long worn. This one is for you, then." He slipped it over alan's head.

"Balan, be wise. Methinks ye be fit to rule here. ove for a woman is on ye, and she loves ye but has ad her head turned a bit by a stranger. She rules Moytura. . . and now ye rule her, for she cannot emove her Chain of Danu or order its removal. Keep hem both in place, Balan, and rule both Riora and he people of Danu! All will be happier for it—aye, iora included!"

Balan was staring as the two men left him in quest f Dithorba's quarters in the palace. Gazing after hem, fingering the silver chain and its sigil, Balan ommenced to smile. . . .

Dithorba was not happy at being roused from hi
sleep. Had the potion not worked? Aye, Corma
assured him, and he explained. Then he stated hi
intention, and made his request, and Dithorb
agreed. One by one he mind-conveyed the saviours o
Moytura to the tunnel just outside the precincts of hi
land.

"I shall say nothing, Cormac mac Art. But five i
Moytura have had knowledge of the Chains of Danu
Tarmur Roag, and the queen herself, and the lor
Balan, and my apprentice. Nor will he say aught o
it, an Balan is. . . wise."

"And Riora *can* not."

"Aye."

"Advise the queen, Dithorba. . . and the king."

"Fare well, Wulfhere Skull-splitter. Farewell
Cormac mac Art. Danu shed her light on you, both.
And Dithorba Loingsech was not there.

The two men walked, not without weariness o
them. When at last they came to the mouth of th
cavern in the hill of Bri Leith, they saw that it wa
night outside. Nor were they saddened; retreating
little way, they lay down on unyielding earth an
stone, and they slept as thought they were in the fines
of palace beds.

"Cormac," Wulfhere said on the morrow as the
emerged from the cavern, "ye do realize. . . with *him*
gone forever, we have no hope of returning to ou
own dimension."

"Aye. We must be seeing what this land holds for
pair of scarred sea-wolves, Wulfhere!"

A few paces down the hill under the misty sun o
Eirrin, they glanced at each other, and they looke
back.

The Doorway to the People of Danu had vanished

Wulfhere shook his head. "Here we be, and the Doorway gone, and with all we've done, it's nothing we have to show for it but these two cloaks woven of cloth made by *worms!*"

Cormac mac Art but smiled, and as he walked the Chains of Danu that had been worn by Tarmur Roag and Dithorba clinked in the pouch at his belt.

Sign of the Moonbow: epilog

Yes, the Tuatha de Danann were real—or a real legend, anyhow.

The Celts have no creation myth. There is a story—and certainly with mythic additions, at least—of the succession of invaders who vied to become The Irish. That tale or series of tales is *Leabhar Gabhala Eireann:* the "Book of the Conquest of Erin" (or Ir-land or Ireland), usually called simply "Book of Invasions." Not even the Irish can agree, not even scholars can agree, as to who the first people on those shores were. *Was* it a Greek, time out of mind?

First there seem to have been the *Fir Bholg,* or Firbolgs; whether they shared the land with the "Lower Demons" or "Demons from Below," the *Fomhoire* or Fomorians, is not clear. The Fir Bholg seem to have been in control when the new people came, well before 1,000 BC. These were the *Fir Dhomhnainn:* the Tuatha de Danann, which means simply the people of the (goddess) Dan or Danu or Dana, more latterly called merely Anu. These people appear to be related to the Briton tribe of the

Dumnonii—a Latinized name.

The de Danann culture was considerably higher than that of the Firbolgs, and they were unusually skilled in crafts—if not in arts. As a result, they swiftly gained a reputation for magic, sorcery. . . in the same way, though more seriously because of the era, as Thomas Edison was and is called a wizard.

Dan/Danu/Dana/Anu is a mother of the gods, "she who nurtures well the gods," whose sons Brian, Iuchar and Iucharba are the *fir tri ndea*: "men of the three gods." (Three was ever a sacred number among the Celts, as among so many earlier peoples—probably because of the male genital triad, which has given us the trefoil arch, the French emblem, and many other triple thises and thats). A deity of plenty, Danu was the mother goddess that was so necessary. Even the Christians, with their lonely and presumably celibate deity "borrowed" from the Jews, were forced to elevate the carpenter's wife Miriam to the Holy Mother Mary.

Danu evolved into Anu. She still lives in County Kerry, in a way. There, the two long mounded hills that resemble the breasts of a reclining woman are called *Da Chich Anann:* the Breasts (or Paps) of Anu. They rise to a height of some twenty-two hundred feet, only a few miles southeast of Killarney.

Long before Saint Bridget, whose mythos borrows so much from preceding deities, the Irish believed in their goddess Brigit or Brighitt or Bhrigid (don't tell your priest or your Irish grandmother), who shares some of her legend with Danu. Danu is partially intermingled too with the Morrighu or the Morrighan, a war-goddess who fought with weapons and gave instructions in warfare to various heroes—and drearily predicted the results of and to some extent presided over battles.

251

Take them in your hands and mix them, kneading, some elements separating, some falling out, others intermingling so that, like clay or various colors, they are only just distinguishable; Danu/Dana/Anu/Bridget/the Morrighan. (The h's you find cluttering up Irish words are pronounced, as little huffs of breath, semi-vocal). Thus the Danans gave much to the lore and beliefs of Erin/Eire, and provided a portion of its deities.

And so they came oversea, and twice met in battle the Fir Bholg, and at Moytura the newer invaders put final defeat on the Firbolgs.

In that great battle, the de Danann king, Nuadha, lost his hand to the Firbolg hero, Sreng. As the rules then were that kings had to be physically perfect, Nuadha resigned his reign to the Danan champion Breas or Bres (which means "the Beautiful") of the Fomhoire. Bres ruled seven years—badly. During that time a genius artificer named Creidhne made for Nuadha a hand, all of. . . silver!

Thus was born Nuadha Airgheadlamh, Nuada of the Silver Hand, and he reclaimed his throne to enter legend. (I have ever been going to do something with that story, that concept, which I love. Now I am told Mike Moorcock has done. Blast!)

Naturally the Fir Bholg survivors went off muttering about the de Danann necromancers; the newcomers had after all won, and surely it was by sorcery that they had done and that their king sported a hand all of silver. (Temptation is on me to use the cliche "solid silver." But surely it was hollow, that argent hand, else Creidhne must needs have invented a pocket for Nuadha to carry it in!)

Nuadha Silverhand was succeeded by Lugh ("the Shining One," a sort of Irish Mercury), who was supposedly the son of Manannan, son of the Sea, the great seagod. As Lugh was an expert at *all* crafts and some arts as well, he was called Lugh Sab Ildanach—Source of all the Arts. And the People of Danu, cultured and highly civilized and superbly skilled in crafts, ruled the isle, and their kings slid into apotheosis and legend.

And time passed, and then came the sons of Mil.

These were Celts who were said to have left the Emerald Isle long before (it's more heroic that way), passing through Greece(?) and Spain, and thus gaining dark hair, though retaining eyes of blue or gray. They are often called the Milesians, which seems useless; these were the Gaels. (*Gailioin* or *Gaedhal*—do you know anyone named Gathel?— after a remote ancestor, Gaodhal Glas, a contemporary of Moses). Perhaps their leader was Mil or Miledh, latinized to Milesius, and perhaps not. Perhaps his wife was named Scota and perhaps it was Teamhar/Tamar, and perhaps it was neither. I have let Cormac consider another logical possibility, in *Sign of the Moonbow*. They came, well before the birth of Jesus later called Christ, to the isle that would not be called "Ire-land" for another 1300 years or more.

The Gaels seem to have come in two waves, or to have landed twice—possible, of course, when one remembers both Jamestown and Plymouth Rock and how we kids got them and their dates, thirteen years apart, confused back in the third grade! A great storm arose as they approached the isle, and they decided it was sent by the de Danann mages. Supposedly by evoking *the land itself,* as though it was a sentient entity, and friendly to them, a Chosen People, the Gaels conquered the storm and landed.

The Book of Invasion says that they made landing on Behltain or Beltinne, the first of May, an important Celtic holy day. Such a convenient and auspicious date would appear to be a later, fanciful addition, though coincidences fo occur. (How nice of Charlemagne to have been crowned Holy Roman Emperor on Christmas, AD 800!)

We might pause to point out that *de Danann* is pronounced—approximately—"Day DOV-nan" and Gaedhal is "GAY-thl."

The Gaels, products of so many years and divers civilizations and lands, landed at Bantry Bay. And again there was war for the land the Romans would call Hibernia and Iuvernia/Juverna—and never never conquer.

The Gaels are still there, and so we must agree that they won.

Yet they called their defeated foes mighty wizards, and came nearly to worship them as gods, members of a mystic mythos that grew and grew. Particularly for the time, the outcome of the (probably long and drawn-out; Erin's geography makes it most difficult to conquer—and hold) Milesian-de Danann conflict was an unusual one indeed. The two people seem to have struck a strange bargain for sharing the land of Eire, so that the de Danann were neither wiped out nor forced to flee. *The story says*—crudely put—that the Gaels received the upper portion of Eire and the de Danann the lower portion—the subterranean one!

To each of the de Danann chiefs was supposedly assigned a *sidh,* or "fairy" mound. The Danans became the *Sidhe,* and they are still referred to that way by the Irish. Sidhe, pronounced "She," gave way over the years to the *Ban-Sidhe,* the banshee, whose awful cry warns families of the imminent death of a member.

Even as they descended into the earth beneath Erin, the de Danann ascended into godhead. The de

Danann ruler, the Dagha, became *Olla thain* (the Great father) and Ruadh Rofhessa: the Mighty Oe of Great Knowledge. The Daghda was now a god, even as Crom and Bel/Behl!Baal was. (Yes, Crom was indeed a god of Ireland, just as Conan is an Irish name).

Many of the stories we call "fairy tales," we know, began very seriously indeed, or referred to very serious matters. And so with the Irish legends of the Little People, the leprechauns. . . They live beneath the earth, and are highly skilled, remember? Aye, it's to those cutesy little bearded guys that the People of Danu, across the centuries, have been reduced.

And I always wanted to write about them, not as cutey-poo little guys in Kelly green, with red hair (which looks mighty Danish, to me) and clay pipes, but as the exiled de Danann, once possessors of Erin, mages and wizards, possessors of great skills, and magic alike. Now I have.

andrew j offutt
the Funny Farm
Kentucky, U.S.A.

November, 1976